AF436156

This Little Town

To those who find comfort in the shadows, solace in the enigma, and thrill in the unanswered questions. May the pages of this book be your lanterns through the labyrinth of mystery, guiding you deeper into the unknown. Just remember, some secrets are meant to remain veiled, and some truths are best left buried in the echoes of time. Embrace the intrigue, for in these words, the arcade dances with the curious.

CHAPTER ONE

Jorja

I'd stared at the welcome sign that leads into the small town of Grove many times. *Welcome to Grove.* There are no catchy phrases or pretty pictures of the mountains that surround us, or the wide river that runs behind our homes in the suburbs and along the rim of the town. Just those three words. They haven't even bothered replacing the population sign a few of my drunk friends stole a year ago. Not that it matters with a population under six thousand people that never seems to change. No one new ever moves here and seldom have the guts to get out. What exactly were we welcoming to Grove? Tourists? Highly unlikely. We weren't interesting enough to attract any. Serial killers?

Probably. The cops were all too lazy or neck-deep in covering up the dirty dealings with my family to worry about any unsettling shenanigans.

The thought of leaving had always excited me. Wondering who I'd be when I finally threw my cap into the air and bid my adolescent life farewell. The fact I was set to graduate next year was terrifying but made me feel more alive than I ever had—the fleeting chance I'd actually get away from this toxic place. Who was I kidding, though? I'd never get out. According to my mother, the time between now and graduation was enough time to finish learning the family business so I could take my place in the company just as every other blood relative who lives in Grove had. *You'd be stupid to leave, Jorja. You have it made here. Money, friends, and family. Everything you want is at your fingertips.*

Her words played in my head like a broken record, over and over.

Dreaming outside the city limits only led to disappointment. I just complied with the expectations and free ride that had been provided to me. I can't stray to the wonders outside of Grove like my sister did. She betrayed us all, at least that's what my parents had convinced my brother and me to believe. I questioned it sometimes, though. I questioned it a lot. But when I did, it felt like a sin.

I looked at my freshly manicured nails and ripped-up, Balmain, embellished, high-rise jeans. From the open-toed silver heels on my feet to the headband in my hair, it totals up to every bit of five-thousand dollars. I'd thought about selling my wardrobe plenty of times to just run away from this toxic place. Yet, something always kept me there. Maybe it was the secrets. Or the comfort of living in Grove and being the queen bee of Grove High. I owned that place. I can't even imagine what it'd be like in a world where my last name had zero effect on others. Bonovich was only intimidating and appreciated in Grove and the counties surrounding it.

Pressing the heels of my hands into the hood of my gray Audi R8, I sighed heavily. My dad would have had a panic attack seeing me sit on the hood of this car. I got it for Christmas a month before. It just so happened to also be my seventeenth birthday, and my parents went all out. You'd think someone with my status would feel fulfilled and happy, but I wasn't. I longed for a normal life. One where I blended in with the crowd. Despite this desire, I was no different than the family I had grown to hate—I had no problem using my name to my own selfish advantage.

I hopped off the hood and got into the driver's seat. I drove back into town through the black slush that was a beautiful white snow just hours before. It reminded me that even pretty things couldn't stay pretty forever. Not in my world, anyway.

I was supposed to be at cheer practice, but I had cut out of school early. I'd told the coach I had family obligations—no one argued with a Bonovich.

I stopped at the only red light in town and waited for it to turn green. Why this hadn't been changed to a four-way stop was beyond me. The light took forever and sometimes stopped working altogether.

I tapped my fingers to the beat of the song playing when a large truck pulled into the turning lane. I'd seen this truck around school and town before. I remembered the peeling tint on the left side passenger window. I looked once but had to look again when I saw a guy my age in the passenger seat of the black Chevy. He looked oddly familiar. A lot like Tobias True. I would have sworn it was him until my eyes glanced to the driver and saw none other than Tobias True with his hands placed firmly on the steering wheel, staring straight ahead. As my gaze drifted back to the passenger, our eyes locked on one another's. This fine-as-sin, blue-eyed guy staring at me with a stupid smolder at a red light felt cliché. I jumped when a horn honked behind me. The guy laughed, and the truck turned away from me. I quickly pressed on the gas and accelerated forward, my cheeks burning with embarrassment. I didn't stare at guys, they stared at me. Shallow, yes, but I didn't ever want to give any guy my attention unless they deserved it, or I planned to use it to my advantage. That applied to everyone. I kept my circle small for reasons I couldn't say out loud. To be my friend came with a price many weren't willing to pay. I lied often and covered up those lies with more lies because I had to keep my family safe. No one could ever truly know the real me.

After pressing the call button on my steering wheel, I said, "Call Becca," loud enough for it to hear me. Becca knew me best out of my five friends, but only because she lived next door. Cheer practice should have been over, but the phone still rang several times before she answered.

"Did you bail on us again?"

A sheepish smile crept up on my face. "I had things to do."

"Uh-huh. Yeah. Anyway, you'll have to work extra hard to learn the new routine. It's intense."

"Just send me a video of the moves and counts, and I'll figure it out. I always do." I turned down the county road leading to the outskirts of Grove toward the suburbs where I lived.

"I will. Or I could just come over and show you myself. Are you free tonight?" She started to laugh, and as it turned into an exaggerated giggle, I knew Beck was close by. Those two had been friends with benefits since junior high. I didn't understand why they played this game and didn't just make it official.

"Let me guess, it's Beck?"

"Yeah," she said wistfully. I could already see her twirling her auburn curls around her finger.

I laughed. "Come over after dinner."

"Perfect! What's on the menu tonight?"

I chewed on the inside of my cheek as I thought. "Mom is on a health kick again, so I'm sure it's something with baked chicken."

"Ruth could make dirt taste good. I'll be there."

We both laughed before she hung up.

Stopping at the gate that protected Grove Hills, I pressed the button. I smiled as Bill, the gatekeeper, popped up on the screen.

"How's my little Princess Jorja today?" His Southern drawl sounded so thick even though he'd lived in the northern parts of Colorado for the past twenty years. His graying hair reminded me of how close to retirement he was. He had protected our gated community since I was in kindergarten, and he seemed old then.

"Living the dream, Mr. Bill."

"Aw, come on now, darlin'. You are in the prime years of your life. You know I married the love of my life at your age. I miss her a great deal."

I smiled softly. "I'm sure you do."

He pressed a button, and the large black-iron gates opened. I waved, and he tipped his hat just before I drove inside. I turned off the radio as I drove down my block. Our house sat at the end of a cul-de-sac, apart from all the others. It was large, and old—remodeled to the standards of my mother—but the oldest house amongst the others. We had large, black-iron gates of our own, which were currently covered in snow. Our home was built in the 1800s and is the focal point of Grove Hills because of its placement on the highest hill that overlooked the town.

I looked to my left and saw the Ellisons outside talking with the UPS man. The Ellisons were the Karens of our little community. Nothing could live up to their standards, and their son, Peter, made my skin crawl. He'd always stare at me and steal things from our home when my parents had dinner parties. Peter took a medium-sized box from the delivery guy and his mom and dad were talking, most likely complaining about something. When Peter's eyes landed on my car, I flipped him off. His eyes narrowed, and I laughed as I passed by.

The driveway split into two, and we used it as one way in and one way out like a drive-through restaurant. After making your way around the circle drive, you could keep going right to get to the garage.

I parked in my normal spot, the middle stall between my mom and dad's vehicles. After getting out, I grabbed my bag from the backseat and headed inside while scrolling through Instagram. Several message notifications caught my attention, and I opened the first one as I came into the kitchen and set my bag on the large open bar.

"Are you hungry, Miss Bonovich?"

I looked up from the phone and smiled at Ruth, our housekeeper. "I could really use one of your strawberry smoothies."

Her smile looked forced, gritting her teeth. She hated working for us. I blamed it on my mother, but she'd never admit she was the cause of her dismay. "But it's cold outside. Wouldn't you like something warm?"

I shrugged. "No. Gotta have something cold like my heart." I patted my chest.

She didn't disagree but gave me a slight agreeable smirk.

I went back to my messages when she started getting things together.

I saw an odd name. *@Rtrue360*

The message read: **When did you learn to lie like you do, Jorja?**

I had to read it three more times to make sure my eyes weren't playing tricks on me. My heart raced like I had just avoided a car accident, the shock of the blow nailing me right in the gut. Air filled my lungs, and I held it there until it burned so badly, I had to let it out. There were many things I lied about. *Too many.* When most parents are teaching their kids morals and how to live life as an honest person, I was being taught the direct opposite. I had no choice. I had to protect my family. I quickly deleted the message and blocked the asshole who had the nerve to send a message like that. Of course, rumors spread like wildfire through the town about what people *thought* they knew about my family, but not a single soul had proof of anything. My parents paid big money to keep that stuff buried deeper than the bodies our grave digger puts in the ground.

For a moment, I thought about telling my parents or grandparents, but they had enough to worry about. I wanted to ask Brian, my older brother, if he knew the person or if he had gotten the same message. I decided against all the above. If I made a big deal about it, I'd only bring more attention to it, and I'd look guilty of something. I was guilty of nothing. Now, my family, that was another story. Their decisions had nothing to do with me. I just kept their secrets.

CHAPTER TWO

Jorja

I expected just another day at school today. Boy, was I wrong. The guy I met at the red light yesterday afternoon had a name—Rush, the twin brother of Tobias True. According to Wren, the know-it-all of our group, he and Tobias were the product of a divorce where the parents took one kid while the other took another. It made me think of the movie *Parent Trap*, minus the happy ending. Rush's mother died recently, leaving him no choice but to move in with his brother and their father.

Rush True. I rested my chin on my fist as I stared at the back of his head. The guy who sent me a message on Instagram, or at least I assumed so with the similarity of his name and username on Instagram. The entire day at school, I so badly wanted to find him and corner him, asking him who the hell he thought he was. Instead, I did my best to avoid him. I wanted to pretend it didn't happen. I liked living in my lies. I did a great job of avoiding him until the seventh period. Math. I hated math, but today I surpassed the level of hate I felt for it, and no adjective that could describe my disdain existed. I decided the universe and God Himself must be against me when the only open seat sat directly in front of me. Becca once sat there but had to get her schedule changed last week to get out of French, which she failed, and put in a STEM class instead. *Damn you, Becca.*

Not a thing Mrs. Stevenson said registered. Math, though I hated it, came easy for me. I caught on fast, and my memory was damn good. I never had below a one hundred in math. As crazy as that sounded, it was true. But today, the day Rush True strutted himself into this class, became the day I'd struggle with the content for the first time in my life. The way he sat up straight reeked of confidence. I hated that I allowed myself to enjoy the way he smelled, like sweet pine. Our house had a study with solid pine walls. The smell of books and pine made it my favorite room.

He smelled better than that.

When he turned around to face me, I sat up straight and froze. I felt stupid for allowing him to have this effect on me, but *damn.* He looked older than a typical junior. His height alone would make you think he had to be at least in his first year of college. His jawline was more defined, his blue eyes were full of wisdom. His dark hair was covered in a hat when I saw him yesterday, but it was cut to perfection and combed neatly to the side today. He smiled, and as expected, perfectly straight. I tried to pick apart his ethnicity, settling on white mixed with a hint of Latino.

I cleared my throat and teetered the pencil between my fingers. "Can I help you?" I narrowed my eyes at him.

"I need a pencil." He looked at the one between my fingers and then met my eyes again.

"I'm sorry, fresh out. This is my last one." I set the pencil on my silver, glittered notebook.

His eyes flicked toward the pencil then back at me. My eyes dared him to try to take it. He wet his lips and smiled. I waited for him to say something, but he didn't. He turned in his seat and tapped Beck's shoulder in front of him. Moments later, Beck started digging through his backpack and handed him a pencil. I narrowed my eyes at Beck, and he shrugged in confusion. Hopefully, he chalked it up to me just being in a bad mood. I really didn't want to explain that stupid message.

I sighed and rested my chin on my fist again, trying to pay attention. Geometric properties with equations were something I had already mastered in my AP course the year before. It appeared she was just reviewing it before we moved on to harder things. I let out a breath I didn't realize I was holding, relieved that I wouldn't have to pay attention.

I peered around him, as furtively as possible, and saw his phone face-up on the right upper corner of his desk. I grabbed my phone and decided to unblock him on Instagram and message him. If his phone notified him when I sent the message, I'd be able to prove my suspicions as true. Once I found him, I typed a message that said, **leave me alone,** and hit send. Just as my luck would have it, Mrs. Stevenson took notice of his phone on the desk, and before I could see a thing, she instructed him to put it away. Immediately, he dropped his phone into his open backpack before I could even hear if it vibrated. I set my phone on my lap under the desk. When it vibrated, I looked at Rush who had been busily taking notes, then at my phone. There was a response from **@Rtrue360**, and with it left my suspicions of the hottie in front of me.

Why would I leave you alone when I've only just started? Welcome to hell, Jorja.

My cheeks burned with anger. My stomach swirled with nerves. I stood, causing Mrs. Stevenson to stop talking and the entire class of twenty students to turn and face me. Normally, I loved an audience, but I just needed to leave.

"C-Can I please be excused?" I asked in a small voice. My lack of confidence caused confused looks from around the room. All except the boy who smelled better than my father's study. He held an amused grin, almost patronizing me. He knew something, and my gut told me he was a part of the Instagram bull somehow, even if he wasn't the one sending the messages.

Mrs. Stevenson's eyes questioned me a moment before motioning her hand toward the door. I put my purse on my shoulder and left the classroom.

With my core tight and my chest high, I jumped backward with my arms close to my ears, ensuring I wouldn't land on my head if for any reason I failed at my back handspring. I kept my legs together, landing perfectly on my feet. I stood tall and groaned when Coach Roquel shouted, "Again!" I did ten more until she decided my already perfect back handsprings were to her liking. I hated practicing in the basketball gym. The wood floors weren't as kind to my feet and hands as the football field.

When she moved onto Wren, I went to my duffle bag and pulled out a bottle of blue Gatorade. Becca came and nudged my side. When I looked at her, she motioned her head to the bleachers. Beck took his usual spot, but next to him wasn't just Tommy like normal. Today, Rush sat with them. They were laughing and having a grand ol' time which confused me even more. Tommy grabbed Rush's shoulders and shook them a little as they both looked in my direction. Whatever he said to him made those stupid blue eyes light up and sent butterflies soaring through my stomach.

"Someone is interested in Jorja," Wren said in a sing-song voice as she came over, rubbing her left wrist. She broke it last spring, and it still bothered her when doing stunts. I noticed the freckles sprinkled across her nose and cheeks more today. She and her family visited their beach house regularly when they were sick of the Colorado winters. They got back two days earlier, and the sun always brought her freckles front and center.

"He's taunting me, I swear." I put the top on my Gatorade and set it back inside my duffle. My short athletic shorts and sports bra normally didn't bother me. Now, I felt naked, like he was undressing me with his eyes. Guys did this stuff all the time, and I enjoyed letting their minds wander. Guys were so damn easy, but something about Rush made my skin burn. I couldn't decide if I liked it or if it terrified me.

"It didn't take long for the guys to include him," Becca said before we all stopped what we were doing. I mean *everyone*. The girls on the squad all drooled and stared in awe as a Rush look-alike walked into the gym. I heard whispers of Tobias's name around me.

We watched as he looked around. When he spotted Rush, he walked up the bleachers and started talking to him.

"That's his brother," Wren whispered.

I rolled my eyes. "Oh, really? And what gave you that idea?"

She stuck her tongue out at me. "Tobias, well, Toby, he's crazy. You know, the quiet kind that never says a word to anyone. So unlike Rush." I looked at her, wondering how she decided she could shorten Tobias's name and talk about them as if she were friends with them and knew them.

I couldn't believe I had never noticed Tobias like this before. Probably because he didn't talk much like Wren said. I also didn't really notice anyone at all. However, Tobias and Rush were those guys you should notice. If you were a girl at all you would notice guys like that. I really needed to start paying more attention to others around me. I felt like I had just reached the top of a mountain and was enjoying the view. With the movement of looking at his watch, his arm flexed a little. The definition in his arms caused my eyes to linger longer than they should have.

Becca giggled. "It's not right being that fine."

I closed my mouth, and my shoulders shook with laughter. "Don't let Beck catch wind of that. He'll be jealous."

Becca shrugged. "The joys of not dating. He has no control over what I do."

I bet the same wouldn't apply to him. Especially if she knew about the secret we shared.

"Did you have any idea he existed at our school this whole time? I mean, I've seen him around but not like *this*," I asked, looking at her. I needed to change the subject of Beck or that skeleton would be lurking its way out of my closet to torment me all over again.

She scrunched her button nose. "I mean, I've seen him around but usually in a class sitting in the back all quiet or in a crowded hall where all faces just blend together. Now I wish I would've paid more attention."

"He's talked to you before, Jorja. You completely blew him off. Don't you remember that?" Wren asked, rolling her eyes.

I shook my head.

"Snap out of it, girls!" Coach yelled. She started laughing when we all looked at her. She turned on the music to our dance routine, signaling we better all get our asses onto the floor to practice.

"He's not good enough anyway," Wren whispered as we walked to our places. "They don't have a lot of money. Just middle-class wannabes."

I couldn't understand why I felt so let down by that comment. My parents would never accept them at a dinner party and would have a heart attack if I even thought about becoming interested in one of the True boys. Coach restarted the song—a mash-up of a mix between modern songs and songs from the '90s. I was thankful that focusing on my movements took over my wondering mind as we started to dance.

CHAPTER THREE

Jorja

I slid my report card across the table toward Dad. Mom wasn't there for dinner. Again. I wished I could at least pretend to be surprised, but I wasn't. I'd probably get a call later to go pick her up from one of the bars two counties over. Grove didn't sell alcohol, one of the only dry counties left in the state. The county officials thought it'd keep drunks off the road, but it only made it worse. They'd go get lit two towns over and then drive home.

I picked at my green beans. I usually loved them, especially the way Ruth made them. Her secret: onion powder and brown sugar. The combination sounds horrific, but they were completely and deliciously amazing. Tonight, I just wasn't feeling it because I knew I'd be in trouble for the ninety I got in science. Anything below ninety-five I got the look followed by the talk of striving for perfection. He wouldn't believe me when I told him it wasn't my fault. It was my lab partner—he was too busy staring at me to care about the group project.

I looked at the empty seat across from me. Normally, Brian would have been there. Dad had said he had to handle some "business" and would be late. Business meant drugs, not a thing to do with funeral home things. Brian had to take me with him on one of his runs once. I was ten, and he was supposed to make sure Ruth stayed with me. Miscommunication led to him having to take me with him. I still hadn't told my parents about that and never would. I wasn't allowed to have a thing to do with the dirty dealings of my family. Women stayed out of that and didn't ask questions. We took care of the books for the funeral home.

I looked at Dad when he remained quiet for too long. He held the report card in his left hand, and in his right, a short glass with a few sips left of whiskey. Pappy Van Winkle aged for twenty years—his favorite. I almost told him about the weird message I got but talked myself out of it. To occupy my mind, I started to do the math in my head about how much the few sips in his glass were worth as he lived in his eerie silence. One bottle of seven-hundred-fifty milliliters costs around four-thousand dollars. So, that'd be roughly twenty-five ounces when converted. He had about three ounces in the cup. Three ounces divided by twenty-five ... I tapped my right index finger against the wood grain as the numbers moved around in my head. Four hundred and eighty. He was drinking four-hundred-and-eighty-dollars' worth of whiskey at that moment.

He set the glass down and looked at me. "Good job, Jorja. I'm proud of you." His brown eyes, in contrast to my blue, went distant as he stared at the large picture of my great-grandfather that hung over the fireplace in our dining room. He picked up the glass once more and took a long drink. He set the report card down and then looked at his food. "How's your day been?"

I looked over my shoulder and around the room. Is this a joke? I opened my mouth to speak but closed it and huffed. Dad chuckled and put a bite of steak into his mouth. I had no idea what to say.

"Jorja, I'm very proud. I know your mother and I aren't really involved until it comes time to showcase your learning. I have been busy with business and your mother, well ... she's been preoccupied. It wouldn't be fair for me to scold you for something I'm only involved with at the end of a semester or progress report time."

That was probably the kindest thing he had ever said to me in my teen years. When I was younger, we'd build forts and he'd read to me. I wasn't exactly sure when or why all of that changed, but it did.

"It was a group project that landed me that ninety."

He smiled softly. "I've never liked group work."

I returned his smile. "It's the worst."

His phone rang, and that was the end of the longest conversation I'd had with my dad in forever. I watched him walk out of the dining room. He spoke so low I couldn't understand a word he said. I took a few more bites of my green beans as I stared at Dad's glass. The tiniest bit of whiskey was left in the bottom of it, so I took it and shot it back quickly. It was the first time I had tasted the nasty stuff. I shuddered as I set the glass down and smacked my lips, quickly reaching for my glass of water to wash away the bitterness. I looked toward dad's vacant seat, sighed heavily, and pushed the plate away.

I stood and walked past the kitchen to the stairs leading to my room. I avoided my phone the entire evening, but I needed to text Becca to see if she wanted to hang out. I couldn't let a good Friday night go to waste. I fell back onto my bed and scrolled until I found her name. I hit call and put the phone to my ear.

"Hey, I was just about to call you!" She sounded out of breath, and I could hear stuff being moved around.

"What are you doing?"

"Running around like crazy trying to get ready." I scrunched my nose. "For what?"

"I guess you didn't get the group chat message?"

I took the phone away from my ear, put her on speaker, and pulled up my messages. "I'm looking now. I haven't been around my phone until just now." I pulled up the new message from our group chat.

Tommy: Bonfire at the lake. Be there in twenty.

I looked at the time. The text came through ten minutes ago.

I put the phone to my ear. "Want to ride with me?"

She laughed. "That's what I was gonna call you about. Want to pick up Wren and Jena on the way?"

I scoffed. "Jena is hanging out with us again? I thought she was still pissed at Wren."

"Apparently, not. Jena is at her house, and when I asked Wren how the hell that happened, she said they worked it out."

"That was fast. It was just three weeks ago when Wren caught Jena with Tommy."

She chuckled. "Tommy is a free man and will continue to be unless he meets someone who can calm him down."

I rolled my eyes. "That'll never happen. I'll see you in a bit." I hung up and quickly went rummaging for my cream, Sherpa pullover. Once I found it hanging in the back of my closet, I put on a pair of my black, fleece-lined leggings and black-fur snow boots. I tugged the pullover over my head on my way to the bathroom.

Aside from Dad's study, my bathroom was my favorite place to be. On my fifteenth birthday, my parents had my entire suite renovated. My room had a drastic makeover. I now had a walk-in closet, movie area, office area, lounge area with a stone fireplace, and a bathroom fit for a queen. My room had never been this big, but my parents had walls knocked out and joined my room with what once belonged to my sister. They insisted that I needed it since I'd hit my teen years. Honestly, I think they just needed to get rid of my sister's room so they didn't have to walk past the door that'd be a constant reminder of her. It felt weird at first, knowing I had taken over what was once hers, but the bathroom was to die for, and I quickly got over it. I had barely known her before she ran away— I was only four when she left— so nothing really felt sentimental.

The large bathroom had a wall-length counter that was part sink, mirror, and vanity/make-up area. That wasn't the best part, though. The bathtub sat in the center, becoming the focal point. I'm not even sure you could call it a bathtub, though. It was slightly larger than a hot tub, always full of fresh hot water that filtered out like a pool. It was centered in front of another fireplace, with a crystal chandelier that hung above it. Toward the back wall was a walk-in shower made of stone with a large round shower head that mimicked rain. I didn't have a problem admitting I was spoiled. Getting what I wanted became a security blanket for me. I could accept all the bad and ugly things my family did because at least I had everything I needed and more.

I went to the mirror and touched up my eyeliner and mascara before opening the drawer with my beanies. I found the black one with the gray puff ball at the top and put it on. I ran my fingers through my hair all the way to the ends that met my stomach. My loose curls were still there, so I didn't bother re-curling them.

On my way out, I shut off the lights and went to find Dad. I found him in the study that Rush smelled better than, angry that I had the brief reminder of that guy. Dad was staring at his computer screen, hands folded against his mouth. His drawn-in eyebrows signified he was deep in thought and if I said I word, I'd bother him. I shut the door quietly and found Ruth to let her know I'd be going out.

"I'll let him know," she said as she cleaned the kitchen counters. She didn't turn to look at me, but that was her. She wasn't very personable. She simply did her job and that was that.

I headed out to the garage, got in the car, and drove to get the girls.

CHAPTER FOUR

Jorja

Driving to the south side of the lake we claimed as ours wasn't the easiest to get to. You had to drive up a curvy road higher than the mountain our town was settled on. It started snowing again, but not heavily. Just enough of a gentle flurry to need the windshield wipers. Wren sang her heart out to the song on the radio, and Becca and Jena were begging her stop before our ears bled. I laughed as her singing got louder. That laughter faded fast as we pulled onto the gravel area to park and I saw Beck, Tommy, and their not-welcome plus one. I threw the car in park and the girls shifted forward with the sudden stop and grew silent as their eyes landed on Rush.

"I mean, damn, though." I cut my eyes at Jena through my rearview mirror. She smiled. "You can't deny he's hot. What's your deal with him anyway, Jorja?"

My lips parted but no words formed. I didn't even know what my deal was with the guy since I couldn't prove he had been the one sending me the messages. I killed the engine. "I just don't like how quickly he's made his way into our group. You know I have trust issues. The last time we let someone new in, we found out they were using us and had us all pissed at each other over lies. I just don't want a repeat of that."

No one argued as we got out of the car. I shoved my hands into the pockets of my pullover and kept my eyes on the ground as I walked over to one of the large boulders surrounding the fire. That spot belonged to me. I pulled myself up and sat down, letting my feet fall over the side. If you looked straight ahead from the boulder, you could see most of our town and the lights and smoke coming from chimneys. I looked toward the vehicles when I heard music start playing from Tommy's truck. He assumed the role as DJ and bartender on nights like these.

I felt his eyes on me without even having to look. Set in my determination to get answers about those messages, I decided the best thing tonight would be not to speak to him but also to keep a close eye on him. I may not have been happy he was there, but at least he was nice to look at.

He came over with a cup filled with steaming liquid. He offered it up to me. I could smell cinnamon and apples when the wind blew the scent in my direction. I knew it was laced with spiced rum, Beck's specialty. As badly as I wanted some, I remembered I drove tonight and by the looks of the cups in their hands, I would probably need to drive everyone else home as well. It'd be better than us all sleeping in our cars and trucks like we'd had to before. My parents didn't know that happened, but when Brian found out, he was pissed. I got a good two-hour-long lecture over it.

You can't stay out like that, Jorja. You're a Bonovich. People talk about us enough as it is, and who knows what could've happened! You could've been eaten by a bear or froze to death!

I remember laughing at him. I slept safely in my car with the heat on that night. His worries were irrelevant. And people talk even when there is nothing to talk about. Lies were made up about my family all the time. No one would know if it were true or not. Even if they did know, what did it matter? Me sleeping in my car hurt no one.

Don't roll your eyes at me. I'm older, and I know things. I know things about Grove, the people, and everything in between. We lost ... Brian wouldn't mention our sister's name. It was forbidden. *Just trust me. If you trust no one else, trust me, Jorja. Can you do that?* I remember nodding, giving him a silent agreement. I may be a lot of things, but I wasn't one to back down on my word.

Rush pulled the cup back from reaching distance and took a sip of it. "So good."

"If you were giving that one to me, where is yours?"

His eyes widened with amusement. "You can't assume this was for you."

"You held it in my direction."

"With every intention of pulling it back if you reached for it."

"Are you always this fun to be around?" I snapped, putting my hands into the pockets of my pullover. I forgot gloves. I remembered they were sitting on my dresser next to the picture of me and all my friends that were there tonight, minus one, of course.

"Why do you hate me so much? I'm new here and your friends have been so nice. Did I do something wrong? If my brother was ever an ass, that's not my fault. He can't help himself."

Yeah, Jorja, why do you hate him so much?

"I don't hate you, and until you moved here, I honestly forgot your brother existed. I just don't like people. I keep my circle small, and you came without any warning at all." I was failing terribly. I told myself I wouldn't speak to him and just watch and try to figure out what he was up to.

He took another drink. "You sure you don't want any?"

I shook my head and looked at my friends. I noticed Beck and Becca were missing and immediately knew not to look toward Beck's truck. I made that mistake once before and the windows hadn't fully fogged up yet.

"I will be the one driving all of you home, so I'm fine." My nose felt like ice. Something warm to drink would be so nice. One cup wouldn't hurt. The second would be the issue. "Actually, I'll take just one. Just a half cup, though. My face is cold."

He placed the cup in my hands.

He folded his arms in front of him. "You're not driving me home."

"If you drink too much, I will." I held the cup close to my face and the warmth made my nose tingle as it thawed out. I took a sip and instantly felt warm. I closed my eyes to revel in the moment.

"Nope." I looked at him and found myself having a love-hate relationship with his stupid smirk. "Won't need ya to. My brother is picking me up."

"Oh, really." I made sure I didn't sound convinced.

"I tried to get him to stick around tonight, but he wouldn't."

I drank some more. It was basically apple pie in liquid form and so good. "I'm not surprised."

He raised a brow. "What's that supposed to mean?"

"You pretty much called your brother an ass, and he's a loner. I'm not surprised he didn't want to stick around with my group of friends. We're not exactly the kindest people either."

He laughed and nodded.

"You agree, yet you're here tonight?"

"I was invited, and I'm new here. Tommy invited me. I've heard things about you and your friends, but I don't get intimidated easily."

"Then you just might fit in with us after all." I took another drink, and when he smiled, I had to look away out of fear he'd see how much I enjoyed it.

"Before you go thinking that my brother is some terrible guy, I need to set the record straight. He is careful when it comes to people. He looks at life on a way deeper level than most, and it does make him a loner. But he's not a bad person. He's my best friend."

"And you're not a loner like him?" I remembered being told his mother died, forcing him to move here with his dad and brother. I wondered why he didn't act sad or withdrawn. My parents may be screwed up, but I love them, and I'd be crushed if something happened to them.

"I can be at times, but he and I are different in that way, I guess. I figured moving to a new school isn't the time to be a sometimes-loner, though. I need to make friends and stay busy."

"Because you don't want to be sad?" I honestly didn't mean to say that. It wasn't my place to bring up his mother. I thought of things I could say to try to retract my words, but from past experiences, that would have only made it worse.

"I'm not sad."

I could feel the pity in my eyes as I looked at him. "I didn't—"

"It's fine. I'm sure you're referring to my mom. People die. It's a part of life." He said it like it was salt on a fresh wound but pretended it didn't sting.

"We don't have to talk about it. I'm sorry for what I said."

He looked at the cup in my hands. "I'm going to get another drink."

I watched him walk off and noticed what he was wearing for the first time since seeing him. His tan Carhartt jacket and matching beanie were most likely from the sporting goods store downtown. They sold things like that. Brian always liked shopping there and, come to think of it, he had that same coat and hat.

I got off the rock and walked over to Tommy, Wren, and Jena. They all looked at me like they were waiting for something. I looked behind me and around the area before meeting their eyes.

"What?"

"We saw you two talking," Tommy said as he nudged me with his elbow and winked.

"People talk." I looked over at Rush as he poured himself a drink from the large thermos in the back of Tommy's truck. "Also, why the hell did you invite him tonight without asking us all first?"

"He's actually a really cool guy, Jorja. My parents are friends with his dad, and I've been talking to him before he ever started school and moved here. We've hung out a couple of times when he's visited his brother and dad."

I narrowed my eyes at Tommy. "And you didn't tell us about him?"

He chuckled in a knowing way. "Would you have been more welcoming?" He knew I wouldn't have. He just didn't know the suspicions I had about whoever was sending the messages. Only Becca knew my family owned more than a funeral home. Even then, the extra parts she knew were filtered, so she really didn't have a clue. If I had tried to explain anything at all to Beck, Wren, Tommy, and Jena, it would've been a revelation no one was ready for.

Rush came over to us with a new drink in his hand. "So, is this what we do? Sit around and talk while Becca and Beck make out in the truck?"

I laughed and took another drink. "Pretty much."

"Damn. I thought there would be some big party. I've heard rumors about your parties."

Wren tilted her head to the side and flashed her famous flirtatious grin his way. "Who told you that?"

"Tommy," Rush said, motioning toward him with his cup.

I raised both brows before glaring at Tommy. "And what else did he tell you about us?"

Rush put the cup to his lips and smiled against the rim before taking a drink. No response and that grin were enough of a response to remind me to have a talk with Tommy later.

Tommy held his cup up and nodded. "I do throw a kick-ass party from time to time. But this is our spot. We come here to just be together with our favorite people when we don't want all the noise."

"Don't think you're a part of the favorite category. You're on a trial period," I quickly interjected.

"You know you have to pay for things once you've used up the trial period, right?"

I blinked a few times as I stared at Rush. "Unless you cancel them before the renewal date."

A few "oooh" sounds from my friends filled the air.

"I've never had any dissatisfied customers before, sweetheart."

I could feel the heat rush to my cheeks. My mouth opened but shut quickly when I realized I didn't have a comeback.

"Dayyyummm, Bonovich, no one has ever rendered you speechless before," Tommy prodded, making everyone else laugh.

I downed the remaining contents of my cup. "Shut up, Tommy," I mumbled before holding my cup out toward him. I shook it a little until he took the hint and went to his truck to pour more. I didn't know what to do with this feeling Rush caused or what it meant exactly.

"Did I piss you off?" Rush asked quietly as he leaned in close to me.

"No," I mumbled.

"Do you want me to leave?" he asked in the same hushed tone.

I met his gorgeous eyes. *Yes.* "No."

"Thank God." Rush's smile felt so genuine, making me think he really didn't have anything to do with the messages at all. Or maybe it was the alcohol fogging up the logical parts of my brain.

I was so focused on Rush that when Tommy turned up the music and the bass hit just right, I jumped a little, almost tripping over a stick. Rush gently took my hand to steady me.

"Did you say you wanted to dance?" he yelled over the music with that ridiculously contagious grin.

My brows furrowed. "No, I—" My words fell short when he pulled me close to him until our bodies were pressed together. His hand was held firmly against my lower back, not allowing distance between us. When his hips started moving to the beat and he started singing every word to the song playing. I threw my head back laughing. Maybe he truly just wanted to make friends and a new life here in Grove. Maybe the username was purely coincidental.

However, I weighed heavily on *maybe*.

CHAPTER FIVE

Jorja

I woke up in someone else's bed. Last night we all ended up drinking entirely too much. Holding true to my promise of not sleeping in my car, I vaguely remembered Rush asking Tobias to give me a ride. What I didn't remember was ending up here, wherever I was. I sat up and rubbed my forehead and realized I was in an extremely large, gray sweatshirt emblazoned with Grove's High. My hands were swallowed by the sleeves. I tugged on the bottom of the shirt until it reached just above my knees. I looked around, squinting to try to focus on something that would give me a clue as to where I was exactly. The blackout curtains only gave enough light for me to see it was definitely a guy's room. A pair of boxers were near the dresser and the covers were dark. The familiar smell of sweet pine invaded my senses, and I cursed. *No. No. No.* I still had my panties and bra on, hopefully meaning I didn't do what this scene could imply. I looked to my right, and no one was there. I swung my feet over the side of the bed and dug my toes into the carpet before standing. I went to take a step forward and tripped over someone, causing me to faceplant onto the floor. I groaned as I rolled onto my back. The person started to stir.

"Jorja?" Rush's voice sounded deeper than usual and full of sleep.

I sat up slowly and ran my fingers through my hair. "I didn't see you there. Sorry. Ummm, what exactly am I doing here? In your bedroom?" I ran my fingers through my hair, ignoring the throbbing in my nose.

"Well—" he laughed and stretched as he sat up "— you insisted we not take you home so you wouldn't have to explain yourself to your parents or brother. I took your phone and messaged your parents and told them you were staying at Becca's. My brother drove everyone else home. I'm gonna need to find out what exactly is in that cider."

"Why didn't you just take me to Becca's? She's my neighbor. If my car isn't at her house, my parents will know I'm lying."

He yawned. "Becca is at Beck's. She didn't go home. Watching her sneak into Beck's window was rather entertaining. Have I mentioned how confusing it is their names are so damn similar?"

I laughed a little. "You get used to it." I rubbed my head and looked down at the sweatshirt. "This isn't my shirt," I whispered.

"No, it's my brother's."

"And my clothes are ...?" My eyes were more adjusted to the dark, and I could see him a little better. His bare chest was a work of art. I quickly looked back down at the sweatshirt.

"So many questions so early in the morning. Let's go have coffee and something to eat before we get into all the details." I looked at him as his eyes went to the bed. "Or we could just go back to sleep for a little longer."

"Or you could just give me my clothes and take me home."

He started laughing, which annoyed me. "You don't remember anything about the ride to our house?"

"I'm really not interested in the details, Rush."

"But the details are so fun."

I rolled my eyes. "Whatever. Please, just tell me where I can find my clothes. I need to go get my car and go home." I hated that he found so much humor in this. All my plans about him went south with that second cup of cider. I didn't trust him, and now I was in his room and in his brother's shirt. I tried to remember everything about last night, but I didn't remember much past dancing with Rush and Tommy daring Rush and Beck to jump in the freezing cold lake. Which they did. The more I drank, the fuzzier the details of the night got.

"Your clothes are in the hall bathroom. I can show you where that is. You started taking them off, saying you were burning up. While I was thoroughly enjoying the show, my brother and I couldn't let you humiliate yourself. Toby quickly took off his sweatshirt and threw it over your head. I made sure you got to my room, and once you hit the bed, you were out."

I hid my face in my hands and groaned.

He chuckled. "You have a very promising career in stripping."

I dropped my hands and narrowed my eyes at him. "Just tell me where my clothes are." I stood and wrapped my arms around myself.

He got up and stretched then motioned for me to follow him, leading me down a small hallway and nodding his head toward a door. "Here's the bathroom. I'll meet you in the kitchen. Just keep walking down the hall and you'll see it." He opened the door and turned on the light. I saw my clothes folded neatly on the counter near the powder-blue sink that was majorly outdated.

"Where's my cellphone?" I had tried to avoid looking at him in the light of the hallway, but my eyes had trouble listening.

"You had it when you went to sleep. I'll go look in my bed."

"Okay." I went into the bathroom and shut the door. I looked in the mirror and noticed the eyeliner and mascara had smudged around my eyes, making me look like a raccoon. I pulled my hair into a messy bun with the rose-colored, velvet Scrunchie I religiously wore around my left wrist. I helped myself to one of their washcloths that they kept on a wooden shelf above the toilet. I washed my face and rinsed my mouth out with water then quickly dressed, but my boots were nowhere to be found.

I pulled the Scrunchie from my hair and it fell around my face and shoulders like a blanket. I ran my fingers through it, working on the lightly tangled mess until it was better than it was. I put the Scrunchie back on my wrist, picked up the sweatshirt, and made my way out of the bathroom and down the hall.

I found Rush in the kitchen cracking eggs into a metal mixing bowl. Still no shirt and his black boxers were showing with the way his gray sweats rested low on his hips. I heard the coffee pot hiss as Toby walked past me. He wore dark jeans and a white Fallout Boy hoodie. His hair was tousled like he just woke up, put on his hoodie, and didn't bother with it anymore.

I knew they lived with their dad, but I didn't see him. Maybe he was still asleep. I wondered if he would be pissed that his son had a girl in his bed last night, and I hoped like hell he didn't witness my apparent stripping session.

I walked over to Tobias and held the sweatshirt out toward him.

"Thanks." I could feel my cheeks heat up. I felt so small and childlike around him. Maybe it was because of how he looked down at me like I was a nuisance. "I'm sorry."

He took the shirt. "You're sorry?" His voice sounded husky and seductive without even trying. He had one of those voices that would make a girl melt by just saying the simplest of words. That was the first difference I noticed between Rush and him. Rush's voice was deep but with more of a rasp to it, like he smoked every now and then. "Why are you sorry exactly?"

My words clogged up in my throat. I didn't know how to answer that. I was sorry that they'd had to take care of me when I was sure he would have rather been sleeping or doing whatever Tobias did on a Friday night. I could have told him that, but I felt too intimidated to form the words. I didn't know how to react on this side of the spectrum. I normally did the intimidating. I looked at Rush when he called my name. He gestured toward the table.

"I really don't want to be a bother, Rush. If you could just take me to my car, I'll head home and get out of your hair."

He looked over his shoulder at me as he stirred eggs around. "After we eat, I'll take you to your car. You're not bothering us. I promise."

The look on Tobias's face would beg to differ. I sat down at the table and felt extremely out of place. I looked around the tiny kitchen with outdated appliances. They were this yellow color, straight from a 70s home magazine, and I wasn't sure if they were meant to be that way or just took on that color because of how old they were. The cabinets were wood with black rusted handles and the walls were covered in outdated, yellow daisy wallpaper.

"Are you done judging our home yet?" I took my eyes off the wallpaper and shifted them to Tobias. I didn't remember him taking a seat across from me. He slid a coffee cup in my direction before taking a drink of his own. If I drank coffee, I don't think I'd accept any from him. If looks could kill, I'd have been dead.

"I don't drink coffee, but thank you anyway. Also, I'm not judging your house. I'm just taking it all in. I might be judging the wallpaper, though. It's ridiculous." I smiled, trying to lighten the mood.

"My grandmother put it on the walls when this place belonged to her and my grandfather. It's sentimental, something you might not understand. I'm sure things that aren't flashy and beautiful hold no sentimental value to people like you."

"Toby, shut up, man. Whether you agree with her lifestyle or not, it's not her fault she lives better than we do."

Something in Toby's eyes changed. Softer maybe, but still full of something. Like he knew something about my family. He looked at me like he had me all figured out. Rush, the guy who had driven me insane the whole first five seconds I met him was actually likeable compared to his brother.

I stood forcefully, causing the chair to screech backward against the wood floor. "Did you happen to find my phone, Rush? I'll have someone else come pick me up and take me to my car."

Rush moved the pan to a back burner and wiped his hands on a towel. "Yeah, it's right here." He went over to the counter near the fridge and picked it up. I'm surprised I didn't spot my pink glittered case earlier.

I walked over and took it. "I appreciate all you've done for me, but I'm gonna go. I'm sorry if this whole situation upsets your dad and you get in trouble." I quickly texted my brother. "Where am I exactly? I need to let my ride know where to pick me up from."

"My dad works nights. He won't be home for another two hours. Even if he were here, he wouldn't mind. He's cool like that. You're at 1714 Oak Street. If you turn right at the truck stop and keep going straight, you'll turn at the first stop sign. We're the third brick house on the right."

I nodded and went to leave but stopped. "Where are my boots?"

Rush pointed toward the living room. "By the front door. I can go ahead and bring you to your car if that's what you really want. No need to call someone else."

I shook my head. "No, I've been enough of a bother." I gave him a look that warned there would be no arguing.

I headed to the living room, not giving Tobias another glance. People had a right to their opinion, and I knew he wasn't the only one with negative thoughts about me and my family, but that didn't give him the right to be mean. Maybe he was the one sending those messages and he made an account with Rush's name as a cover-up. That'd make sense. I put my boots on and called my brother when he never texted back. I opened the door, went outside, and sat on the middle step of their front porch while I waited for him to answer.

I pulled the phone away to look at the time. Seven in the morning. He was probably still asleep. I put the phone back to my ear, hoping I'd get lucky and he'd answer. Nothing. I dialed Becca next. She didn't answer but Beck did.

"Hey, Becca is asleep. You okay?"

"Thank God someone answered. Where are you?"

He yawned. "At my house."

"I need someone to come pick me up from Rush's house. He insisted he bring me to my car, but I'd rather have no more favors from him or his brother."

"You're at Rush's?" He started laughing. "Did you show him how much he is gonna love it here?"

"Can you be serious for two seconds and not think like a guy? Nothing happened besides me humiliating myself and getting death glares from his brother. I want to leave."

He laughed some more. "Alright, I'll be there soon."

"Do you know where he lives?"

"Yeah, in that crap hole of a neighborhood near the truck stop. I'll wake up Becca, and we'll be on our way."

I looked around at the other houses. He wasn't wrong. This was the side of town no one trick-or-treated at, no matter what social class you belonged in.

"Hurry." I hung up and put my phone and hands in my pullover pockets. I realized I was missing my hat, but I'd die before I'd go back into that house and have to see Tobias again.

CHAPTER SIX

Jorja

The rest of the weekend I remained low-key. I finished homework and vegged out on Netflix movies. I even turned off my phone and pretended like I didn't exist. Becca came over at one point, but I told my mom to tell her I was sleeping. I was in a horrible mood all weekend after how Tobias treated me. It shouldn't have bothered me, though. He wasn't someone important to me, and his opinion didn't matter.

As I walked into the lunchroom, everyone stopped eating and talking to stare at me. I looked down at my white pleated skirt and black, long-sleeved crop top. My stomach was showing, but that wasn't unusual. Neither was my too-short skirt I should have gotten dress coded for but wouldn't. I checked my black, ankle-cut wedges. No toilet paper stuck to the heel like what happened to Becca a couple of months ago. I knew not a hair moved out of place and my makeup was on point because I had just left the bathroom to look myself over.

My eyes scanned the crowded cafeteria until I found my friends. Becca stood and hurried over to me. She grabbed my arm, almost causing me to drop my lunch bag and pulled me out of the cafeteria into the empty hall.

"What the hell is going on?"

"I'm assuming you didn't get the group message sent over Snap?" she whispered, and her eyes shifted around the hall to make sure no one could hear us. I wasn't sure why she was acting that way. The way everyone stared at me, everyone knew something I didn't. She sighed heavily and started scrolling through her phone. "I screenshotted it." She handed me the phone.

When I saw the picture, my hands started to tremble. It was a fake grave; one you'd buy from the Halloween section at Walmart to decorate with. It was wedged into the snow with what I hoped was fake blood dripping all around it. In black sharpie, it read, **Here Lies Jorja Bonovich's Reputation.** The date was four days from now. My heart raced and my mouth went dry. I shoved her phone in her direction, and she took it.

"Who posted that?" My cheeks flamed with anger.

"It's Rush's name as a username, *@Rtrue360*, but he swears he didn't have anything to do with that. He said he doesn't even have social media," Becca whispered.

"And you believe him?" I hissed. I put my hand to my forehead when I started feeling lightheaded. God, how stupid could I be? Not that I trusted him, but I danced with him Friday night. I laughed with him. I slept in his bed. Not on purpose, but it still happened.

Beck put his arm around Becca's shoulders and looked at me. When did he get here? "Tommy said he was sitting right beside him when he got it. Everyone in the class got it but Rush. Tommy said he didn't even have his phone. It was in his backpack."

I felt like I needed to cry or throw up. Maybe both. "I've gotten two odd messages on Instagram from *@Rtrue360*." Might as well put that out there since whoever the person was decided to go public. "Where is Rush right now anyway?"

Beck looked toward the bathrooms. "Bathroom. Who the hell did you piss off, Jorja?"

"No one that I know of. Well, maybe one but not intentionally." *Tobias.* I swear my eyes filled with venom. My footsteps thundered against the tiled floor as I stormed into the cafeteria and started looking for him.

"Who are you looking for?" Wren asked, catching up with me.

"Tobias," I got out through clenched teeth.

"He doesn't have this lunch. He has B lunch."

I stomped my way out of the cafeteria and down the junior hall. I opened every door to every classroom until I spotted him. By now, all the teachers were in the hall, as well as students. The teacher stopped teaching mid-sentence and began to scold me, but I pressed on until my palms were planted on his desk. I leaned down to meet his eyes.

"What the hell did I ever do to you?" I growled.

"I'm going to need you to leave my classroom and report to the principal's office, Miss Bonovich." I heard the teacher's voice but ignored him.

Tobias kept his eyes on mine. He looked unamused. "Is there a particular reason you're barging into my chemistry class all pissed off?"

I pointed my finger at him. "Oooh, don't you play stupid! You're sending those messages posing as your brother!"

He looked shocked. "What?" he said quietly. "You're causing a scene, Jorja."

"Jorja Bonovich! Out!" I heard the teacher shout and watched his fist hit the intercom button. "I'm going to need the principal. Now, please!"

I felt defeated when I saw just how innocent Tobias looked. The utter confusion on his face would have been hard to fake. I stood, straightened my skirt, and walked out of the classroom, hearing catcalls and the teacher telling them that was enough and back to work. I barely made it into the hall before meeting the principal, Mr. Thomason. I held my arms out as if I were about to be cuffed and brought into jail.

"Not in the mood for your little games, Jorja. And don't think you'll sweet talk yourself out of this one. To my office, now."

I sighed and followed him down the hall. I didn't frequent the office, but when I did end up in there it was always because of something I did when letting my temper get the best of me. I always remained calm unless someone pushed me over the edge. The last time something like this happened it was over a comment made about their dad having sex with my mom and he asked if I was easy like her. I had that huge football player slammed against a locker so fast he didn't have time to react. Poor guy still hadn't lived down the fact a petite thing like me handled him like that. Not many knew that my dad put me through self-defense classes from the age of ten until I was sixteen years old. He also made me get my boater's license four days after my sixteenth birthday. You know, just in case I had to dispose of a body if anyone crossed me wrong.

When I got to the office, Mr. Thomason pointed to his door. I went inside and sat down on one of the leather chairs across from the desk. He went to his filing cabinet and pulled out a dark green folder. He sat down and began writing on a yellow Post-It note, and when he was finished, he set down his pen and stuck the Post-It on the inside of the folder.

"What exactly initiated your outrageous behavior?"

I folded my arms over my stomach to hide the bare skin. I swear his eyes lingered there a moment. "Someone sent out a message to a lot of people. I don't know exactly how many got it, but by the look on everyone's faces, it was every single student in the cafeteria. Becca screenshotted it. It'd be easier if you just called her in so you could look at it. I had a feeling I knew who sent it, so I went looking for him myself."

"And do you know exactly who did it?"

I shook my head. "No. I thought I did, but I think I was wrong."

"If you have even the slightest suspicion you should let me know. We take cyberbullying very seriously."

"I'll only tell you if I know for sure. I don't want to cause anyone trouble who truly has nothing to do with this. Seems I've already done that."

He nodded. "I will call Becca to the office and take a look at the message."

I stood and started to walk but stopped. "The message is from the username @Rtrue360 but Rush True doesn't even own a social media account according to Tommy and Beck. So don't assume it's him."

"Thank you for the information." He stood and walked past me and opened the door. "Notify me of any more trouble instead of handling it yourself next time, okay?"

My lips curled. "So, I'm off the hook?"

"Nice try. I know you have cheer practice after school, so you'll have before school detention. Be here at seven and report to the cafeteria."

I tilted my head to the side. "We have before-school detention?"

"We had to figure something out for our athletes and noon detention doesn't seem to bother anyone."

"Ah. Makes sense. Just tomorrow?"

He nodded. "And I'm serious, Jorja. Let me know if you have more issues. I will be contacting your parents."

I started to walk again but stopped quickly. "No. No. No. Pleeeease don't do that, Mr. Thomason. They are so busy, and you know when they get involved how crazy things get. Please. I'll be here in the morning, and I swear the moment I have a suspicion, I'll come straight to you. Please." The insistence in my voice had to convince him, and if that didn't work, I hoped my pitiful eyes would do the trick. "Please," I spoke quietly.

He let out a heavy sigh. "Alright, but the moment I hear one more thing, I'm notifying them."

"Thank you!" I left the office and looked at the clock on the wall in the office. I had time to get my things out of my locker and get to sixth period. I was going to be starving by the time school ended.

I walked into class and sat at my desk in the front next to Tommy. The teacher sat at her desk grading papers. I looked at Tommy. "What are we supposed to be doing?" I looked around at the other students who were writing something.

Tommy looked at the board, and I saw a writing prompt. The instructions were to write about the strangest dream we had ever had for the entire class period without a word. Mrs. Foster was notorious for doing this to us when she was behind on grading. I took out my binder and grabbed a few pieces of paper and a mechanical pencil.

Tommy nudged my foot with his. "Everything okay?" he whispered.

"Fine," I answered as I wrote my name on the top of my paper.

"Everyone is talking about how you confronted Rush's brother about it. Why do you think Tobias is to blame?"

I set my pencil down and looked at him. "We're not talking about this here." I looked over my shoulder at the full class. I looked at him again and watched his eyes scan the room.

He looked at me again and nodded. "Want to meet up at your house? I think we all need to talk about what happened today."

I nodded and went back to the assignment. He was right, we did need to talk about this. Someone was seriously messing with me, and when you messed with one of us in my circle of friends, you messed with all of us.

CHAPTER SEVEN

Jorja

I didn't mean *all* of us when I agreed for everyone to come over, but there sat Rush on my favorite chaise lounge like he owned it. It was apparent he would be coming to everything we did from now on. I didn't like how he managed to wiggle his snarky self into our group so easily, but Tommy and Beck needed another guy around, I guess. They had always been outnumbered by us girls.

"Did you do anything to anyone at all? I know you can be oblivious to how you actually treat people." Jena hadn't said much of anything for the past twenty minutes as we analyzed it all. I almost called her out on her remark because it offended me, but I also found myself thinking about telling her that her chin-length, black hair would look so much better with loose waves. The boxy straight look made her look like Uma Thurman when she played on *Pulp Fiction* and looked tacky. My shallow thoughts only validated what she said.

"I haven't spoken to anyone other than all of you lately." I stopped talking when I took notice of how Rush eyed my room and belongings in awe.

"You should see her bathroom," Beck said as he stood. "Come on, I'll show you!"

I narrowed my eyes at Beck and Rush as they went into my bathroom. "How is this helping anything?" I asked, looking at Tommy.

"Damn, this is nice," I heard Rush shout dramatically.

I huffed loudly and looked at Becca. "Should I just ignore this asshole or turn it in? I don't want my parents involved. I'm sure it's not a big deal and someone is just messing with my head. If my parents get involved, they'll hire an army to bring this person down."

"This person obviously wants attention, but not on them. On you. Maybe your parents or your brother upset someone and they are trying to get to them through you. So, maybe telling your parents isn't a bad thing. You know people are always talking about your family." Becca shrugged at her suggestion. "I don't really think there is a right or wrong solution. Whoever is doing this needs to be stopped or it is just going to keep making you miserable."

"You have to wonder how far they are willing to go," Wren added from the white, fur rug in the center of the couch and chairs. She was lying down on her back and never looked up from her phone.

We all looked at Rush and Beck when they came back to the lounge area. I watched as Rush walked over to the fireplace and warmed his hands. During the cold months, I don't know of a day that all the fireplaces weren't up and running. Ruth made sure the gas logs were lit in all of the rooms and my bathroom. The only real fireplaces that required firewood were in my dad's study and the living room downstairs, but she managed them as well.

Rush looked at me over his shoulder. "Anyone come to any assumptions as to why they are using my name?"

We all shook our heads.

But what if Rush is playing us all? "Rush," I said sweetly.

He turned all the way around and kept his eyes on me. "Yes?"

"Can I see your phone? To put my mind at ease that you truly don't have social media and there are no signs of suspicious activity?" I held out my hand and moved my fingers in a gimme gesture.

He nodded and took his phone out of his pocket. He unlocked it and handed it over. He had no social media apps as promised. I opened up his photo album to make sure no pictures of a grave with my name on it were there, and there weren't. I even checked his recently deleted images. There were only pictures of the mountains, a few selfies of him with Tobias with the mountains behind them, and a few of him with guys and girls our age from what most likely were at his other school.

"Scroll too far and you might get into pictures you don't want to see." The corner of his mouth lifted a little when I looked at him. "Or maybe you do."

I rolled my eyes and kept scrolling. Photos of what I assumed of his mother were there. She appeared middle aged with the same blue eyes he and Tobias had. She was really pretty and had a kind smile. My chest tightened at the thought of how much he probably missed her and how he could possibly keep playing it off like he was fine. When I scrolled more, he was right. I cleared my throat and handed him back the phone. Nudes from girls were typical of any guy our age, so I wasn't surprised.

"Did I check out okay, investigator?" His playful grin held my attention for a moment.

"For now, but—" I stopped talking and we all looked at my phone on the coffee table as it dinged with notifications several times before settling down.

"I feel like the time I took a pregnancy test and feared looking at the results," Jena said from the loveseat, causing us all to look at her with wide eyes.

"Well, there goes that little secret," Tommy mumbled from beside me.

Wren cut her eyes at him.

"It was negative," Jena added.

"You three don't start up that mess again." I sat up and reached to grab the phone. "Impeccable timing, asshole," I said quietly as I saw three new messages from @Rtrue360.

Everyone was on edge, waiting as I read through them.

One....

Two....

Three.... I'm gonna kill your Audi.

We all jumped at the sound of my car alarm going off from the garage. I dropped my phone, but Rush picked it up and read the messages out loud.

"Call the cops, Jorja. This idiot must be on your property!" Becca's voice shook.

Tommy and Beck raced to my wall of windows and pulled back the sheer white curtains.

I couldn't remember ever feeling fear like this before. I'd worked in the funeral home, helping the mortician embalm bodies and helping families pick out coffins as if I were selling a car. I'd done a dead woman's make up before funerals all alone in a cold room. I didn't fear intruders. Strangers to our gated community didn't get past Mr. Bill. Our home was secured with the best of the best, or so I thought. Fear wasn't an emotion that frequented my mind. Until then.

I got up and ran to my nightstand where I kept my extra car key. I hit the panic button several times before the car alarm silenced. I looked at Rush who still had my phone. I held my hand out toward him, and he walked over and placed the phone in my hand. I had the sheriff's office saved in my contacts; my parents required it to be there as long as I had a cellphone. They prepared me for things no teen should have to prepare for. I never thought I'd have to use it, that they were being overly dramatic. I put the phone to my ear and waited.

I watched Beck, Tommy, and Rush leave my room.

I covered the microphone. "Where are they going?"

"To look at your car," Becca answered first.

I really didn't want them to go down there just in case it wasn't safe, but I knew for sure Tommy and Beck wouldn't listen to me.

"Sheriff's office, this is Deb. Can I help you?"

I uncovered the mouthpiece. "This is Jorja Bonovich. I believe someone came onto my property and vandalized my car."

"Are you sure? Did you see the person? You guys have that place locked up tighter than Fort Knox."

"No. The alarm went off after I got weird messages from someone."

"Explain the messages."

I started getting frustrated. Could she just notify the deputies and have them come out? "It'd be easier to just show the police."

"I will send someone out."

"Do you need my address?"

She laughed. "Everyone knows where the Bonovich residence is." She hung up the phone.

"Well?" Wren prodded.

I sat slowly onto my bed and lowered the phone to my lap. "She's sending someone out." I rubbed my temples. "So much for keeping it on the down low. My parents will know for sure now. And when my brother finds out ..." I groaned and fell back onto my bed, covering my face with my hands. "This is going to get stupid crazy really fast. And my poor car! I hope it's not bad. I'm too scared to look."

Becca sighed. "I'm sure we will get the full report when the guys come back up."

I sat up and looked at her. "Someone was on my property. What do they want from me?"

"Maybe your suspicions are true about them trying to get to your parents or even your brother. They want to expose something." I kept my eyes on Wren as she spoke. She went on and on about all the things it could possibly be. The people in this room knew very few things about my family, but they didn't know it all.

I stopped listening to her rambling and started going down the list of things I'd been trained not to discuss. Last year, someone who bought drugs from my dad had a bad reaction. They died. It was said that my dad did it on purpose so he could double dip in his businesses. Guy buys a ton of cocaine—money for Dad. Dude dies and now needs a mortician, funeral, and burial—money for Dad. My dad wouldn't purposefully hurt anyone like that. He dealt big money drugs, but his supply came from the cartel in Mexico. He wasn't a part of the actual production of it. He just got it here through casket deliveries and had a few people, including my brother, dealing it in Grove and surrounding areas. I used to wonder how they got away with it around here and other towns, but one night my curiosity got the best of me, and I spied. It was genius actually. They buried it in graveyards in freshly-dug graves and sent out code names and coordinates of the location in a way that wouldn't be traceable by authorities. Everything was done well after dark when everyone was asleep.

I guess there could have been many things for this person's behavior to make sense. My mind kept going back to one thing, though.

Why Rush True?

Why *his* name?

CHAPTER EIGHT

Jorja

My car would be in the shop for several days while they ordered new headlights, taillights, sunroof, windshield, and driver's side window. I rode with Becca to and from school for two days until my parents started having Brian take me. Dad decided that if this person was crazy enough to come onto our property and hurt my car, they'd be crazy enough to hurt me. He made Brian my personal bodyguard until further notice. I didn't mind it, though. It was nice seeing him in the mornings and afternoons. I was thankful for it being Friday, the start of the weekend after an oddly exhausting week. Being at school felt off, not knowing if my stalker was walking the same halls. That's what me and the girls deemed him or her. A stalker.

I looked at Brian as he drove toward home. He was letting his beard grow out, making him look older and wiser even though he was only nineteen. He couldn't grow much facial hair in high school while all the other guys he hung around did, so he said he'd embrace it for as long as he could.

"I'm sorry Mom and Dad are making you do this."

He looked at me before looking at the road again. He drove with one hand on the steering wheel and the other checking his phone every five seconds. I guess that's what drug dealers did. Couldn't miss a pickup or drop-off. I looked at the window and chewed on the inside of my cheek.

"I hope they find this person, Kid." He had called me Kid for as long as I could remember. It used to bother me since he wasn't that much older than me, but now I just roll with it. If he ever called me by my real name, I immediately knew something was wrong. "I plan on finding him myself, and when I do—"

I whipped my head in his direction. "You won't! Brian, promise me right now you won't. I don't want you mixed up in any of this and risking your own safety. You have so many targets on your back as it is. Just leave this one alone. It may not even be a guy. Maybe it's a girl."

His silence was the only confirmation his mind was made up and there'd be no talking him out of it. I was sure he had part of his crew already on the hunt for answers. Being a part of a family like mine comforted me in a sick way. Knowing I had villains protecting my back made it easier to sleep at night. They were ruthless and didn't play fair. If they found whoever it was, they'd be dead, and I meant that with zero exaggeration. My brother used our grave digger and his boater's license a lot. Sometimes I wondered what kind of burden that had to be to carry the death of someone in your hands.

"Hey, Brian?"

He looked at me. "Yeah?"

"Did you know Tobias True when you went to high school? He's in my grade, but before Rush came, I didn't pay attention that he existed at all."

He looked at the road again. His eyebrows met his nose. "Yeah, but he's just some loner kid who doesn't talk to anyone. Why'd you ask?"

"He seems to have something against me, but maybe it's more than that." I started fidgeting with a diamond bracelet my grandmother had gotten me one Christmas.

"Are you saying you think it's him doing all this?" I watched his hand that wasn't on the steering wheel feel his side for his gun.

I looked at him and frowned. "No," I said quickly. "I mean, I don't think so. He didn't seem to know about any of this, but don't go hunting him down just yet, Brian."

He relaxed some and let his hand rest on his thigh again. "Aren't you friends with his brother Rush?"

"I don't know if I consider him a friend, but he hangs around us. It's so weird this stalker is using Rush's name. What do you know about Tobias? You looked pissed at the mention of his name."

"I was just preparing myself for you to tell me he was a prime suspect to all of this. That's all. And are you sure Rush is telling you the truth? You know you can hide apps and schedule things to send at different times."

My chest tightened. "What?"

"Yeah, I figured you would know that, but I forget you're not really tech savvy." He pulled up to the gate, waved at Mr. Bill, and drove through the gates once they opened. "I'm not saying he's guilty, I'm just saying you need to watch him, and you have him right where you need him. Get close to him. As close as you can to figure him out. Maybe his brother, too."

"How close?"

"If it were me, I'd do whatever I needed to for answers. I'm not saying let the guy in your pants or anything, but make him trust you. Make him think you're completely into him. Use that Bonovich seduction charm you were born with." His smirk was laced with evil.

I laughed. "This is the weirdest pep talk I've ever had."

He chuckled and pulled into our driveway. He drove around to the garage and parked on the far left. I hated not seeing my Audi in the middle.

He killed the engine and looked at me. "I don't know why I didn't think of it before, but if his brother is being an ass and doesn't even know you, and Rush is inching his way into your group of friends so fast, I'd consider them both an enemy until proven otherwise. Just don't let them know they're under your radar."

"He was in the room when my Audi was attacked."

"And what if he put his brother up to it? It's just so weird they are using Rush's name. Unless R stands for something else. I'm sure they aren't the only Trues in the world, but they are the only ones in Grove and surrounding counties that would know anything about you. I had my people check already."

His people were pirates, ruthless and great at getting information. "Just don't let *'your people'* do anything stupid just yet. This has gotten so out of hand already, and I feel like it's just begun."

"Just keep all suspects close. It's better to have them under your nose and thinking you're naive."

I rubbed the tension in my forehead. "How would Tobias get into our community to hurt my car if it was him?"

"Maybe he has friends who live here or came through the woods surrounding our subdivision. There are so many possible scenarios, but we can't narrow anything down until you dig deeper and not trust everything the person says."

"This is so insane. If this person is determined to be secretive, don't you think he'd use a different name?"

He shrugged. "Maybe that is exactly why they are using Rush's name, Jorja. Keep the attention on the Trues and off them. They are confusing and scaring you and that seems to be the purpose. Just don't trust these guys with your life but get to know them. Get close but be careful. I know you know how to defend yourself, and if things go AWOL, you tell me, and I'll handle it."

The thought of him "handling it" made me shiver.

"When Mom and Dad figure out who he is they won't like me hanging around with someone from that side of town."

"I think they'll be fine if you tell them your motives. Don't mention this to your friends either. They may blow your cover. And who knows, maybe it's one of them."

Tears burned my eyes at that revelation. I couldn't fathom it being one of them, but it had to be someone who knew things about me. Or at least they claimed to. They haven't come out with anything they actually know yet which made the burning in my stomach intensify tenfold.

"Sorry, Kid. I know this is heavy stuff, but people like us can't trust anyone. From my experience, everyone just wants to use people like us to get what they want."

I ran my fingers through my hair wishing I could just be a kid again when I was oblivious to most things that came with being a Bonovich. "So, does this mean you're saying everyone has to become a suspect at this point, and I can't call anyone a true friend?"

"You stick around here and work with our family and that's exactly what I'm saying, Jorja." His brown eyes were as serious as I had ever seen them.

It started to make more sense why our sister, Olivia, left. She hated all the secrets and lies. She craved normal, but normal had a big price to pay. My parents wrote her off as if she never existed. We had no idea where she was or if she married or had kids. She'd be twenty-eight now. Nothing but vague memories were all I had left of her. I always thought it would feel so lonely to not have your family, but now I realized just how lonely life is for a Bonovich if you can't trust anyone except those in your family. But ... could I even trust them? If it came down to me or the cartel, I knew deep down my parents would always choose the cartel. They were slaves to them, and that was a curse that ran several generations deep.

CHAPTER NINE

Jorja

I woke up in a weird headspace. As I ate breakfast and watched Ruth doing her monthly deep clean, I labeled her as a suspect as well. She was there every single day and knew things we probably didn't think she did. I'd watched *Princess Diaries Two* enough to know that maids claim to know everything. Her whole body wobbled side-to-side as she scrubbed the baseboards below the kitchen cabinets. If it were her doing this, and she was as thorough on revealing secrets and making someone's life a living hell as she were at cleaning and cooking, I'd be doomed. The message I'd gotten the night before was the most worrisome yet. I tried not to even think about it, but it kept me tossing and turning all night. I'd be operating on fumes today after only two hours of solid sleep.

Ready for round three? If you don't admit that your nice car and clothes are from dirty money on social media for everyone in Grove to see, I will share the photos I have of you and Beck. I bet your friend Rebecca will be thrilled to see those. You have until midnight.

I forgot about my eggs for a bit and now they were cold. I pushed the plate to the side and started scrolling through Instagram. This person could hurt my car a million times, and it wouldn't hurt as bad as this would. Becca was my best friend, and such a thing would crush her. Her and Beck may be on and off again, but he's still *her* on-again-off-again mess. What happened had been a mistake, but I let it happen, nonetheless.

Beck and I were hanging out working on a parade float to represent Grove High School in the Halloween parade. It was late and everyone else bailed. He and I wanted to stay and get it done so we wouldn't have to make another late night of it. We had been fighting a weird sexual tension that entire summer. A bucket of royal blue paint got spilled and lucky me slipped and fell in it. Beck attempted to help me only to slip and fall, too. I never in a million years would have thought I'd come close to having sex with Beck, especially not on the paint-covered concrete floor of my garage. We swore to never speak of it again—practically naked and covered in blue paint. I'm just thankful things didn't go as far as they could've.

One thing the message provided me was the comforting fact that it couldn't be Beck. This person had pictures, and Beck was a bit preoccupied with me to be taking photos. It couldn't be Becca because she was too sensitive to not have already called us out on it if she had caught us. The ideas of who it could've been taking the pics were whirling around like a tornado. What if Tommy, Wren, or Jena came back to help and caught us making out and stripping out of our clothes? What if Rush was visiting Grove and had a friend there ... *Wait.* Tommy said he knew Rush before he moved down here. That meant Rush could've been visiting Tommy's and his house is just down the road from my house. Or Tobias and Rush could've both been there. Tommy never told us about Rush, but why?

I set my phone down and checked on Ruth's progress. She had started cleaning the upper cabinets. I wanted to ask Brian what to do, but I already knew what he would tell me. *A Bonovich never rats out a Bonovich. Snitches get stitches, always remember that. I don't care if we're blood or not.* He told me that when I saw him shoving a brick of cocaine into a potato sack. He then told me how much it was worth and how seven of those blocks paid for my car. I didn't understand how my parents and grandparents hadn't been victims of a drug bust. It was more than obvious a funeral home couldn't meet the supply and demand of our lifestyle. However, the rumor that our family has been loaded from smart stock investments isn't a total lie.

I sighed and stood. I thanked Ruth for breakfast and headed up to my room. I thought about the two choices I had. One, I could stay quiet about our "dirty money" and go ahead and tell Becca myself before this asshole released it. Two, I could tell one of my family's dirty little secrets. If they got caught, I'm still a minor so I couldn't get in trouble for anything. They'd most definitely be taken to Federal prison and lose everything they owned. Brian would go down, too. Then it'd get even uglier when their division of the cartel found out. They'd be after me or Olivia if they could find her. There is no telling the things they would do to us to ensure my parents and brother didn't give up their names to the narcs. I'd been given that speech enough times to know the consequences of spilling the beans.

I knew what I had to do, and it was gonna hurt. I called Beck.

"Hey, what's up," he answered. He sounded out of breath.

"What are you doing?"

"Working out at the moment. Did you know I can press one-fifty now? I'm an effin' beast." His voice got deeper with his boasting.

"That's great, but we have a problem." Tears burned at the rims of my eyes. I wanted to find this person and put my boater's license to use.

"Oh, no, why? Do we all need to come over? I can go pick up—"

"No. No one needs to come over. I have to go talk to Becca about what happened between you and I that—" my voice broke "—that night in the garage, Beck."

"Why? No! We swore to keep that a secret forever, Jorja! Why in the hell would you want to out us like that? I get it weighing heavy on your conscience because it does me too, but we know it would cause more damage than good! We can be pissed at ourselves forever before I hurt her like that!" His voice was so loud it was like having him on speaker. I held the phone farther away from my ear as he continued to yell, but his words were now unintelligible from the distance that saved my eardrum. The tears started to flow. I hated how all of this was starting to hurt those around me.

When he calmed down, I put the phone back to my ear. "Beck, I have to protect my family. This person, whoever it may be, threatened me with something I can't let happen."

"What the hell did they threaten you with?" His voice was calmer, but still full of fear and hurt.

I swallowed hard and wiped my eyes. He didn't know about the drugs, at least not all the fine details. He figured it was marijuana when he and the others confronted me about my family dealing drugs last year. It all blew over when Colorado stopped making it illegal.

"Things I can't talk about. Beck, I'm so sorry."

"I'll tell her. You have enough going on as it is." He always tried to play hero when things went wrong.

"No!" I cried. "I will make it my fault somehow. I will figure out how to tell her without her hating you, too.'

"You don't—"

"I do. Let me handle it."

He fell silent for a few moments. "We're going to find whoever it is and stop them, Jorja. And when we do …"

I didn't know if his mind went the same direction as mine did when he stopped talking, but I doubted his mind was as dark as mine. I did hope he was right about finding them though. They needed to be stopped.

I didn't know what else to say because sorry would never be enough, so I hung up and stared at my phone. I had to try to do something before midnight if I could. My gut kept going back to this all being Tobias with the way he treated me. He seemed like a big enough asshole to try to pin this all on his brother. Plus, Brian said he knew him. Maybe Brian did something to him that he didn't tell me about. He definitely had a chip on his shoulder when it came to me. He was the only one that I knew recently to show any disdain toward me. He may have acted innocent when I had barged into his classroom, but he could just be a really good actor.

I texted Rush.

Me: Whatcha' up to?

Rush: Well dad just got called into work so our plans to hike got squashed. Why? Everyone wanting to hang out or have another Who Dun' It meeting?

Me: What does your dad do?

Rush: He's a cop in Grove. I'm surprised you didn't know that.

Me: I don't keep up with who the cops are.

I didn't. Most of them were either in cohorts with all the sleazy things my dad was a part of, or they were lazy. I had never heard of Officer True, so he was mostly likely one of the lazy ones who sat around in the office watching TV.

Rush: So, why'd you text, Jorja?

Me: Well, I haven't been the most welcoming so I thought we could hang out.

It took him more than a minute to reply.

Rush: Ok, sure. I can ask my brother to use his truck since the movers still haven't brought all of my things, including my truck. I know you don't have a car right now. What do you want to do? Hang out there, come here or what?

Me: Did you say you guys were going hiking before your dad got called in?

Rush: Yeah, we were.

Me: Then let's go hiking.

Rush: Don't take this the wrong way, but you don't exactly seem like the type to go hiking.

He wasn't wrong. I liked the outdoors when we had bonfires or spent all of our days at the lake during summer. I wasn't into hiking because of bears, loose rocks, and all the other things that could possibly go wrong. But I was desperate. I needed to find out more about him and Tobias. I was desperate for any leads that could reveal the one doing this.

Me: I'm actually a fabulous hiker.

I had the right boots and coat and things for hiking, but never wore them that I could remember. At least I'd look the part.

Rush: You're a liar.

Me: You won't know if you don't come pick me up.

Rush: Let your scary guard man know I'm coming to get you.

I laughed and was happy I was still able to under the current circumstances.

Me: Mr. Bill takes his job seriously. Lol I'll let him know you're coming.

Rush: I'll be there in twenty minutes. Wear good boots, not those Ugg things you wear. They're too slick on the bottom.

Me: You pay attention to what I wear on my feet?

Rush: Maybe.

My lips curled a little, and I quickly ignored the flutter in my chest. This was a mission, not a time to be letting some guy play with my emotions.

CHAPTER TEN

Jorja

I looked ahead at Rush as he walked the rocky trails as if it were as easy as breathing. I was in shape and had to be for cheer. I also ran track every spring, yet there I was, out of breath and having to take a break. I blamed it on altitude, but Rush was quick to call me out on living in the mountains my entire life. He looked over his shoulder and chuckled as he stopped and turned around. When he made it to me, he took his backpack off and set it on a large boulder. I watched him pull out two water bottles.

"You know," he said as he handed me a water bottle, "for someone who hikes you sure aren't prepared. No water, or backpack ... I still think it's adorable you tried to bring your purse like there'd be a mall at the top."

"I think I can drop that pretense now then." I smiled before taking a long drink of the water. "It's the dead of winter. Why is it so hot?" I set the water down in the snow and took my scarf off.

Rush looked at his thin black jacket and jeans. He wore gold mirrored sunglasses and the same tan Carhartt beanie he'd had on the night at the lake. "The bright snow makes it hotter than you think because the sun reflects off the snow, not to mention all the movement warms you up." He flexed his gloved hands. "It's important to wear something warm, but you dressed like you're going hiking at Mount Everest and plan on trying to survive a night or two. Those snow pants alone will bake you like an oven up here." His riotous laugh filled the air.

I put my hands on my hips. "I've been skiing."

He shook his head. "Not a damn thing like skiing."

I huffed, and he burst into laughter.

"You're making fun of me!" I balled up some snow in my gloved hands.

His eyes darted toward my hand. "I dare you to throw that at me."

I threw my arm back and forced it forward, lugging the snowball toward his chest. He dodged it dramatically, falling and rolling. When he made it to his feet, he threw two snowballs in my direction. I squealed when one hit me on the left shoulder and the other barely missed my face. I bent down, in such a hurry to build a quick snowball that I was blindsided by the one Rush threw, plastering the side of my face. I stood up straight, my mouth wide open.

He moved his sunglasses to the top of his head. "What are you gonna do about it," he said, taunting me with his heartbreaker grin.

I finished with the snowball I was forming and stalked toward him. He started backing up with a smirk and hands up in surrender. I made sure I kept him backing up until his back slammed into a tree. He wasn't going anywhere in enough time to dodge the snowball straight to his face. He tried to move, but I smashed it in his face like a pie. He started sputtering snow, his laughter igniting mine.

He wiped his face on the sleeve of his jacket. "Nice one."

I curtsied. "Why thank you." When I noticed he was still pinned against the tree because I was so close, I cleared my throat and took a step back so he could move but he didn't. "Aren't you going to move?"

He took my hand and gently pulled me toward him. His mouth inched closer to mine, and I closed my eyes, my heart pounding in my chest. I heard him gasp, and instantly my eyes opened to see his eyes fixated on something behind me. I froze.

"Don't. Move," he whispered.

I did the exact opposite and whipped around, startling a bear digging through Rush's backpack. "Rush, it's a bear," I whispered. I had lived there my whole damn life and not once saw a bear that wasn't in a zoo. It was twenty yards away. Maybe less.

"No duh," he whispered. "And I told you not to move!" I felt him grab the back of my jacket and tug. I backed up slowly until my back pressed against his chest.

"What do we do?"

"Wait until it forgets us and finds the sandwiches. Once it's interested in those long enough to distract it, we'll make a getaway."

I nodded and stayed close to Rush. I gripped the side of his jacket hoping he knew what to do if this thing came after us. Just as he had said, the bear found a paper sack and pulled a sandwich out. Rush grabbed my arm, and we started backing up slowly as quietly as possible. It was hard to have complete silence with the crunch of the deep snow. Once we finally made it a safe distance, I looked at him.

"Aren't they supposed to be hibernating right now?" I shrieked, and my whole body began to tremble.

"Not in places like this where it's a public hiking trail and campgrounds surround it. They have a constant food source from picnics, trash, and apparently backpacks." He frowned.

"You sure know a lot about this stuff, don't you?"

He looked at the braid in my hair, and my eyes followed his hand to the bottom of it that fell just below my chest. He dusted snow from it then looked through the trees where we could still see the bear eating the sandwiches. "Yeah, it's one of my favorite things to do. It's the only thing I have in common with my dad, so it helps to have something to talk about and do with him."

"That's nice." I wanted to mention our almost-kiss but decided against it. It was probably a bad idea anyway.

He nodded and sighed. "That backpack is a total loss. I guess let's just make our way down a different trail and find our way back down. I don't want to get caught up here without food and the things I have in my backpack just in case anything bad happens."

"Like get eaten by a bear?"

He chuckled. "No one is getting eaten by a bear today." He gestured with his head toward the woods ahead of us. "Come on."

We started walking, and I stayed right beside him. I watched him closely, reading him like a map of uncharted territory. He pulled his sunglasses back over his eyes, but not before I noticed the redness around them. It looked like he had spent all night crying.

"What is it, Jorja?" he asked without looking at me.

"Sorry." I felt my cheeks heat up. "Do you lie about not being sad?"

His steps slowed some, and I matched his pace. "I haven't lied to you about anything."

"Sorry to be forward, but your mom recently died, Rush. How are you not sad?"

"Just because I don't lock myself in my room and cry every second of the day doesn't mean I'm not sad." He held back a branch so I could walk through the heavily wooded area. I was ready to get back on the path.

I blinked a few times. "Oh."

"Look, I appreciate you trying to get me to open up and talk about it, but I don't know you like that, and I won't even talk to my dad or brother about it. I do better keeping to myself about these kinds of things." He never made eye contact with me once.

"I'm sorry for bringing it up."

"Don't worry about it. I get it. I'm sure it's weird seeing someone who just lost their mom act as if life were normal. It's just how I deal with it. I still smile and have fun because she'd want me to. She'd be pissed if I moped around, especially in the company of a beautiful girl."

I had been enjoying my time with him so much I forgot I was on a mission to rule him out or prove him guilty. It was odd going from thinking it could possibly be him to praying like hell it wasn't. I was finding that being around Rush was something I wanted to do more often.

"You okay?" he asked, nudging my side gently with his elbow. "That bear shouldn't follow us. There's plenty in my backpack to keep him occupied."

I smiled and shrugged. "Just a bunch on my mind." I still had to break the news to Becca about Beck if I didn't figure out a new plan and fast.

"The messages you've been getting and your car?"

I nodded. "If someone wanted to expose my family, why do they have to go through me?"

"Expose your family of what?"

I shook my head. "Nothing I can talk about. Actually, I'm not even sure why I said that to you in the first place."

"Your family owns Bonovich Funeral Home, Jorja. I'm not sure what they would actually be able to expose your family of. Unless you guys were murdering people to keep business going."

I hoped he was truly naive to all the rumors flying around and not just playing stupid. Either way, I needed to make him feel like I trusted him and give him a little bit of info. "My mom screws half the town's men. I'm sure some kid is pissed she caused their parents a divorce. She's notorious for that."

His laugh came through his nose. "You're serious? How does your dad feel about that? They still married?"

"Brian and I call it more of an agreement than marriage. My mom would take everything my dad owns and ruin him financially, so he stays with her and lets her do whatever she wants." That was what my dad said, anyway. Brian told me he heard Dad tried to hire a hit man to have her killed a few years ago, but he ended up backing out of it because some of his most loyal customers enjoy her favors. Mom was just another one of dad's chess pieces on the checkerboard of sales. It was weird getting information like that at the age of fifteen and being numb to it. I didn't even know if I fully believed that or not.

"That sounds miserable. I can't imagine being married to someone who spent more time in another man's bed than our own. You can't be careless with the time you have with the one you love. Our days are so limited."

Hearing him talk about marriage and commitment like that made my heart swell. I looked at him and noticed his sunglasses were back over his eyes. "Sometimes people don't marry for love."

"Which is terrible."

I tilted my head to the side as I looked at him. "You think about marriage?"

He shrugged. "Sometimes, don't you?"

I chewed on the inside of my cheek as I thought about that. I didn't think about marriage. Honestly, I had always had this weird feeling I was going to die at a young age. My parents blamed it on growing up around the funeral home and caring for the dead. I have this irrational fear that if I try to plan my future too much, I'm jinxing myself.

"That must be a no with that look on your face."

I looked at him again and laughed. "I guess so."

"You're really hard to figure out, you know that?"

I shrugged. "I've heard that a time or two."

"Yet everyone wants to be with you or be you. I don't get it. Don't take this the wrong way, but you're considered royalty. Not like Snow White royalty but like Maleficent."

My lips curled ever so evilly. "Good. That means they fear me. I have them where I want them."

"And you're proud of that?" I wish I could see his eyes under those glasses. It'd make it easier to understand where this conversation was headed.

"It's easier being feared than liked. It makes people stay out of my way and leave me alone."

He chuckled but it sounded cold. "Do you hear yourself right now?"

"Loud and clear, actually. It's just who I am. I don't try to be someone I'm not, Rush."

"That's a damn lie. You hide behind your shiny things, bitch persona, and pretty face. You have to have a reason you like people out of your way. Maybe you're protecting them from something, so you keep everyone at a safe distance, yet you suffer because you're lonely."

I cocked my eyes in his direction, feeling naked under his assumption. What exactly did this guy know about me? That thought was enough to bring me back to the reality of why I was with him right now in the first place.

"And what do you think I'm protecting people from?" I stopped walking, crossed my arms, and looked at him.

"I haven't found that piece to the puzzle yet, but just hearing you talk, the way you avoid anyone you don't know and the uneasiness in your eyes proves you're troubled with things that are too much for anyone to make sense of."

I cut my eyes at him. "And you know how?"

"Because I hide skeletons of my own." He held my gaze for a few moments before looking toward the trail. "Wanna head back to the truck or keep going, just a different way?"

My mind was stuck on the mystery of the things that troubled him. "Umm, I'm getting kind of hungry so we could go grab lunch. And please tell me your keys weren't in that backpack."

He chuckled and started walking. "Nope, they are in my pocket."

I caught up with him. "Good." My mind went back to the skeletons, though it shouldn't. I had enough of my own to worry about.

CHAPTER ELEVEN

Jorja

I looked at the time on my phone for the billionth time since sitting down to eat at Chuck's, our local BBQ place. It was *the* place to eat and always had a wait. Unless, you were a Bonovich, of course. Chuck and his wife were regular customers of Brian's. As soon as Rush and I walked in, Chuck himself told the others waiting that we had a reservation. The looks of disapproval and annoyance made it obvious they didn't believe him, yet no one argued. He had us seated and already put in an order for the fried pickles I liked within minutes of entering.

Rush put his hand on top of mine and pushed gently until my hand with the phone was on the table.

"You know it's rude to be on your phone when you're with someone."

I looked up at Rush's playful grin. "Sorry." I placed my phone face down on the table and folded my hands in my lap. The rock in my stomach was growing with worry about the outcome after telling Becca about Beck and myself. I also worried that Rush was somehow going to be a part of all of this and our hanging out would come to an end. He's attractive, sure, but something about being with him puts me at ease. And whether I wanted to admit it or not, I wanted him to kiss me earlier.

"You're really letting this person get to you, huh?"

I frowned and narrowed my eyes in his direction. "Wouldn't you? They hurt my car, they are trying to reveal things they most likely know nothing about and probably aren't true. And now they are trying to get me to admit—" During my quick rant I almost let words fly that I shouldn't. I looked toward the front doors where people were waiting and huffed. "It's getting out of hand."

"I agree, but you're letting them dictate this whole thing. Maybe you should do something about it rather than run scared."

I looked at him. Hopeful that maybe he'd have a productive suggestion. "And what exactly do you think I should do?"

He shrugged. "Something. Anything."

"That's hard when I don't even know who it is. They claim to know things and those things could really hurt my family, Rush."

"So, what kind of things are they?"

"If I wanted it out there'd be no reason for anyone to torment me."

"Must be some really juicy information."

I folded my arms in front of me. "It's just personal. Everyone has their secrets."

He nodded. "And skeletons."

I raised a brow. "What are you implying? We already had a conversation similar to this."

He chuckled as he took a drink of his water. He set the cup down and stirred the ice around with his straw. "You really suck at hiding that you have things to hide."

"And you're really good at giving me a headache."

"Sorry, I just wanna help, and it's hard when you're all secretive. I'm usually pretty good at giving advice, but I have to know what's going on first."

Maybe telling him wasn't such a bad idea or maybe he was fishing for secrets and he was considering this hanging out a mission to do just that. I still hadn't ruled him out completely, but seeing what he'd do with this information, that I'd most likely have told Becca tonight anyway, would help see what kind of guy he really was. He was basically Switzerland in our circle of friends right now until he did something wrong to tell me otherwise.

"If I tell you …" When he leaned forward a little, I laughed. "I said if. Calm down."

"It's better than no."

"If I tell you, you can't say a word. I want to trust you, but trust is something I struggle with."

He sat back when the waitress set the basket of fried pickles and ranch on the middle of the table. When she walked off, he leaned forward again. "Jorja, I know you have no reason to trust me, but I really won't say anything. I want to help. It's just unfortunate for me since this asshole chose to use something close to my name."

I rubbed my forehead, suddenly feeling hot and my stomach in knots. "I'll write it down." I opened my purse and pulled out a pen and paper. I wrote down that they threatened to out Beck and me if I didn't tell everyone my dad bought me things with dirty money. I slid it over to him and chewed on my lip as he read it.

He slid it back in my direction. "What happened with Beck?" he whispered.

I felt nauseous. "We … almost had sex. I mean, super close. It didn't happen, but we made out and clothes were coming off …" I stopped talking when my eyes got hot with tears.

His eyes widened. "Oh. And he and Becca are ..." He nodded. "Gotcha. Wow. Ummm ...Well, tell everyone about the other. Everyone knows it anyway."

"But they don't have proof. If I say it, I could get my family in a lot of trouble," I whispered.

"So, then you take the heat for them and tell Becca before all of Grove finds out."

Tears filled my eyes. The thought of Becca hating me hurt.

He nudged my foot under the table. "Hey, at least you have me ... right?"

"Rush, these are the people I've grown up with. My friends. No offense, but I don't know you like I know them."

The look in his eyes was so sincere it comforted me a bit. "Maybe she won't be upset. Was it an accident?"

I hated talking about this here. That's why I wrote it down. I reached across the table and took the paper. I started marking out the confession. "I wish I could say it was an accident, but it wasn't. Knocking a glass over without noticing is an accident. We knew exactly what we were doing and didn't stop."

"They aren't even together. Sooo, technically ..."

I shook my head as I scribbled out the words more making sure they were illegible. "That's not the point, Rush. They are and they aren't. The 'they are' part is what matters right now."

"Well ..."

I looked at him waiting to see what would come after his long pause. He took a fried pickle and dipped it into the ranch before taking a bite. I could see curiosity and maybe a hint of sureness in his eyes.

"Your family is toxic, you do realize that, right?"

He wasn't wrong, but it still pissed me off coming from a guy that didn't know me at all. "That's the rumor."

"Do you plan on following their trend, whatever *that* may be? I know what I've heard, but like everyone else, I can't prove it, so I don't know the truth from a lie."

He was the first person to ask me that question. I had asked myself that question a thousand times a day, but always replayed my mother's words and decided I'd stick with the life I knew. But hearing him ask it brought out a different feeling inside. Hope.

"I like to pretend I won't," I admitted in a whisper.

I knew by the look in his eyes that those words confirmed my family truly was toxic. That the lies I told and the secrets I kept were worse than I liked to admit even to myself. His eyes softened when tears fell down my cheeks.

"Maybe this is the opportunity for you to break the chains your last name has on you."

I wiped my cheeks. "You swear it's not you doing this?"

"It's not me. I wouldn't do something like this."

I believed him. "And your brother?"

"I highly doubt it. Behind his tough and hidden persona, he's kind. If he wanted to confront someone about anything, he'd go straight to them and not be all theatrical about it."

I remembered Toby's comments to me in their kitchen and knew that had to be true. He had no problem speaking his mind. I put my head in my hands and let out a shaky breath.

"I guess you need to decide whose secrets are worth keeping. Your own or your parents."

I sat up straighter and looked at him. "I really hope you meant it when you said I'd still have you through all of this."

"I wouldn't have said it if I didn't mean it."

I nodded and looked down at the basket of pickles. I wasn't hungry anymore but knew I needed to eat something. I grabbed another pickle and drowned it with ranch. As I chewed, I thought about what he said about my parents' lies or my own. For now, I'd take the heat because outing my parents could turn deadly. That involved more than my parents and brother. So many others were involved who had families of their own. Granted, it was all their fault for becoming involved, but so many were involved by association. Like me.

"I'll tell Becca. In the meantime, I'm going to try to figure out how to outsmart this person. Find out who they are and what they want exactly."

"Jorja found her balls." He started cracking up, his shoulders moving up and down.

I laughed a little and kicked his foot under the table. "I don't have balls; I'm just finding my backbone. That sounds better."

"You sure? I could always check and be sure you don't have any." My mouth fell open, to which he threw up his hands and said, "Kidding."

I laughed when I heard him whisper, *sort of.*

I shook my head and smiled. "All jokes aside, will you please help me?"

"I thought that's what I'm doing, Jorja."

I grinned and started eating again. I swore if he was lying to me and somehow fooled me, I'd put that boater's license to good use with zero hesitation.

CHAPTER TWELVE

Jorja

When Becca knocked on the door, I felt like I was going to throw up. I ran my fingers through my loose curls and opened the door. I tried to smile but couldn't.

"You okay?" she asked as she scrunched her nose. "You look nervous."

"I am."

"Is there another plot twist with creepy-stalker?"

I started walking, and she followed. "Something like that."

When we made it to my room, she took her normal seat on the loveseat closest to the fireplace. I didn't sit. Instead, I paced in front of the fireplace.

"Becca, they threatened to reveal a secret I've been keeping if I didn't say what they wanted me to." When she started to talk, I shook my head to stop her. "Please, just let me talk. You'll hate me forever, and I just want to get it over with." I paused for a moment to take a steadying breath. "Becca ... ummm ... uh ... Beck and I ... we made out back in the fall when we were working on that float. We didn't have sex or anything. It was just ... close. I made him swear not to say anything, so please don't be mad at him. You and him were having one of your fights and weren't dating, not that it doesn't matter. It was wrong. It just happened, and we let it go too far." As horrible as this situation was, it did feel good that she knew now. Like an illness I was finally cured from.

She opened her mouth to speak but didn't. Her lips pressed firmly together, and her eyes narrowed at the floor. I stopped pacing and stood still, waiting for what I deserved.

When her eyes met mine, she started to cry, and it gutted me. "Why didn't you just tell me then?"

Tears fell down my cheeks. "I have no good answer for that except that I'm a coward."

"Did you practice that line?" she asked, cutting her eyes at me.

"No ... What?" I frowned.

"Do you think saying you're a coward will make me feel better?"

My heart raced, and it took me a second to form words. "Becca, no. I'm being honest and that's the best description for what I am."

She stood. "We're done."

"Becca." More tears pooled in my eyes.

"Done!" she yelled and wiped her eyes. "Friends don't keep things like that from friends, Jorja! You're nothing but a spoiled little bitch who has to have everything even if it doesn't belong to you!"

I wanted to get defensive. I wanted to yell back and start listing all the wrong things she's done like leading Beck on and screwing other guys when they weren't dating, but I didn't. Listing her wrongs wouldn't right mine. Diverting this problem to make her look bad would only make me look worse. I deserved this. She had every right to hate me.

"Do you have anything to say?" She cried more.

"I am so sorry, Becca. Even if you don't believe it, I am."

"Liar! And even if you are sorry, it's too late for that."

I watched her leave my room and stood there a moment to calm myself down. I didn't deserve a shoulder to cry on, but Rush offered his if this went the way I knew it would. Before texting him, I texted Beck to let him know I told her.

Me: She knows. She hates me. I'm sorry.

Beck: I know she already texted me and told me to never speak to her again. I can't lose her, Jorja. I'm sorry, but we can't hang out until I fix this with her. Maybe not ever. I love her more than anything.

Me: I know. It's ok. Win her back, Beck. I'll be ok.

Tears hit the screen, and I wiped them off on my jeans. I dialed Rush's number, and when he answered, I lost control and started sobbing.

"On my way," was all he said before hanging up.

I pulled my sleeves over my hands and wiped my eyes. No one was home, not even the housekeeper. I had already added Rush to the approved list to come through the gate, so I went downstairs to wait.

When he got there, I opened the door and found my way into his arms after he made it past the threshold. How I grew to trust him so fast baffled me, but I was thankful that in the midst of assuming he was guilty, he completely surprised me and may very well have been the only one I could count on through this.

He rubbed my back. "I'm assuming it didn't go well."

"She hates me. Beck is having to avoid me to work things out with her. Wren and Jena love drama and will most likely side with her. Tommy will play both sides, but if Beck tells him to avoid me, he will. And you—" He stopped me before I could finish the thought.

"You have me, Jorja. I'm not going anywhere."

"Why are you being so nice to me?" I sniffled.

"I'm not sure right now is a good time to discuss that."

I looked up at him, noticing his shirt was soaked with tears. I patted his chest even though it was pointless. "What do you mean?"

He chuckled and ran his thumbs across the skin below my eyes, wiping tears away. "If it isn't obvious, then I really need to work on my dating skills."

I chewed on my lip. "Oh." I wiggled out of his hold and took a step back. He was right. Right then wasn't the time to discuss this even if I wanted to. I couldn't think about dating anyone at the moment.

"I understand, Jorja. I do. We don't have to talk about it."

"I didn't say that."

He wet his lips and smiled as he put his hands in his pockets. "*Oh* was pretty clear. I swear it's cool. No worries. I'm your friend before anything else, and my intentions are pure. I'm not being here for you in hopes we'll take things further."

I felt heat rush to my cheeks. "I didn't say that either."

A hint of curiosity and excitement flickered in his eyes. He cleared his throat. "*Oh* implies a lot of things. Anyway, let's talk about why I'm really here or not talk at all. We could just watch a movie or something to try to calm you down."

The mention of calming down made me notice how badly my hands were shaking. "I need to figure out what to tell them now. Do I tell them I told Becca, or do I wait for midnight to pass and they post about it so God and my momma will know?"

"I say tell them and ask exactly what it is they want and are trying to accomplish."

I chewed on the inside of my cheek. "Don't you think they would've already told me?"

"I don't think they plan on playing fair. You're gonna have to stop cowering down like a scared little dog."

I frowned. "Sooo, about that movie ..." Just as the words left my mouth, the door opened, and Brian came in.

He looked at Rush with that over-protective-brother scowl on his face. "You Toby's brother?"

Rush nodded and put his hands in his pockets. "We do have the same face."

"Rush, this is my brother, Brian." I smiled when Rush held a hand out to him but Brian didn't take it. Typical. "He's a friend."

"That's what they all say, but I know how a guy's mind works." Brian hung his keys on the hook next to mine near the door. I never remembered to hang my keys there. They always ended up at the bottom of my purse.

Brian took his attention off Rush and looked at me seriously. "You okay? You've been crying."

"It's just a lot and now Becca hates me."

Brian rolled his eyes. "You knew that'd happen."

I didn't like how cold my brother was being, but it probably wasn't geared toward me. He probably had a million drug deals and other issues on his mind.

I nodded. "Yeah ... still hurts, Brian."

He shrugged and pointed at Rush. "Don't do anything stupid or you'll answer to me."

It was my turn to roll my eyes. "Real cliché ..."

"I mean it." Brian used his index and middle fingers to point at his eyes and then at Rush's before walking toward Dad's office. He worked there from time to time when business got serious.

I laughed and took Rush's hand and started leading him toward the stairs. "Let's go upstairs." I let go of his hand when my foot hit the first step, I looked over my shoulder to make sure he was still following.

When we made it to my room, I watched him stand awkwardly, looking around. His eyes went to my bed and then to the sitting area.

I grinned. 'Rush, you've been here before."

"Yeah, not alone with you. I don't want to make the wrong move and you think I'm here for other reasons."

I raised both brows. "I thought we already established that."

"We did." He walked over to the large sofa directly across from the fireplace and sat down.

I shut the bedroom door and went and sat on the couch next to him. I took my phone out of my pocket and my thumb hovered over the screen as I debated my next move.

"You gonna text them?"

I looked up from my phone and met his eyes. "Can you do it?"

He held his hand out, and I put the phone in it. I covered my face and peeked through my fingers as he texted. He looked at me through his lashes, smiled a little, and then peered down at the phone again. I let my hands fall when he set the phone down.

"What'd you say?" My voice shook.

He handed me back the phone. "Well ... first I called them every name under the sun. Then I told them they can't win this. I also asked why they were doing it and what they wanted to accomplish."

My stomach tightened. I felt like I might puke. "You're just gonna piss them off worse."

"Pretty sure they're already pissed off about something or they wouldn't be doing this in the first place." He leaned back against the couch and folded his arms behind his head. "I know this is off topic, but would your parents be pissed I'm here?"

When I realized I was chewing on my nails, I stopped. "They don't care and are too busy to notice." I looked at my phone when it started going nuts with notifications. I saw a few from Tommy, Jena, and Wren. I opened Jena's first and didn't even finish reading it because all she did was call me a bitch and tell me how horrible I am. Wren's wasn't any different. Tommy sent me a middle finger. Nothing from the one who caused all of this. I was so comfortable living in the lies I told for my family and the ones that didn't hurt my friends.

Rush took my phone, and I watched him power it off. "No more tonight."

I reached for it, but he moved it higher out of my reach. "Rush! What if they text back?"

"You've had enough for one night. Whatever is coming next can wait. Try to clear your head the best you can and relax."

Tears started to fall again. "I'm not so sure that's possible."

"We can try." He moved his arms and put his hands on his lap. Well, except one. His left hand took my right.

He had no idea how much saying *we* meant to me. He was right, as impossible as his suggestion was. I sighed sadly and wiped my eyes with my free hand. I looked down at our intertwined fingers and tried not to overthink it. I just let it be and rested in the fact that I wasn't alone, and the guy I doubted the most was the only one who gave a damn at all. Even if I was a ho like Wren called me.

It was as if he sensed my need for him, and he tugged my hand a little before pulling me close to him and holding me against his chest. "We are all bad people, Jorja," he said quietly as he played with my hair. "Some are just better at hiding it."

I closed my eyes tightly, causing more tears to spill down my cheeks. "What do you know about bad, Rush? You've been nothing short of perfect, and I gave you such a hard time at first."

"With good reason. I came into town at the same time all this started. You were protecting yourself. It made sense."

I stayed close to him, relaxed against his chest, and tilted my head up to look at him. He was attractive, almost perfect, but him in this moment couldn't be described. I couldn't recall a time when a guy sincerely cared about me other than my brother. All the other guys wanted one thing. Rush wanted more than just this, that was obvious, but he wasn't pushy. He was just sincere and there. Two things I never knew I'd begin to crave from a person.

CHAPTER THIRTEEN

Jorja

I woke up covered with my gray fluffy throw blanket and a pillow under my head on the couch. It was dark except for the orange glow of the chandelier seeping through the cracked bathroom door. I slightly remembered drifting off to sleep mid-conversation with Rush. I was asking him about his old school and friends there, his mom, his dad, all while strategically avoiding the mention of his brother. He missed his friends. He was quiet and reserved when it came to his mom, but he did say he missed her so bad his heart physically hurt. After that, he went on to talk about hiking and how he shared the love for it with his dad.

I sat up and yawned as I squinted my eyes to try to make out the dark room. I didn't see Rush anywhere, and judging by the darkness outside my window, it was late. I moved the blanket and stood, stretching a moment before walking out of the room. I could hear my mom and dad talking as I made my way downstairs. I couldn't make out what they were saying until I got closer to the living room. I stopped walking and stayed hidden around the corner when I heard my name mentioned in hushed tones. I pressed my palms and cheek against the wall.

"Maybe we should just tell her. She deserves to know before he tells her."

Her meant me. I could feel it even though they didn't say my name.

"Marrisa—" my father's deep voice was hard to cover even in a whisper "—she keeps all of our secrets and tells our lies. She is a product of the life we hate but are forced to love. I lost one daughter. I cannot lose another." The way his voice broke made me want to peek around the corner and see if my father was capable of crying.

"This bastard is tormenting our daughter because of you! The least—"

"Lower your tone," he warned.

"I will not be told what to do. I'm a grown ass woman, Jerome!" Her tone sent shivers down my spine. I hadn't heard my father called anything but Jerry except for the time my mom told me his real name when I asked when I was younger. "You can put a stop to the madness. You could tell her and handle them on your own."

I had zero idea what they were talking about, but I had never thought highly of my mother until then. Whatever he was hiding, she was sticking up for me.

"And you show you're concerned now? You have spent almost every night away in other men's beds when she needs you here right now. To be a damn mother for once!"

I jumped when I heard the sound of a slap. I closed my eyes and knew she had hit him. I tried to tell myself to go back to my room, but I couldn't walk away.

"To appease your business! They're business calls, and if I wasn't so far into this mess I would've left you the moment I found out I was pregnant with Jorja! If you hadn't made me lie about who she should really be calling—"

"I'm her father!" he shouted, then the sound of glass shattering against a wall made every muscle in my body constrict. "If she knew an ounce of the real truth, this asshole will get her to speak and we'd all be dead!"

All the oxygen left my lungs. I wanted to get away and not hear another word, but my feet wouldn't listen. A few moments of deafening silence passed.

I hurried to my room and quietly shut my door so no one would know I had been out. I found my phone on the end table by my bed on the charger. I didn't put it there, so Rush must have. I grabbed a duffle bag from my closet and started shoving clothes in it. So many things ran through my head as a steady stream of tears rolled down my cheeks. My dad wasn't my dad. Not by blood. My mother called those other men "business" and it sounded like I was the product of one of her "business trips". All the disrespect I had for my mother was null and void now. It sounded like she did these things for my dad and he had her keep this a secret. I zipped the bag closed once it was packed.

I opened my window and wedged myself out until my feet were planted firmly on the slanted rooftop. I lowered myself carefully until I was sitting and could ease myself toward the edge. I grabbed a branch that stuck out from the large oak tree. My dad threatened to have this tree cut down when my sister had boys sneaking in and out, but I'm thankful he never did.

I made it to the woods and hills that surrounded the suburbs. Going past the gate would cause concern with Mr. Bill. Tonight was his turn for the night shift, and he'd alert my parents immediately. I took my phone from my back pocket and called Rush, thankful I had anyone to call at all. I had thought about Brian, but I didn't want to upset him about any of this until I made sense of it.

"Hello?" It wasn't Rush's voice, but Tobias's.

"Is Rush there? It's Jorja."

He sighed in annoyance. "Clearly, I saw your name across the screen."

I frowned. "Is Rush there?"

"He's asleep."

"Do you normally answer his phone when he's sleeping?"

"No one usually calls him at midnight. I thought something may be wrong. He told me he's worried about you and fell asleep with his phone waiting to hear from you. Are you okay?"

I hated to wake him, but I needed somewhere to go. What I was about to ask would be pushing it when it came to Tobias. He wasn't exactly inviting. "Please don't wake him up, but no, I'm not okay. I'm actually walking through the woods and trying to make it to the highway right now. My parents have no idea I'm gone, and I want to keep it that way." My lips started to tremble, but I remained composed. I didn't want to give him the satisfaction of hearing me cry.

"You're what?" he almost shouted. "Please tell me it's not the woods that surround your neighborhood."

The sound of a stick snapping in the distance made me jump. I wouldn't have thought anything of it, but his worried voice changed that. "Why?" I looked over my shoulder and was thankful the moon was bright enough to illuminate the space around me.

"Ah hell. You are, aren't you?"

I chewed on the inside of my cheek before pressing my lips together. "Mmmhmm."

"You live in Colorado in the mountains. Mountain lions and all kinds of predators are out there. You don't go camping much, do you?" I could hear the sounds of fabric rustling. "And my brother told me about the run-in with the bear on the hike. Stupid ..."

"I've never been camping, and I'm sure I'm not that interesting to whatever is out here. And I'm not stupid." I frowned.

He growled and mumbled something under his breath. I heard a vehicle door open and shut. "I'm on my way. Do you at least know your way to the road?"

Now every little sound was making me jump. Being so upset, my adrenaline was up, and I just wanted out of that damn house. Walking seemed like a good idea at the time. "I do. I think. I should be able to just go straight less than a mile and get to the highway."

"Stay on the phone with me and keep walking." I could hear the roar of an engine. "I'm setting the phone in the seat on speaker, so I'm here. Let me know if anything happens."

"Okay." I thought about hanging up because, honestly, what could he do being on the phone and not here?

As I walked, he'd ask me if I could see headlights coming through the trees at all. When I'd tell him no, he'd say walk faster. At one point, I tripped over a stick which freaked him out.

"Are you okay?"

I sighed. "I'm fine."

"Define 'fine'."

I laughed and kept moving forward. "I have all my fingers and toes. I'm fine. I tripped over a stupid stick."

He huffed. Toby being all protective shocked me, but also gave me hope he wasn't a complete jackass.

"Toby, I see lights. Is that you?"

"I'm about to pull over on the shoulder where you should be walking out, but not there yet. I'm sure you're just seeing other cars driving down the road."

I kept walking, the sound of cars in the distance getting louder. "I never knew this highway was this busy this late."

"It's the main highway," he stated.

I squinted my eyes and could see the road. "I'm so close."

I saw his truck through the trees and felt instant relief, not a feeling I'd expect to feel seeing Tobias. I picked up my pace and finally made it to him. He got out of the truck, walked around to my side, took the bag from my hands, and opened the passenger door.

"Thanks," I said, getting in and watching him shut the door for me. I looked out the rear window and saw him put the duffle in the back end. When he got inside,

I studied him, trying to gauge his expression for any clue as to what he was thinking. He was hard to read, but so nice to look at. Even though Rush and he were identical twins, I didn't have a hard time telling them apart. Rush always had an amused smirk on his face while Toby's stayed in wry amusement.

I chewed on my lip and fidgeted with the zipper on my jacket. "Is your dad going to be upset with me coming over?"

"The only thing he'll be upset over is that I let you walk through those woods alone at all." He pulled onto the road.

"Is that why you came after me? Because he'd be mad?"

"I came because my brother cares about you. Even if I'd rather leave you to the mountain lions, I was raised to do the right thing."

I blanched. "Excuse me? I believe I'd rather walk if you're going to be an ass."

"You asked a question, and I simply answered it. Honestly." I couldn't tell if the rise at each corner of his mouth was because he was enjoying pissing me off or because he was kidding.

"Brutally honest." I huffed and looked out the window.

He shrugged. "Honest nonetheless."

I rolled my eyes but turned to face the window so he wouldn't see the tears starting to form. "I'm tired, and it's been a long day and night. Can you just knock the assery down a notch?" I turned my head to face him after wiping my eyes.

He chuckled quietly. "Yes, I can tone down the 'assery'."

"Why do you hate me so much?" I snapped.

His lips formed a hard line. "I don't hate you. It's just really hard to tolerate people like you."

Both of my brows shot up. "People *like* me?"

"Don't play stupid. Yes, people like you. Spoiled. Unappreciative. Think they are above everyone."

I wanted to slap him so bad. "You don't know a damn thing about me! Maybe if you took the time to get to know me instead of mocking me every single time I'm near you, you'd see I'm not the person you think I am!"

"Actually, I've tried that 'getting to know you' thing, and it didn't go so well. You're probably too self-absorbed to remember that, though."

So much for toning down the assery. I glared at him.

He scoffed. "You don't remember?"

I shook my head. "And I'm kind of sick of being the bad guy lately, so spare me the details if I was a bitch."

His parted lips closed, and he nodded. I sighed and looked out the window again. Warm tears still clung to my lashes.

"We can start over," he said softly.

I wiped my eyes and shrugged, keeping my eyes on the dark blur of trees as we passed them.

"Are you crying?"

I sniffed and pulled my sleeves over my hands and wiped my eyes. "No."

"Jorja."

"I'm fine. I'll be fine." More tears started to fall, and my hands trembled. I could feel myself on the brink of a breakdown. I felt the car shift toward the shoulder and looked at Toby as he parked on the side of the road.

"I said I'm fine!"

He didn't say anything, he just stared at me with a knowing look.

I shook my head and bit my bottom lip. "I'm not fine," I whispered, my voice cracking as I finally allowed myself to really cry.

I was scared for what was to come. I didn't want anyone else to be my dad. I didn't want to be threatened and bullied into revealing things about my family that could get them all hurt. I didn't want Becca to find out about me and Beck. I didn't want to lose my friends. I didn't want any bit of this, and it wasn't fair. Whoever was tormenting me knew I'd be the weakest link. They knew exactly what they were doing, and they were succeeding. Rush wanted me to be strong and fight back, but after the revelation tonight, I wasn't so sure that was possible anymore. Everything was shattering around me, including any ounce of confidence I had.

"My dad's not my dad, Toby." I wasn't sure what possessed me to tell him that, but either way, it came out, and it felt okay telling him. He came to my rescue tonight when he didn't have to. That was grounds for trusting someone, right?

A curse word left his lips in a whisper as he kept his eyes on mine. "I'm sorry."

"Don't be. I feel bad even being sad around you right now when you're still mourning the loss of your mother. That's selfish, isn't it? That's only proving your case of me being a self-absorbed bitch." I wiped my eyes.

His brows drew together. "Just because someone else is sad doesn't mean you don't have the right to be sad, too. We can be sad together. That's not what makes you a bitch, Jorja."

I felt myself smile a little despite his ability to be so kind and mean at the same time. "Thanks, I think." I drummed my fingers against my thigh as I looked at him. His jaw muscles were more relaxed now. "I'm sorry for your loss."

He shrugged. "Thanks, but it's her own damn fault. She got what was coming to her. Prime example of reaping what you sow."

"I don't understand. How exactly did she die?"

His hands gripped the steering wheel on 10 and 2. His eyes focused on the Chevy emblem in the center of the wheel. "Do we need to sit here longer or are you ready for me to get you to my house so you can see Rush?"

"I'm sorry, should I have not asked that?" It was odd to feel embarrassed over an honest question that he basically opened the door to.

"No, it's fine, I just don't feel like answering it."

"Then don't. I understand." I looked out the window.

"I'll get you to the house so you can see Rush."

I felt bad that I had forgotten about Rush. Being with Toby was oddly satisfying. I looked at him and nodded. He put the truck in drive and pulled onto the road.

CHAPTER FOURTEEN

Jorja

When we got to their house, Toby got out and came around to open my door, but I opened it before he could. He handed me my bag and pointed to the side door of their house where Rush was standing. I didn't realize the last time I was here they had a carport or that this was where Toby parked his truck. I was hungover and highly offended that morning, though. Aside from their gaudy bathroom and kitchen and Toby's bad attitude, my focus was on getting the hell outta there.

I looked at Rush as he made his way toward me. His eyebrows were all drawn together, and I hated that I caused such a deep frown. He had to weave himself around a workbench that took up a lot of the space and shoved a drill to the side with his foot that was on the ground surrounded by a box of spilled nails. I was too upset to wonder why they allowed the garage to get this dirty.

"Are you okay?" He pulled me into a tight hug. I clung to him and closed my eyes. I knew I needed him even if that confused the hell out of me, and being in his arms with the feeling of total comfort, confirmed just how much I did. "I woke up and my brother left me a note that he was on his way to get you and he took my phone, so I wasn't able to call you. You should've told him to wake me up. I would have come for you." For a moment I wondered why he left a note and didn't text, but then remembered him saying Toby didn't own a cellphone.

I pressed my cheek to his bare warm chest as he rubbed my back. "I'll tell you about what happened, but first I want to be sure it's okay I'm here."

He pulled back enough to look down at me. "Completely fine. My dad is working the next two days and nights. He sometimes pulls forty-eight-hour shifts and stays at the station where he can sleep unless needed."

My eyes widened. "But you'll tell him I'm here?"

He nodded. "I will, but he won't mind. He's super laid back when it comes to me and Toby."

Toby walked around us and into the house. Rush let go of me and took my bag. "Damn, this thing is heavy. How long do you plan on staying?" He chuckled.

Tears filled my eyes, and it irritated me. I didn't want to cry anymore. "I don't know. Tonight is severely messed up, Rush. It sounds like my parents know who my tormenter is and why they are doing this, but my dad ... who isn't my dad—" his eyebrows shot up, and I shook my head and held up a hand "—I'll get to that part in a minute. Anyway, my 'dad' doesn't want to tell me the truth about what sounded like numerous things while my mother does. It sounds like my dad has the ability to end this all but doesn't want to in fear I will learn the truth."

"Do they know you're here?"

I shook my head and wiped my cheeks. "No."

"Does your scary brother know you're here?"

I shook my head again.

He adjusted the strap of my duffle to sit higher on his shoulder. The sight of him with my pink sparkly bag was enough to make me smile even though my world felt shattered. He looked down at the bag and then at me again, returning the smile.

"Does it bring out my abs?" He chuckled when that statement drew my eyes to his stomach that indeed had an almost noticeable six pack. "Okay, not perfect but yo' boy likes food." He patted his stomach.

I shook my head and laughed as my eyes trailed up his chest until I met his eyes. "Can we go inside? I'm exhausted."

He put his arm around my shoulders as he led me inside and through the house. I couldn't remember which room was his, I just remembered it being down the hall and close to the bathroom. He opened the door on the left at the end of the hall and waited for me to go in before he shut the door behind us. The last time I saw his room it was so dark. The lamp on his desk and one beside his bed illuminated the room enough to see it decorated in emerald greens and grays. His dresser was actually a chrome tool cabinet with drawers and a nice size flat screen sat on the wood grain top.

"Sorry, it's a mess. I'd be lying if I said this wasn't normal."

I looked over my shoulder at him. "It's fine. The green is pretty."

"My mom's favorite color. She bought most of this stuff." He set my bag down near his dresser and walked until he was standing beside me. "I'll take the couch and you can stay in here."

"That one of your dad's rules? I don't mind you staying in here with me."

He cleared his throat, indicating his mind went deep into a smutty gutter. "Probably. I'm also certain your dad would want me to as well."

"My 'dad' can kiss my ass." It was odd how the tone of my voice changed at the mention of him now. So quickly his name left my tongue as if I were saying sewer water. I chewed on my lip. "I really don't want to be alone, Rush."

"I guess I can ask for forgiveness later."

I laughed and felt relieved. I sat on the edge of his bed and slipped off the UGG boots Rush hated. I bent down and moved them so they were neatly beside the head of the bed. I looked at my bag and then at Rush.

"Can you hand me my bag?"

He picked it back up, walked over until he was standing in front of me, and set it on the bed. I looked up at him. "Thank you for being here for me. You moved here at the perfect time. I think it's funny how I wanted to hate you so bad, yet here you stand, the only one here for me. I don't deserve it. I am all the bad things Becca said." I opened the bag and pulled out a toothbrush, sweatpants, hoodie, and hairbrush.

"People change. I don't know a single person who hasn't ever done anything wrong. The good people acknowledge it and fix it." I watched as he moved his pillow from the middle of the bed to the right side.

I stood. "I'm going to brush my teeth and change."

"I'll get an extra pillow from Toby. He sleeps with like fifty, I swear. I don't see the point."

"Maybe he pretends it's actually someone in bed with him because he knows he's a mean person who will probably live alone forever."

Rush burst into laughter. "Maybe."

"But in Toby's defense, he did come help me tonight when he didn't have to."

"He isn't as bad as he puts off."

I smiled softly. "I'm starting to see that. I'll be right back." I went down the hall to get ready for bed.

I went into the bathroom and couldn't bring myself to look in the mirror. I had always favored my mother and just assumed blue eyes and math smarts came from somewhere in the family. That happens sometimes and someone will favor an aunt or grandmother from past generations. Nothing came from him or his bloodline, but some other man I didn't know. I wondered if the guy even knew and he just kept quiet. Or if he lived in Grove at all. I brushed my teeth and tried to think about something else. I even tried to sing the ABC song in my head like I did when I was five and made sure I brushed my teeth as long as the dentist said I should. Nothing worked. My mind kept going back to what I'd heard my parents discussing. They'd freak out when they noticed I'm not home, but I didn't care.

After I changed and braided my hair all to one side, I left the bathroom. I went back into Rush's room and found him lying down with his arms folded behind his head. His eyes were heavy, and a sleepy smile appeared when he saw me.

I put my dirty clothes, toothbrush, and hairbrush back in my bag, zipped it shut, and got onto the left side of the bed. I pulled the covers up to my chest and turned onto my side so I could face Rush.

"Sorry I woke you up tonight," I said quietly.

"When are you going to realize I'd drop everything, stay awake for countless hours, and voluntarily inconvenience myself for you?"

"But why?"

"Because I see *you*. Not the 'you' you let everyone else see. I see someone who genuinely wants to be a better person, but she got the bad end of the stick when it comes to the family she was born into."

"You barely know me at all," I whispered.

He smiled at the ceiling before turning onto his side to face me. He tugged on the end of my braid gently. "And it sure is fun getting to know you."

"With all of my baggage?"

"Have you seen my muscles? I can help carry that heavy stuff."

I rolled my eyes and smiled. "And what about you? I feel bad it's always about me. You lost your mom. I only know you like to hike with your dad, you miss your mom, you can't wait to go visit your friends back home, and you make me laugh."

"What else do you want to know?"

"Are any questions off limits?"

He stared past my shoulder, his eyes growing cold a moment before looking at me. "I don't want to talk about how my mom died."

Of course, now that was a major question I wanted to ask, but I'd avoid it. "Is that it?"

He nodded.

"Girlfriends?"

He chuckled. "If I tell you I have one, would it make you jealous?"

"What the hell do you mean?" I grinned.

"It means if it makes you jealous then you must like me."

"Just answer the damn question."

He laughed some more. "I've had a few. Nothing serious."

"Why are you grinning so hard?"

"Because the first question out of all the ones you could ask me, you asked *that* first."

"Anyway ..." I chortled. "Do you plan on visiting your friends back home?"

He nodded. "This summer. Some of us want to go to college together."

"Where are you planning on going?"

He shrugged. "Undecided. You?"

"Looks like we're going to the same college." I reached over to trace a heart-shaped birthmark on his left shoulder. It was the first time I noticed it. "That's incredible."

He looked to where his birthmark was and then at me. As my finger trailed the shape of the heart tiny goosebumps appeared on his skin. "It's why I went with my mom and Toby went with my dad."

I frowned. "Why would that matter?"

"My mom has the same one, just on the opposite shoulder. She called it fate. My dad called it stupid. She wanted the split, he didn't. He said she was the devil to argue with, so he just did what she wanted."

"I'm sure that sucked so bad for you and Toby growing up."

"I mean, we didn't know anything different so it was our norm. It bothered Toby more than it did me. I didn't see the point of being angry over something that just ... was. My anger or disapproval wouldn't change anything, so I made the best of it."

I loved his outlook on life. Definitely wiser than most our age. "You are definitely the glass half-full while your brother is the glass half-empty type."

He shrugged. "Sometimes. Depends on the situation."

"What makes you angry?"

He raised a brow. "Damn. You ask deep questions. What happened to the easy ones like what's my favorite food or movie?"

"I want to know the things that matter."

"Food and movies matter."

I rolled my eyes and folded my hands between my cheek and the pillow. "You know what I mean."

"Bullies. Bullies make me mad."

"Is that why you're helping me? Because I'm being bullied?"

He adjusted the covers. "Partly. I mean, it opened the door for me to be around you more. And we have mutual friends. It's a bonus you're fun to be around and beautiful."

My cheeks burned. "Have you talked to Beck or Tommy lately?"

"Yes."

"And?"

He shrugged.

My brows drew together. "Rush, what'd they say?"

"They asked me how you were doing, and I told them you weren't doing good. Tommy said some mean things, and I made him eat his words, reminding him how not perfect he is. Beck didn't say much, but how could he? You took the blame for what happened between you two and tried to keep him innocent when you didn't have to. I know you believe a lot of things about yourself, but you also need to give yourself credit for a lot, too. And why don't you comment when someone calls you beautiful?"

"Because I hear it all the time. It feels like that and my family's money are the only reasons why anyone likes me at all. As stupid as it may be, I get annoyed when people tell me how pretty I am. I wish a pretty face and nice car weren't the first things people see and they'd get to know me."

"And how is anyone supposed to accomplish that when you keep everyone at arm's length?"

I felt my walls going up. "My favorite food is pasta. Any kind."

"Oooh hell naw. If you get to ask hard questions, so do I."

I yawned. "I'm sleepy."

"Jorja."

I sighed.

"Be honest with me."

I stared at his dreamy-blues and blinked a few times. "It scares me to be honest, but what scares me most is that I want to tell you everything I've kept bottled up inside forever."

"I won't say a word."

I narrowed my eyes at him. "And how do I know that?"

"I guess you don't, but I give you my word for what it's worth."

I looked at the heart-shaped birthmark on his shoulder again and exhaled slowly. "Maybe someday, but not tonight."

"Let's get some sleep."

I shifted my eyes to his. "Night, Rush."

"Night, Jorja." He reached over to the lamp on his side of the bed and turned it off. I turned until my back was facing him and smiled contently when I felt his arm drape around me, holding me close to him. I had never felt safer in my entire life.

"Ask me all the dirty things going through my head right now," he said quietly against my ear. I could feel his body shaking with laughter. I laughed and used my elbow to nudge him in the stomach. He grunted. "Okay, okay. Goodnight."

"You're a mess, Rush." I couldn't stop grinning.

"I won't deny that. And I'm just kidding, well ... sorta. Goodnight, for real this time."

I closed my eyes and tangled my fingers with his hand that was around me. "Night."

CHAPTER FIFTEEN

Jorja

I cringed at the thought of having to face school head on after this weekend and losing everyone I cared about. Well, everyone except Rush and maybe Tobias. I wasn't exactly clear on where I stood with him yet, but I felt like we had made progress. I rolled over and looked at Rush who softly snored. I smiled, mostly because I never considered a snore cute until then but also because the guy was the only thing keeping me sane while my entire world spun out of control. The recent events were like a helicopter that was crashing, swaying in the wind, the area it'd make its impact uncertain. The impact worried me the most. No one usually made it out of helicopter crashes alive.

I carefully and quietly sat up, moving until my legs and feet hung off the side of his bed. Once my feet hit the floor, I stood and stretched then left the room and walked to the restroom. I opened the door and covered a gasp when I saw Toby getting out of the shower. Quickly, I shut the door and immediately started apologizing.

"Toby! Dammit ... I'm so sorry! I didn't mean to!"

But holy mother of god he is as hot naked as I imagined. Not that I pictured him naked. And I'm totally lying.

I could hear him laughing. "Calm down, it's fine." He continued to laugh.

I thought about bolting and hiding in Rush's room when the door opened and he towered over me, fully dressed but hair still wet. He brushed my right cheek with his thumb, still warm from the shower. "You're blushing."

"With reason!" I snapped.

He grinned. "And my fault. I forgot we had company and a girl at that. I should've locked the door."

I smacked my forehead before meeting his eyes. "I should've knocked first."

"I could be reading your face completely wrong, but something tells me you don't regret it." He looked at the floor and smiled. He cleared his throat and looked past me and at Rush's door. "Is my brother still asleep?"

I nodded. Was he flirting with me? Or taunting me? Or mocking me? Or all three? My heart thudded dramatically in my chest at the thought of each possibility. I'd felt too embarrassed to think of all the reasons it was wrong and somehow cheating on Rush even though we weren't exactly dating. Plus, they're twins. They look alike so I couldn't help but find Toby attractive because Rush is too.

He shifted his gaze back to me. "Are you hungry?" His eyes were a deeper shade of blue today. Maybe it was the poor lighting.

I nodded again.

"Do you like pancakes?"

I nodded a third time.

His eyes crinkled at the sides. "Did you forget how to speak?"

"I just saw you naked and we're talking about pancakes. I need a second ..." I put my hands on my hips, looked at the wall, and slowly let out a breath. I closed my eyes to better compose myself before looking at him again.

His laughter shook his shoulders. "I'm not sure if that should make me happy because I'm so good looking you're speechless, or you're traumatized and I should be apologizing."

I raised both brows. "You seemed so sure a moment ago that I enjoyed it."

"And you haven't corrected me yet. So, which one is it?"

I scoffed. "You're so full of it."

"And you still don't deny it. Interesting." He rubbed his jaw dramatically.

I refused to say another word because he didn't need to know just how attractive I actually found him. I mean, I was attracted to Rush, so it only made sense I'd find his twin just as good looking. I took a step back and he walked into the hall. I followed him to the kitchen and leaned against the counter near the stove as I watched him pull things from cabinets to make pancakes.

He stood in front of me and, without asking me to move, reached above my head then set a glass mixing bowl next to the flour and eggs. He pointed to the drawer behind me.

"Can you hand me the blue mixing spoon out of there?"

I moved and opened it, rummaging around until I found it. I handed it to him and closed the drawer with my hip.

"Wanna help?" he asked, holding an egg in my direction.

My lips parted as I stared at the egg. "Um ..."

"It's just an egg, Jorja. Are you a vegetarian?"

I shook my head and nervously played with the end of my braid. "I've never cooked before." I chewed on the inside of my cheek as I looked at him. This was more embarrassing than seeing him in all his glory, and glory it was. I mean, hallelujah, amen— I looked at him when he cleared his throat.

"You still with me?" He chuckled.

I nodded. "Just waiting for you to make one of your comments about me being spoiled."

He pulled his hand back and set the egg on the counter. He looked hurt which made me wonder if he had short-term memory loss and forgot all the hateful things he's said to me. His fingers tapped the counter for a moment before he made eye contact with me again. He held his hand out to me, and I took it.

"What are you doing?" I asked as he pulled me toward him.

"Teaching you how to cook pancakes."

I grinned. "Really?"

"Uh huh." He moved until he was behind me, and I was facing the counter, staring at all of the things that must make pancakes. Flour and eggs had never been so intimidating. He reached around me and picked up an egg and placed it in my right hand. "Tap it just enough on the edge of the bowl until it cracks. Then peel it apart enough to let the egg fall into the bowl, but no shell."

I looked over my shoulder at him. "Or you could just do it."

The corners of his mouth twitched a little. "Now what's the fun in that?"

I sighed and turned back around to face the counter. "Here goes nothing." I tapped the egg on the side of the bowl, and nothing happened.

He chuckled. "A little harder."

"That's what she said."

He burst into laughter. "She's got jokes."

"There's a lot of things that may surprise you as you get to know me."

"I'm looking forward to it."

I smiled and looked at the egg. I did just as he said but as I predicted, the egg broke, and everything including the shell went into the bowl. We both started laughing and didn't stop when Rush walked into the kitchen.

"Your girl can't cook," Toby teased.

I nudged him with my elbow. "Watch it. With practice I'll outcook you in no time. And I'm no one's girl."

Rush looked hurt by that comment and then his eyes narrowed at Toby, and for a second I was confused until I noticed how close he and I were. Toby took a giant step back to create enough distance to make Rush relax again. I knew Rush liked me and maybe I was falling for him, too, but I hoped I wasn't giving him the wrong impression. With everything going on, trying to form a serious relationship wouldn't be fair to anyone. I wouldn't give up the idea that he and I could possibly work someday, but I also didn't need him getting all jealous, especially over Toby of all people. Something told me that thought was irrelevant, though. The thought of Toby made something course through my veins. I didn't know if I liked it or not, but I definitely didn't hate it. I also couldn't deny that I enjoyed how his body felt pressed against mine as I cracked that egg. I quickly silenced my thoughts and smiled at Rush.

Rush came over and peered into the bowl and grinned "Wow. I've always liked pancakes with a little crunch to them."

I huffed.

He smiled and patted the top of my head as if to pity me. "Don't worry, Toby is a great cook. He'll teach ya."

Toby folded his arms across his chest. "Am I allowed?"

"As long as you keep your hands to yourself."

I raised my hand. "Um, do I have a say in this?"

Both of them looked at me. "Rush, I like you but we're not dating, so chill. Toby, you put your hands on me, and I will throat punch you. Are we clear?" I asked, eyeing them both.

They both nodded, but Toby's amused laugh confused me.

"What?" I asked, looking at him. "What's so funny?"

"You ... throat punching me."

They had no idea the amount of time I spent in self-defense classes. I didn't say anything about it, though. My brother and dad always told me to keep that to myself until it was needed.

"Can someone teach me to cook already? I'm starving."

Rush looked at Toby and laughed. "Good luck."

Toby wet his lips and rubbed his hands together. "Let's do this."

I hated the amount of distance he kept between us, and that was wrong, completely contradicting what I said to both of them and creating a mountain of problems for myself that I didn't need.

I looked at my phone when it came back on. I'd let it die and had to charge it. I have to say, I didn't miss the stupid thing. It was refreshing to just hang out with Rush and Toby watching movies and playing board games. I started to scroll through my notifications and wasn't surprised to see several from Brian, my dad, and my mom. They were all recent within the past hour so I'm sure they had just now noticed I was gone. Sundays were always lazy around our house and typical for me to sleep in until the afternoon.

Rush turned down the TV and looked at me. "Everything okay?"

"My family wants to know where I am."

"What are you gonna tell them?"

I looked at my phone again. "Nothing."

Toby looked at Rush. "I'm sure it won't be long until they call the station if she doesn't respond and he'll figure it out and have to bring her home himself."

I looked at Rush and crossed my arms. "I thought you told him I was here."

"I did."

I raised a brow. "And what exactly did you tell him?"

Toby started laughing.

My eyes widened. "Now I really wanna know."

Rush scratched his head. "I told him you were drunk at a party, and I had to go pick you up and your parents were out of town."

I covered my face with my hand and sighed. "Rush. No, you didn't."

"Did you want me to tell him you ran away? It's his job to return runaways."

I dropped my hand and looked at him. "I guess not, but now he's gonna hate me."

"The whole town hates you, Jorja," Toby reminded me.

"Shut up, Toby," I said, glaring at him.

Rush shrugged. "He'll find out the truth soon enough."

I stood. "Or you could just take me home now so this doesn't become more dramatic than it has to be."

No one argued with me, letting me know that neither of them had a better idea.

"You sure about that?" Rush asked, looking up at me from the couch.

I shrugged. "I guess. I don't want to make this difficult for you or your dad."

Rush stood and tossed the remote to Toby. "Where'd you put the keys?"

"My jacket pocket. The one hanging by the door." Toby looked at me. "Do we go back to hating each other tomorrow at school or are we cool now?"

I frowned. "I never hated you, Toby."

"I have to say, you're a lot cooler than I thought. It's nice to see a different side of you."

I smiled a little. "See you tomorrow." I looked at Rush. "I'll go grab my stuff and meet you out at the truck."

CHAPTER SIXTEEN

Jorja

Rush parked in the driveway and killed the engine. I looked at him with wide eyes. "Ummm, what are you doing?"

"Going in with you. I figured you'd need support when talking to your parents, and I'd like to formally introduce myself. Yesterday, when I left you asleep in your room before you came over, your parents were just coming home. Brian introduced me to them in passing. Your dad seemed a bit on edge, mostly because I'm a guy and alone with his daughter I think, but he still gave me a nod." He shrugged.

"I really don't think right now is a good time to meet them. Crap is about to hit the fan, Rush."

"I'm sure they'd like to know you were with me and safe. All I will do is walk you in, introduce myself, let them know you were safe and leave if that's what you want."

It wasn't a bad idea. I chewed on my lip as I stared at the front door. I nodded. "Okay."

We got out of the truck and Rush handed me my bag. I held onto the strap to steady my hands. I walked around to the back door that we used if not using the one inside the garage and Rush followed me as we made our way through the mudroom and into the kitchen. Brian, Mom, and Dad all looked at me and dropped the phones from their ears.

"Jorja," my mom breathed out as she hurried over to me. She wrapped me in her arms. "You had me worried sick!"

I hugged her back. "I was only gone a few hours."

"Without warning," Dad said roughly. "What were you thinking?"

I moved out of the hug and set my bag down beside me. Brian was eyeing Rush like he was about to slit his throat. "Stop it, Brian. It's not his fault."

Brian looked at me and his jaw relaxed. "Were you with him?"

I looked at Rush and then at the three of them, ignoring my brother stating the obvious. "This is Rush True. Rush, these are my parents, and you've already met my brother."

Dad crossed his arms. "We've met."

Mom smiled a little. "Thank you for bringing her home."

"It's not a problem. It's nice to meet you all again. I just wanted to walk her in and say hello." Rush looked at me. "I'll see you at school tomorrow."

I nodded and watched him leave.

"Jorja Amelia Bonovich, what the hell were you thinking!" Dad scolded. "First a guy leaves from your room during the night and then you sneak out with him?"

Tears filled my eyes as I kept them on the ground. "I've left before with friends and forgot to tell you and came home the next day."

"Not when you have some stalker who has threatened you and damaged your car!" he yelled so loud his voice echoed through the open space.

I glared at him. "Why are you so worried? You know who's doing it. Don't you!"

Mom hung her head and Brian looked at Dad in shock.

"Who's my real dad?" I hated how my voice trembled. I had wanted to sound strong.

"What the hell is she talking about?" Brian asked him. This wouldn't be good. Brian had an outrageous temper.

Dad rubbed his jaw and sighed. "You heard our conversation last night, didn't you?"

Tears filled my eyes. "I need an explanation."

"Maybe we should sit down and—" Mom said before being cut off by Brian.

"Will someone tell me what the hell is happening right now?" Brian looked at me, his eyes pleading for an explanation.

"Brian, this is none of your business. Go tend to the messages on the answering machine," Dad said, trying to sound unmoved by what was happening.

"Is Brian your son?" I asked, though the answer was obvious. Brian looked exactly like him. The only difference between the two were the few gray hairs and faint wrinkles around dad's eyes. Age was all that set them apart.

"This is my family. It *is* my business." Brian moved closer to me and wrapped an arm around me. "What's going on, Kid?"

Dad adjusted the gold watch on his left wrist and cleared his throat. "Blood doesn't change who your real father is, Jorja."

I already knew he wasn't my real dad, but those words just made it more real somehow. It felt like someone cut my heart open and then poured salt on it. "Who. Is. It?" I asked through my teeth. My tears went from a trickle to a steady stream.

"It doesn't matter, sweetie. It really doesn't." Mom was crying now.

"It does matter!" I yelled. I went to take a step forward, but Brian held me close to him.

"Shhh, calm down and let them explain," Brain said quietly as he stared at both of them. "Because they *are* going to explain."

Dad's breathing picked up and his face reddened. "I am your dad. End of discussion."

I shook my head, my vision blurred by the hot tears. "Tell me the truth!"

Dad grabbed the vase of fresh flowers the housekeeper replaced each day on the bar and threw it at the wall. Mom gasped and cried harder as she scrambled to grab things to clean it up. Dad stormed out of the room, and I heard the door to his study slam shut. I looked up at Brian.

He let go of me and started walking toward Dad's study.

"Don't!" I cried.

He went anyway. I started helping Mom clean up then heard Brian banging on Dad's door ordering him to let him in. Mom's hands shook so badly she struggled to clean up the mess. I heard the door slam shut again and knew he was in there with Dad—their tempers combined could be more explosive than a bomb itself.

She gave up and sat down and pressed her back against the bottom cabinets. "Jorja, I'm so sorry you found out like this."

I took the paper towel Mom had gotten and tore off a bunch to lay it on top of the water. I stood and wiped my eyes on the back of my arm. "I'll grab a broom to clean up the broken glass." I didn't want her telling me anything. Dad owed me the truth.

"I didn't want to sleep with the man who is really your father, but this life, well it's messy, Jorja. It's so messy." She cried harder. "This man in particular is a local buyer and your father pissed him off. He sold him a bad batch and cheated him out of some money. So ... your dad made it right by ... giving him something he wanted."

I gripped the broom handle until my knuckles were white and closed my eyes. "You?"

"I have to ... you know ... I have to right a lot of your father's wrongs."

I felt nauseous. Here I always thought Jerry Bonovich hung the moon and my mother was a cheating whore. I felt so stupid for being angry with Mom all these years. I was even angrier that my father allowed me to hate her so much and actually encouraged it by speaking ill of her.

"He purposely got me pregnant. He's a monster, Jorja. He did this to make your father angry."

"The only monster right now is Dad. Please, Mom. Tell me who my real father is." If I gripped the broom any tighter, I'd break it.

My mom had never looked so small. She pulled her knees to her chest and hugged her legs. "Do you know," she wiped her eyes as she continued, "the Ellisons?"

I nodded, and my heart fell to my stomach. "They live three houses down from us. They have one son. Peter Ellison." I didn't like where this conversation was going. I hated the Ellisons. When my parents had dinner parties, they always came, and Peter stole things. He's two years younger than me and a complete idiot.

"Well, your real father is Edward Ellison."

I lost the ability to keep a grip on the broom handle, and it fell to the ground. I expected to feel a certain way—shocked, hurt, or maybe even a bit fulfilled after hearing the truth, but I felt none of those things. I felt nothing at all. It felt like I had hit a wall.

She shook her head. "I'm so sorry. I didn't want you to find out like this or find out at all."

"Does Mr. Ellison know?" I stared blankly at the floor.

"Yes," she answered quietly.

"And he's okay not being a part of my life?" I looked at her.

She shrugged and nodded.

I rubbed my forehead and inhaled deeply. "Oh," left my lips through an exhale.

"It's very complicated. He doesn't want his wife to know. He agreed that your father would be the only one you ever called Dad. Mr. Ellison got what he wanted. Every time your father looks at you, he will always remember the day he crossed him. Those were his exact words when he got the paternity test results. This business is disgusting, and you'd be smart to run away from it like your sister."

"But you told me—"

"I take it back!" She began to cry harder. "I take it all back! I only told you those things because I'm selfish and did as I was told. When I came into this family, I inherited all the dirty things that come with it. I was young, stupid, and intrigued by wealth. I wanted children, and I knew it was a selfish thing to bring you kids into this mess, but I did it anyway. Listen to me, Jorja. You finish school, graduate, attend an amazing college and forget this life. Don't look back. Your sister ... she was smart. She got away from here."

I felt hopeful for a moment. "Do you know where she is?"

She shook her head. "No, but I envy her."

A question kept pushing its way to the front of my mind. "Last night, I heard you say Dad knew who sent the messages."

"We assume we know. It's the only thing that makes sense. We think it's Peter. He must know about you and me and his father. Or it could be his wife, Judy, if she found out. Either way, Jorja, they know things about us that could ruin your father and grandparents. Also, your brother. They'd end up in prison or dead."

"But if it is them, then why would they use the username so close to Rush's name?"

"That we definitely don't know."

"Then after I clean up this mess, I will go ask myself."

She looked around at the mess. "I'll take care of this mess. And don't go looking for answers from the Ellisons. We don't know for sure if it's them doing this."

"It has to be. They live so close that they would've been able to murder my car!"

She stood, careful not to step on glass with her bare feet. "As much as I would love to confront them, we can't until we have proof. Now that you know, we get strategic. Jorja, your father regrets his life decisions every single day. He hates he allowed that man to have his way with me. But you came from all of that, so I don't regret any of it. As messed up as all of this is, you are my little ray of sunshine in the midst of this big stupid mess. Your father loves you, and he kept this from you to protect you."

I felt lost and had no idea what my next move would be. I also didn't understand her need to protect

Dad and try to smooth this over. "I need to process this. I'm going to go see if I can stay with Becca." I sighed. I couldn't stay with her. She hated me. "Or ... well, I guess I have no choice but to stay here."

"I will talk with your father, and we'll give you space while you process this. Please stay home where I know you're safe and cared for. Where you can ask questions and get honest answers. We are family, and we will get through this. Together. I know you're not okay; this is a lot to take in. I wish we had told you sooner, but I have no good excuse for why we didn't except that we hoped you'd never find out."

"Dad's pissed."

She laughed a little. "Yeah. Mostly at himself. He's made really bad decisions, and it haunts him every single day."

I sniffled. "It should." For the first time, I truly realized my mother was the victim to an abusive and controlling relationship. She had gotten into this life knowing what it entailed, but I believe she got more than she bargained for.

She nodded and grabbed more paper towels.

We both cleaned up the mess without another word. What exactly could we say? She was right. It was a lot to take in, and the weight of it all fell on my father's shoulders, as it should. Everything about my life and my family's dealings and bad decisions never made sense to me. However, that didn't change the fact that this was indeed my family, and, inevitably, their problems became my problems. No matter what I did or where I went, my last name would always haunt me. I wished I could find my sister and ask her if leaving truly ridded her of the Bonovich curse.

My phone dinged from my bag, and Mom and I both looked at it. She took the broom from me, and I picked up the bag. I set it on the bar to unzip it and took the phone out.

As if the day couldn't get any worse, there was an unread message from **@Rtrue360**. After the Dad-bomb dropped, you'd think the universe would give my sanity a much-needed break, but **@Rtrue360** wasn't letting that happen. As a matter of fact, they had me right where they wanted me. Broken and on my knees, ready to surrender to whatever it was that they wanted. I just needed to rest and for this to stop.

@Rtrue360: It's too bad your brother is a nice guy. He was just born into the wrong family. Better hug him tight and tell him goodbye. Or... maybe we can work something out. You give me something, and I delete these pictures before hitting send to your new friend's dad.

Rush and Toby's dad.

The photos came through and air caught in my throat. It was Brian placing a few bricks of cocaine in a pile of freshly-dug dirt that was making room for a grave. Brian was never so careless or messy with his work.

How the hell did this person have pictures of him dealing in plain sight?

I responded.

Me: Tell me what you want.

@Rtrue360: I don't know. Seeing your brother behind bars would bring me and so many others joy. It's fun messing with your family. You all thought you were made of stone, and it turns out you're glass and all of you are shattering to pieces. It's hilarious.

Me: Screw you!

@Rtrue360: Now that's a nice thought...

Me: What do you want!

@Rtrue360: Let me think about this. Brian Bonovich behind bars or get something else I want? Decisions, decisions. I mean there are so many possibilities with you, Jorja. I'm basically your puppet master now. I could put Brian behind bars and still get what I want because I know so much it would make your head explode.

Tears spilled down my cheeks.

Me: Just tell me what you want! Please.

@Rtrue360: Tsk, tsk, tsk. So hasty. Calm down and give me a second.

I gripped the phone tightly as I reread every message trying to find a clue as to who this could be. I zoomed in on the pictures to see if I could find a hint, a shoe, anything. Not a damn thing reminded me of anyone I knew. If it was one of the Ellisons, I'd find out. But how? If I made the wrong move, there was no telling what this idiot could do.

"What'd they say?" Mom asked as she gripped the counter and stood.

I wiped my eyes on my arm then turned off my phone and set it on the counter. I shook my head. "It wasn't them," I lied.

She knew I was lying but didn't ask any more questions. "I'm going to go check and make sure Brian hasn't killed your father."

But he's not my father, my brain whispered. I nodded and looked at my phone.

Think, Jorja.

Think.

CHAPTER SEVENTEEN

Jorja

School was as dreadful as I had anticipated. For two days everyone but Rush avoided me like the plague. Cheer practices were lonely, and I started to consider homeschooling if my parents would approve of it. Rush was the only person who talked to me. I liked to think Toby would talk to me too if we had any classes or lunch together, but we didn't. The last thing I wanted to do was go to cheer practice another day where I'd see Becca, Wren, and Jena and their side glances and hushed conversations. Today, Rush promised he'd stay in the bleachers and wait until practice was done for moral support, and maybe I'd feel like at least one person didn't hate me in the gym.

After changing into my leggings and sports bra, I grabbed my water bottle and walked into the gym.

Becca, Wren, and Jena glanced in my direction and started to whisper. I went and stood with the other four girls on the squad. They never spoke to me but were always trying to dress like me and fix their hair like mine. It used to feed my power of popularity, but now it just made me sad. No one needed to be like me. Even they began to whisper. I'm sure they wondered why Becca and I weren't talking. We were usually thick as thieves.

We all made our way onto the court and started stretching. I could feel Becca's eyes on me, so I sat up straight and looked at her, reaching for my toes as I did.

"Are you and Rush dating now?" she asked, her voice small and distant. She mimicked the same stretch as me.

I sat up straight. "You don't have to do this."

She sat up straight, too. "Do what?"

"Make small talk. I understand why you hate me."

She looked at Rush in the bleachers. I looked at him and noticed Beck and Tommy were talking to him. She looked at me again. "Beck told me everything. He explained the entire situation and told me you wanted to make it like it was all your fault so I'd hate you and not him."

I shrugged. "It was a mistake, and he loves you."

She nodded. "I know. I have thought about all the reasons I should hate both of you all weekend. I'm pissed and hurt, but I brought it on myself. I like to tell myself that I wouldn't have been mad if it were a girl I didn't know, but no matter what I'd still be mad. We weren't dating. I've had sex with other guys, not once considering Beck's feelings because it didn't matter because we weren't official or anything. At first it was easier to be mad at you instead of at myself."

"What are you saying, Becca?"

"I'm saying I'm still pissed but we're not going to let whoever is unravelling you come between our group of friends. We're too close for that."

A hint of a smile slightly stretched the corners of my mouth. "I agree. So, we forget what happened?"

She nodded. "Well, sort of. I won't forget it, but we move on."

I wanted to cry and hug her. I wanted to vow to never hurt her like that again, but I didn't want to cause a scene, so I bottled up my emotions and nodded.

"Since we're talking again, you should know the rumor according to Wren is that you stayed the night at Rush and Toby's house and you're screwing both of them."

I threw my head back laughing. "Definitely didn't happen. I did stay there one night, but nothing like that happened unless you count me accidentally walking in the bathroom as Toby was stepping out of the shower."

Her mouth fell open. "You lucky bitch!"

I laughed some more. "Pretty sure my eyes went to Heaven."

"Tell me more!"

I grinned. My Becca was back.

I shook my head. "It was just that, and I shut the door. I was so embarrassed, and then he taught me how to make pancakes."

"So, you and Toby are cool now?"

I nodded but shrugged. "I like to think we are. Toby is ... unpredictable."

"Which brother do you like?"

I raised a brow. "I didn't say I liked either of them."

She motioned her hand toward my face. "Your smile says otherwise."

I looked at Rush and the guys then back at her. "It's complicated. I'm not in the right mindset to be anyone's girlfriend right now. Rush admitted his feelings for me, and I wish I felt the same, but there's just too much going on to distract me from what could be. Know what I mean?"

"And Toby? Did he admit he likes you, too?"

I laughed. "Negative. I think he's just getting used to not completely hating me. He told me that one time he tried getting to know me, and I was horrible to him. I don't remember it at all."

"What if they both start fighting over you?"

"Take that back! Knock on some damn wood or something. The last thing I need is to end up in some stupid love triangle."

"It'd be hot."

I frowned. "It'd be stupid."

Jena and Wren came and sat with us.

"Are we all cool again?" Wren asked.

I looked at Becca and she nodded.

"About damn time!" Jena squealed.

I laughed. "It was just a few days."

"It felt like yeaaaaarrrrs," Jena said, and Wren nodded in agreement.

The four of us looked up when our coach came rushing into the gym. She apologized for being late and told us to continue stretching while she made a phone call. I looked at Becca again as we started to stretch. With the news of the Ellisons, my suspicions of my group of friends left. It couldn't be any of them.

"I think we all need to meet up at the lake and talk. This weekend revealed something huge, and I can't talk about it here."

"Was it Rush's dick?" Jena wiggled her eyebrows.

"Jena!" I squeaked.

"Maybe Toby's, too," Wren added, and her and Jena fist bumped.

I covered my face in my hands. "Oh, my god. Stop."

"You guys stop!" Becca laughed. "Let's get practice over with and tell the guys." Becca looked at Wren and Jena. "Are you both free after this?"

They nodded.

"Why the lake and not your house?" Jena asked.

"Because I don't want to go home until I absolutely have to. It's just weird there right now."

Becca kept her eyes on me. "Why?"

I shook my head when I noticed the other girls trying to listen to us. "We'll talk about it later."

Coach walked back into the gym and blew her whistle at the guys. "Get out of here! I need my girls focused and without you guys distracting them. Three of them have tryouts for college in four weeks."

I had completely forgotten about trying out for a cheer scholarship, something I at least wanted to try to do even if I didn't end up going. College had left my mind completely with all the crap going on. We finished stretching and stood. I waved at Rush as they made their way out down the bleachers.

I noticed his playful grin and wondered what he was up to. I inclined my head to the side when he stretched then took off running, doing a terrible cartwheel, and awkward backflip, before shouting, "Go Bears," in his best peppy voice.

I covered my face, blushing and shaking my head. The entire cheer team burst into laughter. I moved my fingers enough to see him take a bow.

Becca cupped her hands on each side of her mouth and yelled, "Tryouts are in March!"

"As long as I'm the spotter for Jorja!" he yelled back.

"Get out of here," the coach yelled, laughing.

"You look nervous," Rush said quietly from the driver's seat.

I stopped chewing on my lip and looked at him. "What if they don't show up? What if Becca's just feeding me full of crap? I need my friends. I've never realized how much until now."

I wouldn't blame them if they didn't show up. I tried to recall a time when I did anything for any of them that would give them a reason to give a damn about me. The only person I had given anything to was Beck, and even that was wrong.

"I'm a bad person," I whispered as I looked up at the stars through the sunroof of the truck. We all agreed to meet here at nine tonight. That gave everyone a chance to get home, have dinner, then come out here and help me hash out all my problems. "Rush, I don't know how I have any friends at all."

He put his arm around my shoulders. "Well, you're fun to be around." I felt his fingers comb through my hair.

I turned my head to look at him. We were so close with the way he was holding his arm around me. He smiled.

"How am I fun to be around?"

He chuckled. "You just are. I don't think you have to have specific reasons to enjoy someone's company. You just fit with me. And ..." A hint of mischievousness danced in his eyes.

"And what?"

He shook his head with a huge grin. He looked down at the floorboard. "Nah, never mind."

I gave his chest a gentle shove. "Rush! Now you have to say it."

He shook his head again, smiling bigger. "I wasn't going to say anything." He looked at me seriously.

I laughed. "You totally were!"

"I wasn't. I swear."

"Then what the hell was that 'and' and long pause for? I saw it in your eyes, too. You were about to—" My words succumbed to his lips when they pressed against mine. My heart stopped before speeding up, pounding in my chest. He pulled back, before I was ready for him to, and I was left wanting more.

He was still close enough for me to kiss him again. "I told you I didn't plan on saying anything."

My eyes stayed on his lips before looking at him. "Can you not say anything again?"

He suppressed a laugh. "You made it clear you don't want to date, and if we do that again ... Well, it'll just complicate things more."

He took his arm from around my shoulders and pointed toward headlights in the distance. "It looks like they're gonna show up after all." He opened his door, but I grabbed his hand to stop him from getting out. He paused and looked at me.

"Just give me time to figure things out. I'm not exactly girlfriend material."

"My brother filled me in on everything I need to know about you. None of us are relationship material until we find the right one."

My eyes narrowed. "What exactly did Toby say?"

"Your friends are here, and trust me, you don't want to know."

I could hear the sound of gravel under tires and engines being killed.

"Just tell me."

He sighed and rubbed the back of his neck. "Basically, that you can't make a wife out of a ho."

I clenched my teeth. "How long ago was this conversation?"

"When I saw you at the red light for the first time driving around town with him. Remember that?"

I remembered him laughing as he looked at me. That must've been why because of what Toby said. I let go of his hand. "Oh."

"Yeah ... I was like dayyyumm she's fine, and he glanced and saw it was you. He said no. I asked why. Then he said ... well, you know. Then filled me in on all the details."

"Yet you still pursued me?"

"My brother is an idiot, and I like to make my own mistakes."

I raised a brow. "So, I'm a mistake?"

"Probably," he said through a laugh.

I playfully shoved his shoulder. "Hey!"

He laughed some more. "You gotta be somebody's problem, right?" He kissed my forehead. "Come on. They're all here."

I laughed and looked out the window when I heard someone knocking on it. I grinned when I saw Becca waving. I got out, and she hugged me tightly.

"I'm so glad we're okay again. I'm so sorry for hurting you!"

She hugged me tighter. "Just don't do it again."

I laughed when Tommy, Beck, Wren, and Jena all piled in for a massive group hug. I may have not always been a great friend, but right then I swore to be the best friend that they all deserved. I had been trying to find the silver lining in all of this mess and there it was.

@Rtrue360 was making me a better person, as twisted and confusing as that may be.

When we all pulled out of the hug, Tommy went to his truck and came out with two large thermoses. Beck went into his backseat and came over with Styrofoam cups. I looked at Rush who gave me a "go ahead" nod. When Beck held a cup out toward him, he shook his head and explained he'd be the DD. I smiled a little and mouthed *thank you*. After our cups were full, we sat around on the fallen logs we had made permanent benches. Rush, Beck, and Tommy worked on starting a fire.

"Tell it all, Jorja," Becca said before she brought the cup to her lips and tipped it back.

I took a long drink. The perfect amount of warmth and burn. "When you say tell it all ... I think I'm ready to lay it all out there. It's a lot and not just what I found out this weekend. All these lies I've been keeping are eating away at me." And they were. It was like billions of maggots decomposing my sanity. Whether I complied with this idiot stalker or not, I had a feeling they weren't about playing fair. Everything would be out there. I could feel the demise of my family coming on fast and strong. Like this spiked cider. I took another drink.

"Are you sure?" Becca asked, motioning her eyes toward Wren.

"Hey! I can keep secrets!" Wren said, flipping off Becca.

We all laughed.

"Fine," Wren pouted. "Maybe not all the time, but for people I care about I can keep my mouth shut."

I held my hand out and wiggled my fingers. "First, I want to see everyone's phones." When they all looked at me oddly, I clarified. "I want them all turned off. I don't need any of this recorded or the chance of someone else hearing."

Tommy, Beck, and Rush stopped tending to the fire and handed over their phones. The girls followed suit. I made sure they were all off and set them on the ground by my feet.

I went into detail about my parents' business and how they used the funeral business to mask the drug dealings. I told them how my dad wasn't my biological father. I told them who it was, which raised a lot of eyebrows. Well, all of us except Rush. I didn't expect a reaction from him since he doesn't know that many people here. Aside from him, we all hated the Ellisons. But the idea that this tormentor may be one of them had us all intrigued and ready to dig for answers.

I told them about the threats to Brian and how this mystery person still hadn't told me what it was they wanted exactly. I told them how I doubted they'd play fair at all, and it was obvious they had a goal to bring my family down and they chose me, the weakest link, to do it. I told them about all the missed playdates when we were kids, and it was because I was being trained to kill people. Literally. I told them about the boater's license, and that I knew how to dispose of a dead body without getting caught. I told them everything except that my parents and brother deal directly with the cartel. *That* was something I'd never be able to tell because that would get my family killed. Every single one of us and the people sitting with me right now. Rule number one was never tell where the drugs came from. I didn't know exactly who or what they looked like, I just knew where they were from, and when Brian's gone for days at a time, he's meeting up with them for pick up and deliveries. No one interrupted me, they all just listened. It felt so good to just lay it all out there with nothing to hide.

"Have you ever killed anyone?" Jena asked quietly.

"No, but I've helped cover up a scene before."

"Who?" Wren asked eagerly. It freaked me out how excited she seemed about this, but she did love those crime shows and murder podcasts.

"Do you honestly think she can tell who? Idiot," Rush mumbled.

"He's right, I can't say. Honestly, I don't even know who or where we were. I was only eight at the time, and my brother brought me somewhere he shouldn't have. We were hours away from Grove."

"I always thought death never fazed you because you helped at the morgue," Tommy said, shuddering a little. He always hated when I'd tell stories about helping do the dead's make-up or the embalming process.

"I'm sure that has a lot to do with it, but death is talked about like just another normal day at my house. I've been trained to kill if I have to, know how to make sure I don't get caught, and grew up running around the funeral home. It's just a part of life. No big deal." I shrugged.

"Just a part of life? No big deal? It's that easy for you, huh?" The malice in Rush's tone made me instantly regret wording that how I did.

"I'm sorry, Rush. I didn't mean it like that. It's a huge deal when it's someone you know and love personally."

He glared at me for a moment, and I wondered where his mind went. He was angry with me for something bigger than what I said, and it made my stomach tighten. Surely he knew I didn't mean it like he took it. He started tending to the fire again.

I stood and walked over to him. "I'm not downplaying your mom dying as just another day and no big deal if that's how you took it," I said quietly.

I could feel everyone's eyes on Rush and me. He turned his back to me and threw another log into the fire. I didn't know what I had done wrong, but he was clearly pissed.

I touched his arm. "Rush."

He jerked his arm away and wiped at his eyes. "I'm going to look for more wood." He walked in the opposite direction and into the woods.

I was so confused. What the hell just happened? I looked at Tommy and Beck for help. They were dudes. Maybe they'd understand what I did wrong.

Tommy handed his cup to Wren. "I'll go catch up with him and see if I can figure it out." He walked off in the direction Rush went.

Beck cupped my shoulder. "He never talks about his mom or what happened to her. He's never really shown much emotion about it all. Maybe it's all just hitting him. I mean, he's only been here what, a few weeks?"

"But ... did I say something wrong?"

"Not to me, but maybe it just hit him wrong. I'm sure he's just sad and it has nothing to do with you or what you said. Grief is weird. All the talk about death may have just reopened the wound." Beck took a drink. "Let Tommy talk to him."

"Maybe I should go after him and talk to him?" I pressed my lips together as I stared into the darkness past the fire.

"No offense, Jorja, but he walked off when you were talking to him, so just give him some space and let Tommy handle it." Becca rubbed my back. "Tommy's good at stuff like that anyway."

I sighed and nodded.

"I think I have a brilliant idea," Jena said as she stood from the log to the right of me. When she had our attention, she continued. "I think it's time your parents throw another one of their famous dinner parties."

"How the hell will that help?" I asked, laughing. I started to feel the effects of the liquor, and everything was becoming hilarious.

She started pacing in front of us as she spoke quickly. "Your parents have a dinner party. The Ellisons come. Peter and his stupid self will be alone somewhere at some point trying to steal something. I bet he has this whole shrine of things he steals from people's homes. Anyway, moving on. So, they have this bomb-ass dinner party and everyone is drinking and being their fake ass selves, and all of us are hanging out like we always do at these things and ... we corner Peter when he's alone and interrogate the hell outta him. If you know how to kill people, Jorja, then I bet you're good at threatening people." She clapped her hands and jumped a little.

Wren looked unamused. "Or ..." We all turned our attention to her. "We spike the punk ass kid's drink, slit his throat, and find a boat."

It was silent a moment before we all burst into laughter.

"Or ...," Beck said and now our attention on him. "You girls stay out of it and let us guys handle the jackass."

Becca shook her head. "We're not even sure it's him. Jorja said so herself. They don't know for sure. They are assuming. I don't like any of their ideas except for the dinner party. I think it's not a bad idea that we get all the people in our parents' circle together. It has to be someone who knows your parents well."

"What if ... what if it's your sister?" Jena said with wide eyes. "I hadn't thought about this until now. I mean, she went missing. Poof! Gone! What if she's so angry she is taking her own family down?"

I'd actually considered that one night when I couldn't sleep, but it only lasted a second. She wouldn't do something like that. She purposefully got away. She didn't just go missing. She hated this life and wouldn't do anything to get involved with it again. But ... that gave me another idea. "I don't think it's her, but maybe if I could find her and talk to her, maybe she'd be of some help."

"And a dinner party," Jena quickly added. "It's a brilliant idea."

I laughed. "I'll mention it to my parents."

"Are you mad at your dad?" Becca asked, slightly changing the subject.

I nodded. "Yes." I shrugged. "And no. I think I'm just shocked more than anything. It's weird. I was so pissed off at first, but then when I talked to my mom, it oddly kind of made sense why they just kept it hidden. It doesn't make it right or make it less wrong, it just … it's just not something they should've kept from me. That's all. I know my dad loves me, but I do question a lot of things now learning about what all my mom does for this business that he allows and orchestrates." I cringed.

I looked toward the woods again. Through the clearing and the light from the fire I could see Tommy and Rush coming back our way. I stared at him, hoping he'd make eye contact with me so I could try to gauge his feelings, but he didn't. He had an arm full of thick branches and started tossing them into the fire, using a longer one to poke the logs with.

Tommy looked at me and shook his head. I huffed and took another drink.

"So, we're gonna tell Jorja's parents to throw a dinner party," Jena said excitedly.

I listened to them hash out the details but couldn't make out all the words they were saying. My own thoughts were drowning out the sound of their voices as I stared at Rush, completely confused about how his attitude changed so drastically toward me when things had been so easy and good with him. I wanted him to talk to me so we could work through it together, but if he wanted to, he wouldn't have been avoiding my gaze like he was. I looked down at the cup in my hands and frowned. Maybe he'd talk to me on the ride home. I shifted my attention back to the plans being made by my friends and focused on how good it felt to have them back on my side.

CHAPTER EIGHTEEN

Jorja

Tommy hung out of Rush's sunroof, singing a song I had never heard at the top of his lungs. We had already dropped Jena and Wren off, Beck and Becca stayed at the lake and swore they'd just sleep there and not attempt to drive, so it was just Rush and me with a very wasted Tommy. Rush held onto Tommy's left leg as he drove, because if he didn't, he'd probably have killed himself by now. I was so glad I stopped drinking when I did. Rush needed another sober person to deal with this idiot, and I needed a straight mind when I finally got him alone and could talk to him.

"Tommy, get your ass back inside!" I shouted through laughter. As bad as he was frustrating the hell out of me, it was still hilarious.

"We're almost to his house," Rush said as he took a turn, making Tommy's body shift and fall back into the truck right on top of me.

"Hey, gorgeous," Tommy said in a slur as he sat up with his face not even an inch from mine.

"You're so drunk." I pushed his chest so he'd move off me.

He sat down in the middle and laid his head on Rush's shoulder. "Rush rhymes with dick."

Rush chuckled. "You need to go back to kindergarten."

It was good to hear Rush laugh. It gave me hope that he wasn't too terribly pissed off. I covered my mouth when I started to laugh.

"I see you laughing over there," Rush said with a smirk.

Tommy sat up and put his finger in my face. "You should let Rush in. You're all bolted up like a bank at night. He's good for you, Jorja."

The way his words were slurred made me roll my eyes. I laughed because doing anything else would blow my cover. "You need to go to bed and sleep off that cider."

"Okay." He leaned his head back against the seat and immediately started snoring.

I peered around him at Rush. "How much did he even drink?"

He shrugged. "It's Tommy. Probably too much and not enough."

When we got to Tommy's house, Rush parked, and we went back and forth about a plan to get him inside without waking up his parents. We ended up just winging it and going with no plan at all. I stayed in the truck and watched the entire thing go down. Rush had Tommy's arm draped around his shoulders and he had to coach Tommy the entire way inside. At one point, Tommy stopped and threw up on his front lawn. I watched as they went inside, and the door shut behind them.

I sat up to get a better look when I saw Rush walk out with Tommy's dad following. They talked for a bit before Tommy's dad went back inside. Rush rubbed the back of his neck and kept his eyes on the ground as he headed this way. I sat back against the seat when he got in and shut the door.

"How pissed is his dad?"

"Only a little. He's happy he didn't drive."

He put the truck in drive and started down the road. We weren't far from my house, so I needed to talk fast.

"Rush, I'm sorry for whatever I said to upset you. I wasn't thinking about my choice of words, and that's not okay. I feel myself becoming this different person, and I like her so much better than the Jorja that hadn't met you yet."

He rubbed his lips gently with his thumb as he drove. His brows were drawn in, concentrating on every word I said or ignoring me completely. Either way, he was very intent with whatever he was doing.

"I don't know what else to say except that I'm sorry. I really meant no harm in what I said, but it was typical of me to not think of anyone but myself. I really am trying to work on that." I waited two whole minutes before I spoke again, thinking maybe he'd have something to say after that. "I'm so sorry about your mom, and it's a big deal that you're hurting even if you don't show it. I don't mention it because you don't act like you want it brought up. I'm scared to really say anything right now because I don't want to dig myself a deeper hole than I already have. I'm ... I'm gonna just shut up now." I looked out the window instead of at him. I folded my hands in my lap and huffed.

"It—" when he finally spoke, my heart sped up as I looked at him "—it just hit me all of a sudden that she's really gone. That feeling comes in waves. It's weird when someone dies. The world just keeps going, and, for some reason, it feels like it shouldn't. That it should just stop and pause a little while, but it doesn't. You just have to keep living and going on with this ... this new normal, and it's not fair." His voice cracked. "Then when you think you're okay, you're not, and it hits you all over again, and the world still doesn't stop. It just keeps going even though *my* world feels wrong. I feel like I'm just this shell of a human, and I can't catch my breath. I get angry at people for not ever knowing her. That's a really stupid thing to get angry about. She loved bonfires and right before you said what you did, I was just thinking about how much I wanted her to meet you, and we could have a fire, and she could get to know you. I could see her smile and hear her laughing, telling me to hold onto you and fight for you. Then you said that death wasn't a big deal and I just ... I took it personally when you didn't mean any harm. It was just personal at that moment."

"Rush, if you ever need to talk about anything or just want to tell me good memories or whatever it is, you can."

He looked at me, and it looked like he wanted to say something but didn't. He shook his head and looked at the road again.

"What?"

He exhaled heavily. "Nothing. I just want to change the subject, please."

"Okay." When we got to the gate of my house, Rush put the number in I gave him and drove through when it opened.

"Rush?"

"Hmm?"

"Are you angry with me?" I had never felt so insecure before in my life. Not when it came to the opinion someone had of me.

"Not at you, no. More the situation. I don't know why it's hitting me like it is tonight." He continued down my long driveway before parking near the back door.

"Do you want to come in?" I asked while putting my purse strap over my shoulder.

"It's a school night, don't your parents have some rules about that?"

I shook my head. "Even if they did, I don't think they'll enforce any rules right now with how badly they screwed up and lied to me."

He chuckled. "Are you using this situation to your advantage?"

I smiled sweetly. "Wouldn't you?"

"Absolutely."

"Well—" I looked at him through my lashes "—let's go then." I opened the door and slid out of his truck. When he got out and came to walk beside me, I looked up at him. He opened the door for me, and we went inside.

He followed close behind, and I reached back for his hand. When he tangled his fingers with mine, I led him through the dark halls and up the stairs. When we made it into my room, I shut the door and set my purse down on the coffee table in the sitting area.

I turned to face him and frowned at the unsureness in his eyes. "What is it?" I asked quietly as I sat down on the couch and took off my shoes.

"What exactly are we doing, Jorja?" His hands were in his jeans pocket, and he stood so still, like if he moved the floor may break beneath him.

I kept my eyes on him as I thought but didn't say anything because I wanted to choose my words carefully. I set my shoes neatly beside the couch. I was falling for him, and the realization of that made me avert my eyes to my hands clasped in my lap. I was scared to death. I trusted him more than I had ever trusted anyone, and it confused me. I had only known him for a short period of time, but, when he was around, I felt safe and desired for more than my money and looks.

"What do you mean?" My words came out choppy, making me clear my throat.

He scoffed and shook his head, looking toward the wall of windows behind me. "Don't play stupid. I know what I'm doing, and so do you, you just won't say it."

I narrowed my eyes at him. "Rush, I told you, right now—"

"You just want to be friends. I get that. But then I kissed you tonight and you asked for more. Then you asked me inside tonight."

Tears filled my eyes even though I willed them not to form at all. It felt like he was angry with me, and if I didn't say something right he'd leave and never talk to me again. I was never scared to lose anyone like that before. Yeah, the idea of my friends never talking to me again hurt, but this felt different somehow.

This was exactly why I didn't date. Relationships scared me because I always figured my life, my family, would be too much for someone. I always knew that I'd never be able to fully be honest with anyone. I opened up about a lot tonight, but none of them knew everything. There would always be things I couldn't say. If I ever got married, I'd have to tell it all, and that meant they'd be in danger because of the information they knew. If they ever chose to leave me and this family, they'd be killed. It's why I think my sister left. It was the final straw for her. She fell in love, and when she told Dad, he laid down the ground rules if it went further and resulted in marriage. For two years there were hit men looking for my sister. My parents tried to hide that she ran away, but the cartel issued the hit when they found out. They wanted to find her and kill her because she knew too much. My sister was smart though; I'm sure she had it all planned before she ever left that night. I rubbed the chill from my arms when my mind went back to that day I woke up and she was gone. The cries of my mother, the late nights of driving around, and Dad drinking heavier than normal.

"Just tell me what you want from me, Jorja, so I know who I need to be around you."

I looked up from my hands and at him. "I'm so scared," I whispered through my tears.

He cursed under his breath. "I don't want to make you cry."

I wiped my eyes. "It's not you. It's me."

"That's the worst thing you can say to a guy. Are we breaking up before we ever dated?" His smirk and witty response lessened the blow of the entire conversation.

"I mean it, though. It really is me. It's my family. It's this virus of a last name!"

"You're more than that. You let it control you, and you put up walls because of it. Are you always gonna be a little bitch to your last name?"

I glared at him. "What the hell did you just say?"

"I said it, and I mean it. Are you always gonna let Bonovich be your excuse for everything?"

I looked down again and fidgeted with a string on my ripped-up jeans. 'You're right."

"I know."

I laughed and looked up at him again. My eyes followed his every move as he walked closer and closer to me. He knelt down on one knee in front of me so our eyes were level. He tucked my hair behind my left ear, and his eyes never left mine.

"I'm asking this one more time, and then I swear I'll never ask it again. What are we doing, Jorja?"

"I'd love to tell you what you want to hear. But I also want to tell you what I want my mind to say even though it won't align with my heart. We're friends. I'd like for this to be more some day soon, but things are so messed up. and if we do figure this thing out—"

"You mean if *you* figure this 'us' thing out. Not me. I already know what I want."

I smiled and nodded. "Right. How about we don't give answers right now. Let's just let whatever happens happen. I know I need you, Rush. More than anything right now. Just promise me you'll stick around."

"I can see in your eyes you want this just as bad as I do."

"I won't deny that, but right now it's not about what I want. I have some freak trying to ruin my life and expose my family. I found out my dad isn't my dad, but this douchebag I hate is. I just want to work through all of that so when that's over, my mind can focus on other things. You and I deserve to be the center of attention without all this stuff muddying something that feels close to perfect."

"Okay." He smiled a little as he moved to sit on the couch beside me.

"Stay here tonight?"

He played with my hair and nodded. "I will. I just need to be sure I leave in enough time to run home and change clothes."

When he put his arm around me, I laid my head on his shoulder. "You're making me a better person."

He laughed quietly. "No, it's not me. You are just realizing the person you always have been; she was just hiding behind really big walls."

"Why does it feel like I've known you forever?" I picked up my head to look at him.

"It just happens like that sometimes, I guess."

I snuggled closer to him and yawned. "I guess so," I whispered. The slow rise and fall of his chest lulled me to sleep.

CHAPTER NINETEEN

Jorja

The rest of the week was a blur of cheer practice and planning a dinner party with my parents. It felt like we were orchestrating a game of Clue. I always hated that game. I didn't know exactly how I felt about a house full of rich assholes, especially with the man who was really my father and Peter. But that was the point. To get the Ellisons there and slip something in Peter's drink. With the help of my friends, we were going to take his phone. My parents didn't know about that part. They just thought we'd be able to sense the guilt if it were the Ellisons pulling this stunt.

I looked in the mirror at my satin, navy, cocktail dress. It dipped low in the front, creating a large v shape, and the loose-fitting sleeves cuffed tightly at my wrist, stopping just enough before my hand so that you could see the black pearl bracelet. I turned to make sure the back was free of wrinkles, then turned to the front and tugged on the bottom until it rested mid-thigh. I combed my fingers through my hair where I put a few big loose curls at the ends and sighed. I didn't know what would come of tonight, and it worried me. I looked around until I spotted my black stilettos on my bed. I walked over, sat on the edge of the bed, and slid my feet into them. I started tying the bow that went around my ankle just as my door opened and Becca, Jena, and Wren walked in.

I gave them a faint smile. "Hey." I bent down and started on the other shoe.

"Girl, your man just got here and is mega hot in his tux," Wren said, fanning herself.

I smiled at all three of the girls. They all looked stunning. Jena in a tight pink dress, Wren in a floor-length black dress, and Becca in a black halter and short ruby-red skirt that was tight at the waist but fanned out.

I stood and adjusted my black pearl necklace and earrings. "He's not my man."

"You're a liar," Jena said with a playful smile.

"Leave her alone. She'll admit it soon enough." Becca came and hugged me. "We're here for you tonight. We're going to figure this out and end it. I can feel it."

My breath came out shaky as I nodded. "I hope so. Where are the guys?"

Becca fixed a strand of my hair that must've been out of place. "Downstairs waiting for us. Your mom asked them to help with the ice."

"Did that bastard tell you what it is they wanted to keep Brian in the clear?" Wren asked as she fingered the jewelry I had laid on top of my dresser.

I shook my head.

"So, who invited Tobias?" Wren asked as she checked her nails then flipped her hair. "I can just see God in heaven when he created the True boys. He created one, and then was like, damn I'm good at this, look at him, I should create one more."

We all stared at her blankly.

"What?" She giggled. "You know all of you have thought the same thing."

"No," I laughed. "Pretty sure I haven't thought about their actual creation."

"But am I wrong?" She raised a brow and crossed her arms in front of her.

The three of us shook our heads.

She grinned. "And the congregation said ..."

"Amen," the three of us said in unison, causing an uproar of laughter.

"So, did you invite him?" Wren asked me.

I shook my head. "I didn't." My heart felt like it was going to burst from my chest at the thought of him being down there. I didn't know if he was truly on my side. At times it felt like he might be, but it also felt like he was happy, and I deserved this.

The four of us headed out of my room and down the stairs. I saw the guys talking in the large dining area where the table had been removed so everyone could walk around and mingle, maybe even dance if the drinks started flowing right. These dinner parties were never low key. We'd have at least a hundred people here tonight, if not more if they brought guests. My parents hired a DJ, bartender, and a catering company to help host these things. Looking at it now, it felt ridiculous. I used to love house parties because they made me feel superior, and I enjoyed showing off. Now, it felt superficial.

Beck grabbed Rush's shoulders and motioned his head toward me. As soon as Rush turned around, his eyes scanned me from head to toe. My cheeks reddened under his gaze. I didn't know what to do with this feeling or even what to call it; I just knew I had never been looked at like that before, nor had I ever felt more beautiful in my life.

He walked over, and it became my turn to appreciate what was standing in front of me. His well-fitting navy suit and white undershirt brought out his blue eyes. His hair was neatly combed to one side, and he smelled amazing as always.

"You are so out of my league," he said as he wrapped me in his arms. I inhaled deeply before he let go and took a small step back. "I hope it's okay that I brought Toby. I told him what was going on, and he insisted on helping."

I scrunched my nose. "He did?"

Rush nodded and looked over his shoulder. I followed his gaze and saw Toby talking with my brother. I smiled at Toby's choice of clothes. He had on a crisp white shirt, open gray blazer, and dark jeans, which are typically not allowed at these dinner parties. He never ceases to amaze me. Every encounter I have with him, he's always himself, even tonight in Grove Hills, he didn't try to be someone he wasn't.

Rush looked at me again. "Is that okay?"

I nodded. "Of course. We're good now ... I think." I glanced from him to my brother. "I hope Brian is being nice."

"Actually, your brother thinks Toby is me. He freaked out when he found out there were two of us and said he needed to talk to the guy who wants to date his sister." Rush put his fist to his mouth to suppress a laugh. "I bolted, so Toby is taking one for the team."

I threw my head back, laughing louder than I had intended. "Are you serious? Rush! You're so mean!"

He grinned. "Yeah. I can be. So, how does your brother know I want to date you?"

"He noticed we've been spending a lot of time together, and he asked me what was going on. I may have told him more than I should have. I hope that's okay."

"I'm just glad you're talking about it. Must mean you want it to happen."

I smiled and looped my arm with his as people started to fill the room. I scanned the crowd, looking for the Ellisons but didn't see them. They were usually late to everything, so I wasn't surprised. I noticed Tommy and Beck talking to Wren, Becca, and Jena. I tugged on Rush's arm and, when he looked at me, I slid my arm out of his and took his hand, leading him toward our group of friends.

When we made it there, I looked at Rush. "I'm going to save your brother now."

"He's a big boy. He can handle Brian."

I laughed and shook my head before standing on my tiptoes to spot Toby and my brother. Once I spotted them, I headed their way. I whispered "sorry" several times as I squeezed past people in the middle of conversations and almost knocked a glass out of a woman's hand. It was too crowded, and it wouldn't be long until Dad would be offering more space outside on the back patio.

I made it to them, but just as I was close enough to talk to them, I tripped over a man's shoe as he went to take a step, and Toby caught my right hand before I hit the ground.

"I saw this in a movie once," he said as he held onto my arm to steady me. "It ended terribly."

I pulled my hand from his and frowned. "Well, hello to you, too."

He chuckled. "Are you okay?"

I nodded and smoothed out my dress. "Hey, Brian," I said, looking at him with a raised brow. "I see you met Toby. Rush's twin."

Brian's mouth fell open. "Hey!"

I cracked up laughing as Brian narrowed his eyes at Toby.

"I tried to tell you, but you kept interrupting me with your 'ground rules'."

I placed my hands on my hips. "Oh, really?"

"Mmm-hmm," Toby mumbled and nodded. "They're all fairly reasonable, but nothing I'd agree to. Rush probably will, though. He has manners."

"That little asshole," Brian said as he inclined his neck to look for Rush, I assumed. "Excuse me." He handed me his drink and got lost in the crowd of people.

I smelled the clear liquid in the tall glass and smiled. "Lemon drop martini." I took a sip before downing the whole thing. I handed the glass to one of the waiters walking past us.

Toby studied me for a moment with curious eyes. "Do your parents condone underage drinking?"

"They don't pay enough attention to notice."

He grunted and shook his head. "How many rude comments am I allowed to make tonight?"

"Considering you weren't actually invited, none."

He shrugged. "I heard you needed help."

I tugged gently on the front of his blazer. "Are you saying you actually want to help me?"

The look in his eyes gave me a sense of calmness in the middle of all the chaos. "I believe that is what me being here means."

My lips broke into a huge grin. "Thank you, Toby."

"You're welcome."

I stood on my tiptoes as I looked around. I found Rush, and he smiled at me before turning around and talking to our group of friends again. I looked at Toby. "Want to come hang out with us?"

He rubbed the back of his neck and looked over at the group. "Yeah, sure, but your friend Wren won't stop staring at me."

I laughed. "She's harmless. Handsy, but you might like that."

He laughed and shrugged. "She's not really my type."

"What's your type?"

He shrugged and shoved his hands in his pockets. "Ready to go over to your friends now?"

I raised a brow. "Oh, are you gay?" I asked in a whisper. "I won't tell anyone."

"What! No!" He laughed so hard his eyes watered. "No, Jorja. Definitely not."

"You avoided the question."

He nodded. "Good observation."

"Well?"

He bit his lip and grinned before walking off through the sea of people, leaving my mind to wander. I frowned and started weaving through the people until I caught up with him. He stood next to Rush and avoided my eyes. I huffed, and Rush stopped listening to Tommy tell one of his famous stories about pranking the principal every year and how this year would be even better than the last.

"You alright?" Rush asked, looking at me and putting his arm around my waist.

I nodded even though I was still trying to figure Tobias out. Just as I thought I finally found a common ground with him and understood him, bam, he threw a damn curve ball. Again.

Rush shifted as I looked at him, like he was nervous about something. "Are *you* okay?"

"Did my brother say something to upset you?"

I shook my head. "No. Why?"

He rubbed his jaw and shrugged. "It's Toby."

Toby raised a brow, signaling he probably heard Rush, but he didn't comment. Him and Rush looked at their watches at the same time which struck me as odd, but maybe it's a twin intuition thing.

Becca touched my arm. "Hey," she whispered, taking my attention off the boys.

"Hmm?"

She pointed toward the entryway, and I stiffened at the sight of the Ellisons. I wasn't prepared for the feelings I'd feel when seeing them. My stomach tightened, and I quickly looked to the floor. We had made a plan on how this would all go down, but, in that moment, I had forgotten everything. The music that played sounded muffled as if it was underwater, and my whole body felt hot.

"Oh no," Becca whispered. "Rush."

I felt a hand on my back and closed my eyes. "Hey, it's gonna be okay. We've got this. You let us handle it, okay?" Rush's voice remained so calm.

I nodded but didn't take my eyes off the floor. "This is stupid. Why am I freaking out? What if it really is him?" I whispered.

Rush put his mouth close to my ear. "Then we will figure it out tonight and put a stop to this."

My breathing picked up as I nodded. "I need a drink."

He took my hand and placed it in Toby's. "Go get her a drink and take her outside."

When I finally looked up, Toby looked at Rush with accusing eyes. I didn't understand and wondered if I was reading it wrong. Maybe he was pissed Rush was pawning me off on him to take care of. I'd be fine. I could handle it. I just needed a minute to gather myself and focus. I pulled my hand from Toby's grip.

"I can take care of myself. I'll be right back." I ran my fingers through my hair and walked off.

When I made it to the bar in the far corner of the room, I ordered water. I had just taken a sip when Toby came over. "I'm fine."

"Liar." He looked over his shoulder and then at me again. "Why don't we go outside and get fresh air? Rush is right, you need to take a minute or just let them handle it."

I grabbed Toby's arm when I saw Peter coming over. "Save me," I whispered.

I noticed Rush and Tommy walking over and moved behind Toby so maybe Peter wouldn't see me even though he probably already had. He'd at least get the hint that I didn't want to talk to him. It wouldn't come as a surprise to him. He knew I hated him.

"Jorja, it's so good to see you," Peter said, his voice deep and arrogant as always.

I forced a smile. "Hi, Peter. Glad you could come."

"Why would I miss a Bonovich party? That'd be as bad as murder." The way he said murder made my skin crawl.

My eyes shifted to his pockets for a moment to see if I could make out the shape of a phone. I cursed under my breath. No sign of one. I continued to force my smile as I looked at him.

He looked around at Rush, Tommy, Toby, and me. "Four out of five of us here right now know all about murder, don't we?" When his eyes started to shift around the room, I stilled when his eyes focused on something. They were so intent and evil.

All of a sudden, commotion and screams broke out from inside the house. I swear I heard a door slam, but by the way people were acting, it wasn't a door. I had heard a gunshot plenty of times in my life, but not in my home. Adrenaline is a funny thing. You react without realizing you're moving or screaming or crying. I will never forget the smile on Peter's face before Toby grabbed my hand and pulled me from the room. We were running, but I couldn't feel my feet hitting the floor. Peter had said something before I was forced to leave the dining hall. Something about promises, but it was all becoming a blur.

"He's not breathing!" someone yelled, but I couldn't tell where the voice came from.

"Get her out of here!" I heard Rush shout.

But then ... then I saw the blood. I ran through it. I could see the trail of red my heels were leaving as I ran across the tile. I stopped. I didn't want to, I wanted to keep going, but I heard his name. Brian's name was said in the same sentence as not breathing, and that's when I heard my mother's screams. I fought so hard against Toby's hold as I tried to get free so I could get to the body my mother was cradling in her arms. I struggled to fight, so I gave in to Toby's hold and collapsed against him. Sirens sounded in the distance.

Everything after that happened so fast. At some point I had made it outside and was surrounded by my friends. Toby had me wrapped in his arms, his blazer over my shoulders as Rush and Tommy talked to the police. While all of that was going on, medics were rushing my brother strapped to a stretcher into the ambulance. They left, and I begged to go with him, but either Becca or Jena told me I had to answer questions first. Beck was talking to someone, and I heard him say Brian was breathing, but it didn't look good. This was all my fault. I wanted the dinner party to find out who was stalking me. Instead, I had created the perfect storm. The opportunity for someone to hurt my brother. Whoever was messaging me had something against my entire family. Had they planned on trying to kill him this entire time?

"He's going to die," I finally spoke as I stared into the distance. I wasn't talking to anyone in particular, just whoever heard me, I guess. I'm not even sure why I'd said that, it just came out.

I felt warm hands on my cheeks, and my eyes focused on their owner. Toby. "We don't know that yet. Just breathe."

My lungs burned from holding my breath. I inhaled deeply and let it out slowly. He let his hands fall once I started breathing normally. "No one can lose that much blood and live, Toby." I was shocked at the calmness in my voice.

"Let's go!" I turned my attention to Rush as he came hurrying past us. We didn't ask why or where, we all just followed him to Toby's truck. We all got in, and I sat in the back with Becca. Rush was driving.

"But ... I didn't talk to the cops," I said as I stared blankly out the back window.

"I told them you didn't see anything happen. None of us did," Rush said from the front.

My body jerked at the movement of the truck speeding out of the driveway. I turned around and rested my back against the seat. I felt numb. I knew I should have been panicking. I knew I should have been doing more than staring out my window, but I couldn't. I couldn't react at all.

As soon as we got to the hospital, my friends argued on my behalf that I needed to be back there with him, but when they mentioned surgery, the arguing stopped. I found myself sitting in a chair. I'm not sure how long

I sat there before it registered that we were in the waiting room. I didn't pay attention to who all was with me at that point. I rubbed the chill from my arms and stared at the double doors that felt like a thousand miles down the hall. I heard mumbling from a doctor before Rush's determined voice caught my attention.

"I'm O-negative. I can give blood."

"We are in low supply so any donation will help. We can run some tests, but for now we have some O-negative on hand we're giving him, and we've ordered more from the blood bank." The doctor looked at me with a reassuring nod before waving at Rush to follow him. Everything happened so fast I couldn't thank Rush. I watched him go through double doors that now felt even farther away. If they needed blood, that meant Brian was still alive, right? I started to become more aware of my surroundings and looked to the right of me to see Toby leaning forward with his elbows resting on his knees. He turned his head and looked at me then slowly sat back in his seat so we were sitting side by side.

"Is he okay?" I asked. My cheeks were damp with tears.

He took my hand and squeezed it.

More tears started to fall. "Toby, is my brother okay?"

"We don't know yet. He's in emergency surgery, and Rush is giving blood. Those are the only two things I know for certain right now."

I looked down at my feet and noticed I wasn't wearing shoes. 'Where are my shoes?"

"Becca took them off because they were dirty."

"With blood," I clarified, and he nodded.

I sniffed and wiped my eyes. "And my parents? Where are they?" I could feel my energy starting to come back. I went to stand, but Toby held onto my hand, keeping me seated.

"I think that's enough questions for now," Becca said from the other side of me.

"She deserves to know," Toby said.

I looked at Toby. "What?"

"Your mom is here and signing papers. Your dad ... the police took him into custody."

"What?" I repeated.

"When they got there, to your house, whoever shot your brother was already gone, but they had some information sent to them earlier before that happened. They were coming to your house anyway to arrest your dad."

"For *what*," I cried.

Toby hung his head but never let go of my hand. He inhaled deeply before letting it out. He looked at me. "The death of my mother."

CHAPTER TWENTY

Jorja

My eyes blinked open, and I noticed we were still in the waiting room. The night before, when Toby told me my dad was being charged with the death of his and Rush's mother, I went numb. I knew I should've reacted, but I was so tired. My brain shut down, and I just needed rest.

I looked up at Toby from where my head laid in his lap. I sat up slowly, rubbing the tension from my neck. I noticed my heels were lying on the floor on the other side of Toby, then looked down at myself to see my dress riding up on my thighs, so I straightened it out and pulled it down lower on my legs. Toby had his head resting on his arm that was folded on the seat of the chair. My movement woke him, and he sat up. He stretched and grabbed my shoes, handing them to me.

I slipped them on my feet and stood on shaky legs. I looked around the room and saw Becca, Wren, Jena, Beck, and Tommy sleeping. Toby stood, ran his fingers through his tousled hair, then put his hands in his pockets. Everything that transpired the night before started to collide in my mind. I sat in the chair behind me, put my head in my hands, and closed my eyes.

I felt Toby's hand on my back. "Is my mom still here?" I wanted to ask about Brian and my dad, but I was too afraid of the answers.

"She's in the room with Brian."

Tears filled my eyes as I sat up and looked at him. "Is he okay?"

The way his eyes shifted down and he exhaled, I knew it wasn't good. "He's stable but they don't know if he'll make it. They have him heavily sedated so he doesn't wake up and make a bunch of movements. Only time will tell. I'm so sorry, Jorja."

I swallowed hard and wiped tears that wet my cheeks. "Rush?"

Toby started to play with a strand of my hair and focused his eyes on it while he spoke. "He's in a room resting. He gave a lot of blood last night, and they just want to observe him for a bit."

I looked around the room again and Toby dropped his hand from my hair. "Is your dad here? Does he know?"

"He knows, but he's the one who came in and arrested your dad."

I chewed on my bottom lip as tears continued to fall. "Oh. Why do they think my dad killed your mom?" Saying that out loud felt like a punch to the gut. If it were true, had him and Rush known this entire time? The thoughts that came next made my head spin. @Rtrue360 was literally Rush's name. The conversation between Peter and Rush, before my brother was shot, started replaying in my head.

He looked around at Rush, Tommy, Toby, and me. "Four out of five of us here right now know all about murder, don't we?" When his eyes started to shift around the room, I stilled when his eyes focused on someone. They were so intent and evil.

Rush shook his head, "Don't," he whispered as he looked at Peter. I don't think Peter meant for me to hear that, but I could recognize the sound of his voice in a whisper. It was clear they knew each other somehow.

"I don't make promises I don't keep." Peter smiled as the commotion started to break out at the sound of a gunshot.

"Dammit," I breathed out. I grabbed my head. "No," I whispered. I'd stood too quickly and had to steady myself with the arm of the chair.

"What's wrong?" Toby asked as he stood. He reached for my arm, but I jerked away and started backing up. "Did you and Rush know Peter Ellison? Before last night?" I spoke so loudly the others in the room started to stir. My back hit a wall, forcing me to come to a stop.

No response from Toby was enough to answer my question.

"I'm such an idiot!" I yelled.

"Jorja?" I heard Becca say. "What's going on?" Becca looked at me and then at Toby.

Toby started to walk toward me. "I need you to listen to me."

I shook my head as I broke into violent sobs. "Get away from me!"

Becca stood, hurried over to me, and held me in a hug. She was the only thing keeping me standing.

"Rush was trying to put a stop to it," Toby explained calmly. "It was going too far, and then he met you ..."

My entire body trembled. "Stop!" I begged.

"He didn't know you, Jorja. He just knew your dad killed our mother, and he put Peter up to it. But then he moved here instead of living with our aunt and he saw you and then he got to know you. He never wanted to hurt you."

"Just my brother and my dad? That *is* hurting me!" I cried harder. "What you're telling me is he orchestrated this, and you knew about it the entire time?" Rage filled me, and I broke free from Becca's hold, but before I could attack Toby, Tommy and Beck had me by my arms, holding me back.

"I'd just leave, Toby," Beck said sadly.

Toby rubbed his jaw and nodded. "Jorja, for what it's worth, we both care so much about you, and this was all supposed to end. It should've never gone this far, but Peter has his own hate against your family and—"

"Did you not hear, Beck? Leave!" I screamed.

Toby hung his head and turned and left the waiting room at the same time nurses came into see what all the yelling was about. I heard Wren explaining it to them and Jena saying we had it under control. I heard the nurses mention something about me needing to leave, and that's when Tommy literally picked me up and started carrying me out.

"Put me down!" I begged.

"No, I'm taking you home. You need to rest and process everything so you can calm down."

I looked at him, remembering he and Rush were friends way before he had moved here. "Did you know, too?"

He didn't answer.

"Tommy! Did you know too?" The no response caused me to fight against him until I was out of his arms and on my own two feet.

"I didn't figure it out until he had already fallen for you."

"But you knew," I cried.

"He thought he had it handled and would be able to talk to Peter at the party tonight. It was supposed to be over."

"Who all knew, Tommy?"

He put his hands in his pockets and looked down at the concrete.

"Everyone?" My voice came out broken like shattered glass.

He met my eyes. "Before you go and hate all of us, you should know a few things. Becca, Wren, and Jena had no idea. Beck was told only a few days ago because Rush was begging for help. Toby has liked you since kindergarten and told Rush to leave you and your family alone. Rush has fallen hard for you, and because Toby begged him not to let Peter do this before he ever moved here, Rush pulled the plug on the plans and told Peter never mind. Peter wanted to do this. This was all Peter from the beginning."

"If you knew, why didn't you say so! He could've been stopped before it escalated to my brother laying in a damn hospital bed dying! And my dad ..."

"Whoa." He held up his hands. "Don't put me in this, Jorja. I'm the middleman and on no one's side. I thought this would be stopped, and I wanted to let those who started it handle it. Your family and you can hate me for saying this, but they are toxic, and you know it. Their actions and decisions are ultimately what has us standing here in this hospital parking lot, your brother fighting for his life, your dad in jail, and Rush giving blood to the one who drove your dad to pull that trigger to kill his mom."

I shook my head and crossed my arms in front of me as tears fell in a steady stream. "I can't believe this. Why would anyone want to kill Rush and Toby's mom?"

"That's a question you'll have to ask Toby and Rush. They're the ones who need to be okay with telling you that."

I wanted to run. I wanted to just leave and never look at Grove, Colorado again. I wished my sister had left me a *How to Run Away* checklist since she did it so well. I rubbed my arms and looked at Tommy.

"I just want to go home."

"It's a crime scene, Jorja. You can't right now."

I let out a shaky breath. "Oh ... right."

"Your mom did tell me she got a hotel room. Do you want me to take you there?"

I shrugged. "Sounds like I don't have a choice." I looked toward the hospital and then at Tommy. The sun was getting higher in the sky, so it had to be mid-morning.

"You may want to go see if she has the key to the room."

I shook my head. "I can't go back in there, Tommy."

He took his keys from his pocket and handed them to me. "Go wait in my truck. I'll be right back."

I held them tightly in my hand and turned around to look at all of the vehicles until I spotted his truck. I headed that way, wondering what would come from all of this. I tried hard not to even think about it at all, but that was impossible. Everything that happened would haunt me for the rest of my life.

CHAPTER TWENTY-ONE

Rush

An entire week passed without Jorja at school. Rumors were being spread that she'd moved, but Tommy told me that she didn't, and she and her mom were staying at her grandfather's cabin farther north until the investigation at their house came to a close. I called her the moment I found out her brother had woken up from his induced coma and was on the road to recovery, but she didn't answer. Not that I expected her to. I mean, why would she after what I did to her?

I looked at my right arm and rubbed the spot they took blood from for my donation. There wasn't a sign of the needle pricking my skin. but a yellowish bruise still lingered which was better than the dark purple it had been. I'd never forget the time my mother told me my blood type. I thought it was a weird conversation and didn't know why it even mattered, but now I did after helping Brian. The doctor told me they wouldn't be able to use mine right away because it had to go through a whole process of medical terms I didn't understand, but after a week or so it could be used and would aide in saving Brian's life.

"Son, you haven't eaten anything on your plate. You've barely eaten anything all damn week now that I think about it." Dad had worried everything would end up like this the moment he found out I started hanging around Jorja.

I responded with a lazy shrug. I could feel my brother looking at me, but I avoided meeting his eyes. He told me this would happen and told me to tell Jorja when I took her hiking. I had every intention to, but I got consumed with how happy I felt with her, and with her already being so upset, I didn't want to be the one to bring her grief, just happiness. I thought I could make up for what I started with Peter by fixing her problems and stopping Peter myself. I didn't know it would all lead to this. Not to this magnitude, anyway.

I checked my phone to see if she texted me back, unsure why I even held onto the hope she would. I stared at the home screen with no new notifications from her, just my background of a picture of her laughing at me when I snuck in a picture in class one day and she caught me. It would forever be my favorite because that laugh was real. The smile was everything, including the way her nose crinkled when her smile was genuine. Not many got to see that smile from what I observed.

"She just needs space and time to think, Rush. Just give it time." Dad always said encouraging things even if he didn't think things would get better.

I pushed my plate away and looked at Toby. "Can I use the truck tonight? It's not like you go anywhere anyway."

His eyes narrowed. "Just because you screwed up doesn't mean you get to talk to people any way you want. Lose the attitude, asshole."

"You're one to talk. All you've ever done is say whatever the hell you wanted to Jorja, without ever considering her feelings."

His fist tightened around the paper towel he was holding. "With reason. Did you already forget I knew her way before you? How I speak to other people is none of your damn business. How I speak to you directly reflects how you choose to speak to me."

"Would you get off my case?"

Dad slammed his fists against the table causing our glasses to shake and ice to rattle in them. "Enough! Neither of you are going anywhere tonight except to the sink to clean the damn dishes!" He wiped his mouth on a paper towel, balled it up, and threw it in the middle of his plate. "Both of you should know that her dad was bailed out of jail today and is going home until his court date. He's on house arrest, and I'm sure Jorja is far more worried about being at home with everything going on than either of you." He narrowed his eyes on Toby. "And what did I teach you boys about being kind even if it's not deserved?"

"She made fun of the wallpaper in here," Toby mumbled.

Dad raised a brow. "We all know it had way more to do than this god-awful wallpaper."

Toby folded his arms across his chest and looked toward the sink.

Dad stood and looked at both of us. "I mean it. You two stay put. If I find out either of you left this house, you'll regret it. Am I clear?"

We nodded.

Dad left the kitchen, and Toby and I stood, then started cleaning without a word to each other. We didn't have a dishwasher, so, against our will, we had to stand by one another to do the dishes. He washed, I dried. It was almost as if Dad knew we'd end up pissed at one another so he dirtied every dish while cooking so we'd have to do this forever. It made me shudder remembering the time he decided to do that stupid trick where we had to wear the same shirt until we got along. That backfired on him quickly. We ended up ripping the shirt as we rolled around the floor beating the crap out of each other.

"I'm so close to falling in love with her," I said to Toby, breaking the silence and making my feelings clear. Now that I was the bad guy, I was afraid he'd use this chance to make his move.

He pulled the drain plug out of the sink then turned the faucet on. He stuck his finger under the stream of water waiting for it to get hot. When it started steaming, he put the plug back into the sink and added soap. He peered sightlessly into the sudsy water.

"You can't tell me you love her, too," I scoffed. "You may have known her longer, but from a distance. You love the idea of her."

He turned the water off with so much force I winced, preparing for it to bust and water to start spewing everywhere. His eyes narrowed to slits as he looked at me. I could tell he wanted to say something, but he shook his head and went back to washing the dishes.

When he handed me a dish, I started to dry it. "I know you want to say something."

"I have not once said I was in love with her. I have always liked the idea of her because whether she remembers it or not, she did things that proved she's not a total bitch. I've always known that side was in there somewhere."

"In kindergarten," I scoffed.

"She kicked a dude in the balls for taking my fruit snacks. Then again in second grade, the same punk-ass kid thought it'd be funny to pee on my backpack behind the slide. You can laugh all you want, but I've watched her for so many years doing these little random kind things for people that no one ever saw. She didn't even take credit for a lot of it. I've just known there's more to her."

"She's not one of your stupid ass puzzles." I laughed coldly. "And if you wanted to figure her out so badly with your weird stalker crush, why are you such an ass to her? I thought you tried to talk to her and she blew you off."

He set the cup down he was washing. "I don't have to explain myself to you. I told you I wouldn't interfere with whatever the hell it is you two had going, and I still won't. She isn't some piece of candy you can just claim as your own. You're the one who wanted to bring her family down. Do you not remember that? And that I begged you to just leave the Bonoviches alone? Then you saw her that day when we were driving and because she is beautiful—"

"You called her a ho!"

"I would've said she was actually a man if it would've kept you away from her! I knew the moment you saw her and decided you'd tell Peter to forget everything y'all planned that this would all blow up in your damn face! I was trying to keep you and her from getting hurt!"

"I was trying to fix it! I thought I had Peter under control!"

"Yeah, well, how did that work out for ya?"

I threw the towel down and pushed his shoulders as hard as I could then put my face only inches away from his. Both our hands were in tight fists at our sides, and our breathing matched a heavy and fast pace. I was ready to beat the crap out of him. One move from him and it'd be over.

His eyes relaxed some, and he took a step back. "You know what? Do the dishes yourself." He stormed out of the kitchen.

Part of me wanted to go after him, but the other half knew it wouldn't be worth it. So many people were mad at me, and whether I wanted to admit it right then or not, I needed my brother. I also didn't want to admit how right he had been. I tried not to think about how upset my mother would be with how we're acting if she were here, but it crept into my mind regardless.

I looked at the multitude of dishes in front of me, rested my palms on the edge of the sink, and sighed heavily. I asked Dad why they didn't have a dishwasher when I first moved in, and he said dishwashers were a luxury that he didn't want any part of. He didn't want to be a part of any luxuries at all. This house was a dump even though he could afford a place out by Jorja's if he wanted. He said that he knew too many people who lived like that, and he never wanted to be like them or allow his sons to feel privileged. When I asked why, I got the oddest response; a quote from Confucius: *A perfumed butthole is still a butthole.* I don't remember if I even responded when he said that. All I remember was his deep laughter that followed. Dad's always quoting dead people from all those old books he reads.

I shook my head and laughed as I started washing the dishes. My laughter faded as my mind left the past and came back to my current reality. The sting of it burned like salt to a fresh wound. I never got to see Jorja when she found out the truth about Peter and me. Toby explaining the hurt in her eyes was enough to crush me completely. I kept telling myself if I could just get to her and explain myself, if she'd listen to me at all, I could make this right. I dried my hands and took my phone from my back pocket. I'd text her one more time and if no response, I'd leave her alone.

Me: Five minutes, Jorja. Just give me the chance to explain myself. You can hate me forever, but you deserve to hear everything from me.

I set the phone on the counter near the sink and finished washing the dishes, praying like hell she'd respond.

CHAPTER TWENTY-TWO

Rush

Three nights ago, I texted, asking one last time for Jorja to give me a chance to explain. She never responded. I came to school fully prepared that Jorja wouldn't be there, but I was wrong. As she sauntered into first period, I noticed her normally perfectly curled hair was straight and pulled into a low ponytail, no makeup, eyes red and puffy, and she wore leggings, a sweatshirt, and those stupid boots that were terrible for hiking. Everyone stared as she made it to her seat. My heart ached for her normal sexy smile with the nose crinkle. When she noticed me looking at her, her eyes shifted quickly to the floor, avoiding me as she took the seat behind me. Beck, who sat in front of me, turned around to pass some papers back. Had the teacher even given instructions? If she did, I damn sure wasn't paying attention.

I took the papers, kept one for myself and turned around to hand the stack of papers to Jorja. She had her hands folded in her lap and looked down at her desk blankly. I did that. The broken girl sitting before me was a product of my screw up. And, my god, it killed me.

"Jorja," I said quietly.

She didn't look up.

"Jorja," I said again, a bit louder.

She jerked a little when she looked up at me. Tears filled her eyes, and she took the papers. I held onto the papers longer than I should, causing her to tug a little. Her cheeks reddened, and I craved one of her snarky remarks. All I got were tears that trickled down her face. I let go of the papers, mentally fighting the urge to let all the things I needed to say spill out. When I turned around, I realized I had tears in my own eyes. I wiped them on the back of my hand before they could fall.

The rest of the class period was pure torture knowing Jorja sat behind me, within my reach. I wanted to hold her until all the hurt melted away and tell her I'm sorry forever. I told Peter not to pursue anything further, but he had his own hurts that pushed him over the edge. He missed out on growing up with his only sibling because of a secret affair that could never be spoken of. I talked to him five times about leaving her alone since it all began. He just wouldn't listen. All of my anger began to gravitate toward him instead of myself, and it felt good to take the blame off me for a moment.

The bell rang, and I gathered up my things slowly, hoping Jorja might take her time to pack up and we'd be forced to talk. Of course, nothing was going my way. She had her things packed so fast that she left the classroom before anyone else.

Beck turned around and looked at me after zipping his backpack. "Hey, you alright?" It's the first thing he'd said to me that wasn't school related since everything went down.

"It doesn't matter."

We both stood from our desks at the same time.

"I just ... don't want anyone doing anything stupid like hurting themselves or anything." He fidgeted with the strap of his backpack stuck out of the buckle. "Jorja looks terrible. Like she's standing on the edge of a cliff waiting for a gust of wind to knock her down. Know what I mean?"

I swallowed hard and looked down at the floor before looking past him at the students spilling into the hallway. I really didn't know what to say.

"Well ... see ya." His words trailed off as he sighed heavily and turned to walk out of the classroom.

I stood there a moment trying to convince my boots to move in the direction of my next class, but they didn't listen. Instead, I found myself walking through the halls looking for Peter. I turned the corner and found him at his locker. I had told myself I wouldn't do this. Had to talk myself out of it the moment I left the hospital. Seeing Jorja that morning, how broken she was and just a shell of a person, not the girl I knew before this nightmare, ignited a fury I could feel in my bones.

I spotted him at his locker. Just as he shut the door, everything fell silent, and all I focused on was him. I dropped my backpack then grabbed him by his collar and slammed him against the lockers, the loud thud against the metal echoing down the hall. His mouth opened but a word was never spoken because my fist plowed into his face twice. The sensation of warm blood smearing over my knuckles was an indication I hurt him good. It wasn't enough, though. I went in for another hit, but someone pulled me away from him before I could. My brother. As he pulled me farther and farther away, I could feel Peter's blood drying on my hands, and the satisfaction from that made me smile. The sound of commotion in the hall was more audible as my adrenaline settled, and I started to become aware of my surroundings. I was being guided to the office by Toby and the assistant principal, Mr. Langston. They each had one of my arms.

When we made it to the office, Mr. Langston told me to sit down in his office that was adjacent to the principal's. He told Toby to go back to class, and I sighed heavily. I hadn't had any reason to be in there until now, which was a huge contrast from my previous school. Mainly just me and my buddies clowning and stuff, rarely fighting. I saved that for the football field. If I had moved at the beginning of the year, I would've played for Grove. The coach had already been hounding me about playing next year, though.

I looked down at my bloody knuckles then at Mr. Langston as he walked in. "Can I go wash my hands?"

He shut the door and walked around his desk. He sat down and started doing something on his computer. Maybe he didn't hear me.

"Excuse me, Mr. Langston? Can I please go wash my hands?"

His eyes widened, acknowledging that he heard me, but I guess his lack of words was his response. I huffed and pressed my back more into the chair.

"Your father is a good friend of mine."

I raised a brow, unsure of how this had anything to do with why I was in here. "Oh."

"It's terrible about your mother. I'm very sorry for your loss." His eyes remained on the computer as he typed something.

"Thank you. Did you know her?"

He chuckled. "Only all the horrible things your father said about her."

I looked at my hands again. The mention of my mother stung a little, and I felt myself getting angry that he chose to say that about her. I was sure he'd meant no harm, so I decided not to press the issue. "I'm sorry, are we gonna get to the point or ...?" I looked up when the sound of typing stopped.

"The entire town knows what happened with Peter Ellison and the Bonovich family."

I frowned. "They still don't know who shot her brother, sir."

"No, but we all know Peter was the one sending those texts to Jorja since he openly admitted to it. Is that why you thought it'd be wise to knock the kid out? We know you and Jorja have this thing going on. Small town talk."

"I knocked him out?" Toby pulled me away before I could be sure.

He grunted, but I think he was covering up a laugh. "You'll be suspended for ten days for this."

"I figured. Has anyone called my dad yet or do I need to?"

"The secretary is already handling that. So, was that the reason for this occurrence today?"

I nodded. "Yes, sir."

"Did he do something else to her that I need to be aware of?"

I could feel the confusion showing on my face.

"I'm asking because you've been at school all last week and left him alone. Why today?"

It felt like this meeting was getting too personal. "Nothing else happened. It just felt like a good day to knock him out."

I looked out the window behind him. I saw Peter being escorted out by the school nurse to his parents' car. He held a towel over his nose.

Mr. Langston turned to follow my gaze. "They think he has a broken nose."

I grinned but stopped when he turned back around and looked at me. It was odd being so happy causing someone else physical pain. And even crazier to think he and I were once friends. His mom and my mom went to school together, and that's how we knew each other. When I came into town to visit Toby and Dad, he and I would hang out. Toby never really liked him, but he was actually pretty cool until all of this stuff happened. I figured once I told him to drop the whole thing he would've.

"I'll have your brother gather your things and bring them to the office. You can wait out front until your dad gets here to sign you out."

I nodded.

He rested his elbows on the desk, leaning forward. "Also, be prepared. The Ellisons may try to turn this into an assault case. They're notorious for making things a bigger deal than they need to be."

I shrugged. "It'll be worth it."

The creases at the corners and the hard line of his lips pressing together made it obvious he was trying not to smile. He cleared his throat. "As long as you're aware." He stood and opened the door. "See you in ten days."

I stood, left his office, and went into the main office area. I saw Toby sitting in the chair closest to the door with my things and his.

"Why do you have your stuff, too?" I took my backpack and slung it over my shoulder.

His eyes went to my hands covered in dry blood then looked at me again. "Dad told me he was checking both of us out."

"But you didn't do anything."

He shrugged. "I'm not arguing with Dad about it."

We both looked at the door when it opened, and Jorja came walking in. Tears were falling down her cheeks, and she had her arms crossed in front of her. She pretended to not see us and walked to the front desk.

I went to take a step toward her, but Toby grabbed the back of my backpack to stop me. My shoulders sagged as I heard her talk to the secretary. She spoke so low through her sniffles it was hard to understand what she said. I looked at the door when it opened again, and Dad walked in. He noticed Jorja and must've sensed my struggle between staying put while he signed me out or wrapping her in my arms and not letting her go until she felt happy again.

He looked at me with serious eyes. "You and your brother head home."

I didn't move.

"Now," he said through his teeth.

Toby stood and opened the door. I sighed heavily and followed him out.

CHAPTER TWENTY-THREE

Jorja

I looked up from my book and toward the door when I heard someone knock. When Mom had answered the door, I could hear Tommy's deep voice. I put my bookmark between the pages and set the book on the coffee table. I wasn't really much of a reader, but lately, I found it therapeutic to get lost in someone else's messed up world instead of my own. I stood and smoothed the wrinkles from my sweatshirt. I went to head toward the entryway, but Mom and Tommy came walking into the living room.

My heart fluttered. Part of me hoped he had news on Rush and what came of the fight. I heard he really messed Peter's face up which made me smile for the first time since Brian was shot. I tucked my hair behind my ears and waited for Tommy to say something. I noticed his eyes shift to Mom, so I cleared my throat and raised a brow. She took the hint and left the room.

Tommy looked past me and at the book on the coffee table. "You're reading. You must be ill."

I shrugged. "Why are you here?"

"To talk."

"About?" I could feel heat rush to my cheeks. My hands made tight fists around the ends of my sleeves. I lied to myself. I didn't want to talk about Rush at all, and the gnawing feeling at the pit of my stomach told me that's why he's here.

"Rush. What happened. What *really* happened, Jorja."

"No."

He sighed and rubbed the back of his neck. "Please, you need to know the truth."

I crossed my arms in front of me and tried to keep my expression neutral. I didn't want to lose my temper or cry. "I know what happened, Tommy. My brother almost died. I really don't feel like reliving that."

"No, you know what happened from *your* perspective. Not Rush's, and you're killing him by avoiding him."

I narrowed my eyes. "I hope he dies."

"You don't mean that," he snapped.

I didn't mean that. That he was right about. But that didn't change reality.

I huffed and shrugged again. "You're wasting your time if that's why you're here. Did he send you?"

"No, I'm here on my own. I hate seeing you so sad, and whether you want to admit it or not, Rush makes you happy. You've been the best version of yourself when you were hanging out with him, and you can't deny that. You need to know his side even if you won't let him talk to you."

My lips began to tremble. "Because of him, my brother almost died!" I shouted.

"And he won't deny that, but he tried to stop it all! He told Peter to back off before all of this started, but he didn't listen! Peter is the one who chose to do it all. He is the one who continued with something that Rush decided not to have any part in!"

My legs felt unsteady. I could feel myself about to lose control, and I didn't want anyone to see me cry over Rush. I kept telling myself that I just needed to put my walls up again and get back to the place I used to be, where I didn't need anyone. I walked over to the couch and sat down. Tommy followed and sat beside me.

"Jorja, I just can't have you hating someone who made you happy and someone you need through all of this. Especially when he didn't do anything. If anything, he tried to stop it."

I picked at fuzz on my left sleeve to focus on something that would keep me from crying or screaming in a fit of rage. "Even if he didn't do anything and tried to stop it, it doesn't change the fact that my father killed his mom. How can we ever move past that?" I looked at Tommy, and a few tears trickled down my cheeks.

"He already knew that and didn't let that get between how he feels for you. That's obvious. Admit it, you need him."

"I don't need anyone," I said through clenched teeth. And that I meant and believed. As a matter of fact, if I could have just run away and gotten away from this god-forsaken town, I would have been able to create a new me. Like my sister did. Everything she did completely made sense to me in that moment.

"You need all of us right now. You can be stubborn and act like you don't, but we all know you better than that. The only person you need to be mad at right now is your dad. If he cared enough about his family, he wouldn't live the life he does. He brought all of you into this."

I didn't say anything because I couldn't argue with him. Everything he'd said I'd heard and understood. I hated my dad. I didn't hate Rush even if I said I did. How could I? Especially knowing he did try to stop all of this. I tried to tell myself I hated him because it was easier that way. I had to let whatever idea I had of him go. We couldn't come back after this. I'd always be the girl whose father killed his mother. He'd always be the guy that initially wanted to take my family down and use me as the pawn. That didn't sit right with me. Maybe he could move past it all, but I couldn't. No matter how badly I wanted to.

"You should go." I ran my hand down my face and leaned back into the couch. "You shouldn't be involved with me, Tommy. You have big plans for your life after high school. Don't jeopardize that."

"You don't get to tell me what to do."

My lips twitched at the corners a little. "I'm serious."

"Me too. You're one of my best friends. Abandoning you when things get tough isn't an option for me." His smile was contagious, though the movement of my lips still felt foreign.

"Thank you," I whispered. I mustered up every bit of strength to admit he was right. "Fine, I do need all of you right now. I just don't want all of you involved with something that has the potential to mess with your lives worse than it already has."

He looked at the book on the table and picked it up. His shoulders moved up and down with his quiet laughter. "The girl who doesn't read chose to read *The Great Gatsby*?" He held the book up and looked at me with raised brows.

"Because it's awful."

He held an amused grin as he looked at it again. "Then why read it?"

"Because it's so bad that it makes what I'm going through feel not as bad." I shrugged.

"Why on earth would you own this book anyway? It's too long and boring."

"My parents buy me odd stuff all the time. Just proves how much they don't know me."

"And your logic confuses me. Why read a book you don't like when things are so messed up already?" He shook his head and set the book back down. "Doesn't that make things worse?"

I shrugged again and sighed. "Maybe." I decided to talk about what he really wanted to talk about. I couldn't avoid it forever. "I want to forgive him," I blurted out before I could swallow those words. That wasn't what I wanted to say, but it came from the heart and was what I needed to say.

His smile faded, and his features softened. "Then forgive him, Jorja."

"I don't know why I even said that. I'm so confused. It's too soon to even think I could forgive him."

"I don't think you can put a time frame on when your heart is ready to forgive someone." He leaned back against the couch and turned his head to look at me.

I nodded. "You're not wrong." I hated how all over the place I was. One minute I hated him. The next I didn't. It was like a heavy revolving door that just wouldn't stay shut.

He laughed through his nose. "I know I'm not."

"My parents and the attorney say I should stay away from the True boys." I began to fidget with my sleeves again.

"Why?"

"I think they are trying to say one of them shot my brother. I know they didn't. I vouched for them and told them they were with me when it happened. Peter was, too. For some reason, they aren't listening to me, though. But considering their mother was killed by my dad, I can see why they don't want me around them. It's probably for the best." My brow furrowed with that last statement. "They want one of them to look guilty so my dad doesn't."

"That's not fair."

I laughed coldly. "Welcome to my life. Nothing about any of it has ever been fair. Maybe I should just run like my sister did. Start a new life." I didn't even try to quiet my voice when I said that. I'm sure my mom was listening.

"Don't do that." His eyes were pleading with me.

I leaned forward, picked up the book from the table, and found the page I was on.

He nudged my side. "I'm not done talking to you."

"Well, I am. My head hurts, and my emotions are giving me whiplash." I tried to focus on the words on the page but couldn't.

"You're not running away."

I set the book in my lap and looked at his worried eyes. I sighed. "Okay. I won't."

"Promise?"

I nodded. "Mmhmm."

"You're lying, but I won't let you do anything stupid. Do you want to go do something? Get ice cream or pizza? You can't just sit at home on a Friday night."

Getting out of the house and doing something other than sulking was probably a good idea. "Sure. I need a shower and to get ready. I haven't fixed my hair or makeup in days." I stood and stretched.

Tommy stood and put his hands in his jean pockets. "Okay. I'll head home and come back in an hour. That'll be enough time?"

I nodded, walked him to the door and, after he left, went upstairs to get ready.

CHAPTER TWENTY-FOUR

Rush

I drove through town to go to the lawyer's office a few counties over to discuss things regarding my mother's belongings and other things. I didn't know what "other things" the lawyer referred to, but it sounded important. The lawyer wasn't normally open on Saturdays, but since it was impossible for me to get over there during the week, he'd made an exception.

I groaned as I was about to pass the welcome sign. A sign that I'm sure was intended to welcome newcomers looked more like an apology to anyone who found themselves entering this toxic ass place. I turned down the radio when I saw Jorja parked on the shoulder. Her car faced the sign, and she sat on the hood twirling a strand of her hair around her finger. Her eyes were void of any emotion at all, and it made the pit of my stomach ache. I tried to will my foot to keep its heaviness on the gas pedal, but, against my better judgment, I released the gas and eased on the brakes until the truck came to a stop on the other side of the road.

"Rush, you're an idiot," I mumbled to myself as I killed the engine and got out. I saw her jump a little when she heard the door shut, but she didn't turn to look at me. I checked the time on my watch and then shoved my hands in my pockets as I crossed the road. I walked until I stood in front of her car. Her hair and makeup were fixed, giving me some sense of normalcy.

Her eyes were now on her hands folded in her lap. "What do you want?" Her voice sounded so raw. She always had this sexy little rasp to her voice, but now it sounded painful to talk.

"I don't know exactly. To talk? To tell you how incredibly sorry I am? To give you an explanation." I hadn't taken my eyes off her in hopes there'd be a rare moment when she'd meet my eyes.

"Okay."

My eyes widened. "Really?"

She shrugged.

I had chosen my words a million times in my head. Practiced them. I'd even dreamt about them. Changed them and picked more sincere sounding words. I forgot them all when "okay" left her lips. I wasn't prepared to see her so broken and still be able to form words.

Her eyes finally met mine and tears wet her lashes. "Well?" She scoffed when I still didn't speak and shook her head. "That's what I figured."

"Excuse me? That's not fair! Give me a second."

"Fair?" she fumed. "You want to talk to me about being fair? Are you kidding me right now?"

I closed my eyes and sighed. "Sorry. I didn't mean ... I didn't ... I thought I had the words, Jorja. I don't. I don't know what to say or do. All I know is that I'm sorry, and I know that word isn't enough. I don't deserve forgiveness or even this moment with you at all. I'm a mess. I tried to stop all of this. I told Peter not to do this, but he did it. He rolled with it after I had already bowed out. I started it from miles away until I met you. Then I said never mind. He did it. Peter did this."

"What did meeting me change in your mind? My father killed your mother, Rush! That's not okay! You had every right to hate my family and want to ruin us."

Tears filled my eyes and my voice cracked. I cursed under my breath, hating I let my emotions get the best of me. "Not you," I said, unsure if she could even make out the words with how shaky my voice was. "Damn," I whispered as I wiped my eyes.

"I'm not angry with you, Rush," her voice was so quiet and sweet I swore it had to have been a joke.

"You're not?" Testing my luck, I took a few steps forward to be closer to her.

She shook her head and looked toward the woods to the right of us. "No. I wish you had told me, and I'm hurt, but I'm not mad. I was at first, but then Tommy explained things better. Once I got past making it all about me, I started to understand." She pulled her sleeve over her hand and lightly dabbed her eyes, careful not to mess up her makeup. She sighed before looking at me. "When I think about leaving this place, I come here." Her eyes shifted to the sign.

I looked at the sign and then at her again.

She smiled a little, but it faded quickly. "My head is a mess."

"That's understandable."

"I miss you." She covered her mouth with her hands, and I could see the shock in her eyes. I was happy she said it, but it hurt knowing she didn't mean for me to hear it.

"Then stop avoiding me," I pleaded.

She shook her head and watched as a car passed us coming into town. "I can't do that." I started to walk closer, but she held up a hand. "Don't," she stated sternly.

"Why?" I asked, sounding more demanding than I intended to.

"Because we can't be friends. We can't be together. We can't be anything at all." The fresh tears that filled her eyes gave me some satisfaction in knowing that those words hurt her.

"That's not true."

"My dad killed your mom! I will not have you think about that every single time you're near me."

"Jorja, I knew that, yet I still chose to be around you. You're not your dad or responsible for his decisions." I needed to talk about something else. The flashbacks started to come, and I needed them to go away. What Jorja didn't know, or maybe she did, is that I was there when he shot her. He didn't see me. I wasn't fast enough to stop him. He shot her and left before she had even taken her last breath which only took a few seconds. My hands shook, and I needed to think about something else and fast. I looked at my watch and had to rub the tears out of my eyes to focus on the time. I needed to go so I could meet with the lawyer.

"Where'd your mind just go?" she asked quietly.

I looked at her and she was rubbing her arms. "Nowhere that I want to talk about, but I do need to leave. I have a meeting with Mom's lawyer."

"Where's Toby?"

"Home. He didn't want to go." I wanted to kick myself for being jealous she mentioned him.

"Are you busy after the meeting?"

I tilted my head to the side a little. "Why are you asking?"

"I don't know. Forget I even asked that."

"How the hell am I supposed to forget you asked that?"

She smiled a little and shrugged. "You should forget I asked that."

I smirked. "How long exactly are you planning on torturing me like this?"

Her lips formed a hard line. "I'm no good for you."

"Then, I guess I'll spend every single chance I get to prove you wrong."

She slid off the hood of her car and opened the car door. "Thanks for stopping and talking, but we can't do this again."

"Jorja."

"We can't, Rush! I'm in a completely messed up head space."

I took several slow steps toward her. "Me too."

She gripped the side of the door so hard her knuckles turned white. "Just go to your meeting."

I kept moving until I stood directly in front of her.

"What are you doing?" she whispered as she looked up at me through her lashes.

I wrapped her in my arms, and she tensed for a moment before relaxing. She held onto the front of my shirt and pressed her face against my chest.

"I ... I," she stammered before completely breaking and sobbing. I rubbed her back and kissed the top of her head. I'd miss the meeting if it meant doing exactly this right here.

"You can work up all the horrible things you think I think about you in your mind, but I promise you none of them are true."

"But my dad—"

"I don't want to talk about that. It has nothing to do with you and I."

She looked up at me. "It has everything to do with us."

I shook my head and wiped her tears from her cheeks. "No, it doesn't."

"Does your dad hate me?"

I laughed and shook my head. "My dad doesn't hate anyone. He said my mother chose her own life path and those decisions had consequences."

"I'm sorry about your mom."

"Me too, and as hard as it is for me to admit it, my dad isn't wrong. I'm sorry it all ended up like this. I tried to stop it."

She shook her head. "I get it. I do." She wiggled free from my arms. "You should go."

"And when the meeting is done?"

"I'm not sure. I'm so confused right now, and I'm not thinking straight. I was told to stay away from you and your family."

"By who?" I started getting pissed.

"My mom. My grandparents. The lawyer. Everyone in my family. Brian."

Confusion had to be written all over my face.

"They're trying to ..." She bit her bottom lip. "I can't talk about it. We both need to go. People are watching." She got in her car and shut the door. I heard the doors lock but tried to pull the handle to open the door anyway. She started backing away, forcing me to move unless I wanted my feet ran over.

And just like that, she was gone again.

CHAPTER TWENTY-FIVE

Jorja

"Where have you been?" Mom asked me as I came into the living room. She laid down on the couch with a throw blanket pulled to her chin. She'd started feeling bad last night. I think all the stress had finally taken its toll on her.

"I went and picked up a few groceries from town. I told you where I went. Remember?" I had been helping out with things since Ruth quit. With everything going on, she didn't want to be tied to our family at all. Who could have blamed her? I'd wanted to quit my family at times, too.

She blinked a few times. "Oh. Right. Did you get water?"

I wrapped my arms around myself, still able to smell Rush's cologne on my shirt. "Yes."

"Thank you, Jorja. I know all of this has to be so hard on you, and now I'm not feeling good and—"

"No apologies. You agreed we'd get through this together and not apologize for things that aren't our fault."

Her lips pressed firmly together.

"How's Brian this morning?" I leaned against the wall.

She sighed and pushed a few strands of hair from her face. "He tried to get up by himself and almost fell. He caught himself on the end table by his bed. Luckily, I came in there when I did or he wouldn't have made it back to the bed."

"He's stubborn."

She smiled a little. "We all are." Tears clouded her eyes. "Gosh, I miss when you were all little. I felt like I could protect you and keep you safe. Now ... my son was shot in our own home." She closed her eyes.

She was pretty good at holding it together considering all she'd been through. She had carried a lot of the weight of this life over the years, but my sister ran away and Brian getting shot pushed her over the edge.

She wiped her eyes and looked at me. "Go get me water and my anxiety meds, please."

I pushed off the wall. "Anything else?"

She shook her head. "No. But, Jorja?"

"Yeah?"

"Did you *only* go to the store while you were out?"

Lying and keeping secrets were my specialty, but not anymore. I felt too tired to conceal anything right now. "Yes. The store and home." Nothing convincing about the way I said that, but hopefully she was too exhausted to notice.

"Remember, we don't want you going near the Trues." Her forehead creased with worry. "I know you were getting so close and—"

I cut her off. "We've already talked about this. I'm not."

Neither of us said a word when Dad came walking into the living room. I hadn't spoken a single word to him since he got bailed out of jail and brought home on bond. His court date was in two weeks. His lawyer came to our home every single day working on a plan to get him out of all this. He really did shoot Rush and Toby's mom. He had denied it to Mom and me, but I'd overheard a conversation between him and his lawyer when they didn't know I was anywhere around. In a family like this, you learn to be sneaky over the years, a skill I became a pro at by the time I turned five.

I left the room when Mom and Dad started to talk. I couldn't understand her forgiving him so quickly. Everything he'd put her through their entire marriage should have been impossible for anyone to bear. Mom was strong, I'd give her that. But also a complete idiot. She'd believed when he said he didn't shoot Ms. True. I'd wanted to at first, but then I heard him tell his lawyer he shot her because she stole money and drugs from him, and I had vowed to never speak to him again. I talked to Becca about it. She said it was no different than him hiring hits on people even if he didn't shoot them themselves; they still died by his hands. It wasn't that I hadn't realized that before, I just sugar coated it in my mind so I wouldn't think less of him. With everything in the open now, he'd be nothing but a monster to me.

I made it into the kitchen and walked to the counter that housed all of Brian's medications. Mom's were there somewhere, but I had to look at each bottle to find her name because there were so many keeping my brother alive and pain free. I found hers and grabbed a bottle of water before walking back into the living room. I sat both down on the coffee table, doing my best to avoid looking at Dad who was sitting beside her on the couch playing with her hair. I had almost made it out of the room before Dad said my name.

I stopped but didn't turn around.

"I really am sorry you're having to go through all of this." His voice sounded sincere, but he was a liar. If he were sorry, none of us would be going through this at all. He wouldn't have allowed any of us to live this life. He would've left it long ago when Mom wanted to. As hard as leaving it would have been, he could've found a way.

I swallowed hard and waited until nothing else was said before making my exit. On my way to my room, I stopped at Brian's door. It was cracked open enough for me to see he was sleeping. He had been shot in the chest. The bullet just barely missed his heart, and had the surgeon on call not been there that exact moment they wheeled him into the hospital, he would have been dead. Everyone at that hospital was baffled he was even alive when he got there. *Luck.* That was all they could use to describe it.

We still didn't know who shot him, but I knew the investigators were at the Ellisons' a lot asking questions since Peter had been the one causing all of the issues with me. The rumor was the bullet had actually been meant for my dad, which started raising suspicions toward Toby and Rush. Mostly Rush, though. When the investigators asked me where Rush and Toby were the moment it happened, I told them they were with me and vouched for them. Was it bad to have wished it was my father who was shot and the bullet had done its job? That thought alone made me a villain in this story, too.

I made my way into my room and saw my phone sitting on the bed. After seeing Rush earlier, I was tempted to message him. I had been so angry at him at first and hated him a solid two weeks before. According to Tommy, Rush's only intentions before he met me were to shake me up a bit to get me to talk so he could take my dad down. He never wanted any of this to be what it had become. Rush and Peter shared a strong hate for my dad, and I understood why. My dad kept whose daughter I really was a secret which kept a sister from Peter. My dad shot Rush and Toby's mom. No one could have blamed them for devising a plan to ruin the man who wreaked havoc on their lives. I was so tempted to go talk to Peter and get to know him now that I knew he was my half-brother. I wasn't allowed to talk to him, though. Or Rush and Toby. The lawyer had advised me to stay away from them all while the investigation was still in progress. Mom, believing Dad's innocence, was scared that they'd hurt me, too. She was convinced one of them shot Brian, and the bullet was meant for Dad. There was no convincing her otherwise.

I sat on my bed and looked at my phone. I opened the million messages from Rush and started reading them from the beginning. I never deleted his messages. They were all I had of him right then, and his words always comforted me. My thumb hovered over the message I had typed two days before but never sent. I couldn't send it. My phone was being watched, and if they saw me communicate with him, I would have been in trouble. I was sure it was only a matter of time before someone was notified that I was with him that morning. Small town secrets were never secrets. Someone *always* saw. The town was buzzing with the talk of my family and all eyes were on us. They always were, but more so now. I should've just told Mom the truth earlier before someone else did.

But, despite my better judgement, I needed to see Rush. Toby, too. I clicked around until I found Tommy's messages.

Me: Can we hang out?

Tommy could have been my secret door to the guys. No one told me I couldn't hang out with my friends who didn't have anything to do with this mess.

Tommy: I can after I get done helping my dad paint this fence.

Me: Can't you hire people to do that?

Tommy: He said something about teaching me hard work ethic. He doesn't know me at all. I don't need to paint a fence to know how to be a hard worker. Whatev. So, what do you want to do? Want me to invite everyone?

Me: Not in the mood for a large group right now. Just thought it'd be fun to just hang out with you and maybe... two others.

Tommy wasn't an idiot. He'd get the hint.

Tommy: I should be done this afternoon. 6:00 sound good?

Me: Sounds great!

Tommy: Want me to pick you up?

Me: Sure!

Tommy: See you at 6.

Now, I just hoped Rush and Toby would be available.

CHAPTER TWENTY-SIX

Rush

"Why did Tommy want us to meet him in Tillar of all places? This place is basically a ghost town," Toby asked from the driver's seat.

I shrugged. "He just said meet him here at this exact spot." I looked around at the trees and trails that surrounded us. Toby said long ago it used to be a state park but didn't get enough visitors so they closed it. "Maybe he knows our love for hiking and wanted to show us some trails."

"At six o-clock at night? Yeah, right. It's more than that."

I shrugged. "Probably." I hoped he had news about who shot Brian or anything about the case at all. Maybe he was worried about Jorja and wanted to tell me, but he'd just tell me that at school or on the phone. I saw Tommy's truck pulling in. Toby killed the engine, and we both got out to meet him.

I swear my heart stopped when I saw Jorja getting out of the passenger door. Tommy hadn't even turned off the truck before she was shutting the door and running into my arms. I held her close, my heart thudding dramatically in my chest.

Toby stood respectfully to the side with his hands in his jacket pockets. Jorja let go of me and moved until she was hugging him. I cringed when his arms held her instead of mine. I looked at Tommy instead of them so I wouldn't let my possessiveness get the best of me.

"She wanted to see you both but is under close watch, so we had to meet here," Tommy said, grinning. "Why do you look so pissed? I thought you'd be happy."

I rubbed my forehead and gave him my best smile, showing all of my teeth. "I am."

He looked over at Toby and Jorja and then at me again. "Ah."

"Yeah, you see it, too?" I asked quietly.

Tommy was about to say something, but Jorja started to walk our way with Toby following close behind her.

Once she stood closer to me, she smiled. "Hi."

I wet my lips and grinned. "Hi."

She ran her hand through her hair and bounced on her feet a little. "I wanted to see you both but couldn't text or call you to tell you that. The lawyer and investigators want me to stay away from anyone who is linked to this case at all. They still think both of you know who shot Brian, even though you said you don't."

"We don't know." Toby frowned.

She nodded. "I know that. They don't."

"How's Brian?" I asked, absentmindedly rubbing the spot on my arm where I had given blood.

She rolled her eyes. "Thinks he is better than he really is."

"That's normal then," Toby grumbled.

She narrowed her eyes at him, and when he smirked, her features softened, and she sighed. She shook her head and looked at me again. "He's alive and healing, but it's gonna be a long process. Thank you for giving him blood, Rush. Without it, he'd be dead."

My chest puffed out a little. I wouldn't have acted so proud of myself had Toby not been there, but that was straight up bonus points for me, though I was sure I was the only one keeping score. "It's not a problem. I was glad to."

She wrapped her arms around herself and her whole happy demeanor deflated, making my chest tighten. Her eyes shifted from me to Toby and then to the ground. She kicked the gravel around a bit.

"What's wrong?" Toby asked before I could.

"My time's up. I have to leave now. I'm risking getting us all in trouble for being here. I just needed to see both of you even if it was for a second." She looked at Toby, and tears filled her eyes. "I've cried so much lately, it's stupid." She shook her head and wiped her eyes.

"It's not stupid. You're going through a lot," Toby said, taking a few steps toward her.

"So are you and Rush. You lost your mom. My dad killed her. I can't believe either of you are here talking to me at all. This entire situation is so screwed up."

"It is, but it isn't our fault. We didn't do anything wrong. Well, besides my brother." Toby chuckled, looking at me.

I flipped him off.

Jorja cracked a smile. "Yeah, but I understand his reasons, and he did try to stop it from happening. I just want to talk about something else and hang out like things were normal. I hate that this is who we are now."

"We'll get past it," I said, cutting off whatever my brother was about to say.

Jorja's eyes met mine, and she nodded but didn't say anything.

"We need to find out who shot Brian," Tommy said to Jorja.

She sighed heavily. "Yeah. That's part of the reason I needed to talk to you both. If either of you have any idea who did it, please tell me. I was going to ask you to talk to Peter but wasn't sure how that'd go since you broke his nose." She giggled. "What enticed you to do that anyway?"

"When I saw you for the first time since all of this happened at school, I lost it, and all of my anger gravitated to him." I put my hands in my pockets. I wanted to just hold her in my arms, but I knew right then wasn't appropriate. My pockets felt like the safest place for the moment. "I don't know who shot your brother. If you think he'll talk to me, I'll talk to Peter."

"Do you guys want to sit on the tailgates? I'll back my truck up to face Toby and Rush's," Tommy offered.

Jorja chewed on her bottom lip. "I should really get going."

"Ten more minutes. Your parents won't have a clue you're here," Tommy said as he took his keys from his front left pocket.

She looked at Toby and me. We both gave her a nod.

She looked at Tommy. "Okay."

Tommy moved his truck until the tailgates were facing each other. We all sat down. Jorja sat by Tommy on his tailgate, and me and Toby on ours. This felt wrong. She needed to be beside me.

"How did your mom become friends with Peter's mom?" Jorja asked me.

"They went to school together in Grove. They were best friends, and Peter and I grew up knowing each other."

Jorja looked at Toby. "Are you friends with Peter?"

He shook his head. "No. I've never liked him or my mother. Peter's mom is the one who got her into dealings with your dad."

Jorja frowned. "How deep were the dealings? Did she do drugs or just sell?"

Toby looked at me to answer that. I rubbed the back of my neck. I hated talking about this, but she deserved explanations that I should've already given to her.

"Both," I stated. "I don't know everything or how it got started and to the point it had taken her to—ultimately being killed—I just know that Peter's mom introduced her to someone, and she got tied in with your dad. That's all I know. I had already known you were Peter's half-sister. He told me about it and how he found paternity tests in his dad's home office. He was pissed when he found the agreement his dad signed saying he'd give up all rights. He also found a letter from your dad. Basically, a promise that if he ever tried to break the agreement, he'd be dead. Peter was going to take it to the police, but his dad found him with it and burned it. He said taking it to the police would do nothing but put a bullet in his head. All of the cops in town, except my dad, are working for your dad and grandfather. The system is seriously a mess."

Jorja nodded and spoke quietly. "I know. I hate Grove. I hate my dad." She looked at her hands with her eyes squinted. She wiped her cheek. "Sorry," her voice broke. "I swear I'm trying to be strong, but my dad is ... Jerome. I don't think I can call him dad anymore. Anyway, he's trying to plead innocent in the case of your mother's death." She looked at Toby and me. Her eyes turned grim. "He's going to try to frame someone for shooting my brother and blame them for your mother's death as well. He doesn't even care who really shot Brian at this point. He's just trying to cover his own ass. I heard him talking to his lawyer. My dad always wins, guys. But he can't win this time."

"What are you saying?" Toby asked.

She struggled to speak.

"Do you want me to explain?" Tommy asked her.

She shrugged.

Tommy looked at us. "Maybe you two can talk some sense into her because this idea of hers is insane and dangerous."

I looked at Jorja. "Okay, so my answer is already no."

"I second that," Toby said, his brow furrowed, not taking his eyes off her.

Tommy raised a brow. "I told her you'd both say that. She wants to kill her dad."

"Jerome," she corrected with a deep frown.

My jaw dropped. "The hell? No. Jorja, why would you want the weight of that on your shoulders? Why on earth would you think for a second that's a good idea?"

She looked up at me, and I don't think I had ever seen her so serious since meeting her. "Because of *him*," rolled off her tongue with so much malice I could taste the bitterness in my own mouth, "my mother is basically raped weekly to keep his 'customers' happy. He doesn't just sell drugs. He makes dirty deals, and she is a part of that. My older sister ran away because of this life he's cursed us with. My brother is his puppet. I know he hates it, but he can't get away from it now. He's too far in and might as well dig his own grave if he tries to get out. I've been lied to my whole life about who I really am. I could go on and on."

"And then what? He dies and your mother and brother are still wrapped up in this mess even after he's gone," Toby said, sliding off the tailgate and standing. "Your sister will still be gone and there is no telling what would happen to you."

"I don't care what happens to me," she said through clenched teeth.

Toby stood. "Yeah, well, we do," he almost shouted.

She pressed her lips together and looked toward the woods. The sun was starting to set, and it illuminated her face through the trees. Even in this twisted moment, she looked absolutely gorgeous.

"Jorja, you can't tie yourself up in this stuff more. Not in that way," I said calmly.

"It's not your choice. I know what I'm doing. He trained me well. I know how to kill discreetly. I know how to dispose of a body." The look in her eyes told me her mind was already made up.

"And when did you decide this?" I asked.

Toby shook his head as he looked at her in disbelief, obviously fed up with the conversation.

She fidgeted with her hands. "On the way here while talking to Tommy ..." She gasped and looked at Toby and me. "Or ... we could run away ... make a life somewhere else!"

"Who?" I asked, my voice cracking.

"My brother, mom, and me. If they wanted." She shrugged. "I want to break the chains of this last name. I don't want to use this last name as an excuse for my problems anymore. I want it to be gone and done with it. With him dead, it'd be a fresh start."

"Or you could make sure he's found guilty and put in jail for life," Toby said calmly. He sat back down.

"Killing him would be faster," she said as stared at him.

"Jorja, don't do anything stupid. Think this through. I'll help you prove him guilty if I have to. I was there. I saw him shoot my mom," I admitted.

She looked at me. "No. If he knew you saw him, you'd be dead next." Her breathing picked up. "Promise me, Rush! You won't say anything. Swear you'll never tell!" She had started to cry, and when she stood, I did as well and hugged her. "Swear to me, Rush," she begged against my chest.

"Okay," I whispered and rested my chin on top of her head. "I swear I'll never tell. But you have to promise me you'll find another way to put a stop to him without killing him. I won't let you have that on your hands."

She didn't answer, but she had started to calm down.

"We need to hear you say it," Toby said from beside us.

She sniffed and nodded, still keeping her face buried against my chest. "I promise I'll try to figure out a new plan."

"You're not alone. I know we may not be able to talk to each other in public right now, but we can find ways around that. Like tonight. Text Tommy a code word or something, and I'll be there for you in a split second." I held her tighter.

"Me too," Toby said. "I'll even get a phone if you want."

That made her perk up, and she looked at him but remained in my arms. "That might be the answer," she beamed.

He chuckled. "What do you mean?"

"Get a phone! No one knows it'd be your number. You could get one of those prepaid ones and not tie it to a name. That is a thing, right?" She looked up at me. When I nodded, she looked at Toby. "It's genius!"

Toby laughed again. "As long as you put me in your phone under a ridiculous name."

"What? Tobias isn't already ridiculous enough," she teased.

He flipped her off, making her laugh.

"One problem with that," Tommy butted in. "If they see a new phone number come through on the bill, it'll raise concern."

"What if we just get her a prepaid phone and put all of our numbers in it? She could keep that hidden and get in touch with us," Toby said looking at Tommy.

Tommy nodded. "That'll work."

"See?" I said to her. "We're already figuring things out that have nothing to do with killing anyone. No one else needs to die or almost die."

She didn't look convinced but nodded anyway.

"We should get going. Her parents think we're going to the lake to hang out with Becca, Beck, Jena, and Wren," Tommy said mostly to her.

"Hold me a minute longer," she whispered for only me to hear.

I kissed the top of her head and looked at Tommy. "Go ahead and get the truck started. She'll be there in a minute." I looked at Toby next. "Gimme a sec," I said, hinting he go start the truck and let me be alone with her for a second.

He didn't look happy, but he nodded and left us alone anyway. When both engines started, she looked up at me.

"I'm serious, Rush. Don't tell anyone you saw him kill your mom. Swear to me."

I cupped her cheek with my right hand and brushed her cheek with my thumb. "I swear."

She searched my eyes for several seconds before relaxing against me. "Thank you for coming tonight. I needed this."

"Me too."

Tommy rolled down the window and stuck his head out. "Come on, Jorja."

She groaned, and we begrudgingly let go of each other. She took my hand in hers, and I walked her to the door. I opened it for her and watched her climb in. I hated letting her go and back into that toxic house.

I looked past her at Tommy. "Take care of her when I'm not around."

"Always have," he chuckled.

I looked at Jorja. "We'll get you a phone and get it to Tommy."

She nodded. "Thank you."

"We're gonna make it through this."

She smiled a little. "I hope so."

I kissed her forehead and hugged her. "Talk to you soon."

She gripped the front of my hoodie before I could walk off. When I looked at her, she leaned forward and pressed her lips softly against mine. The kiss was too fast, but a kiss nonetheless. She pulled away and let go of my hoodie before I could try to keep it going.

I grinned. "What the hell was that?"

It was getting darker, but I could tell she was blushing from the light inside the truck. "Who the heck knows. I'm confused, remember? My head is all over the place."

I gripped the side of her door. "Then please stay confused forever."

She looked down at her hands and laughed. She playfully kicked at me. "Get outta here."

I laughed and made sure her legs were inside before shutting the door. I watched Tommy drive away before getting in the truck with Toby. I rested my elbow on the door and ran my thumb slowly across my lips where hers were just moments ago.

"Do you really think she'd kill someone?" Toby asked as he started to drive. "Especially the man who raised her?"

"Yes." I wanted to tell myself she wouldn't, but the earnest look in her eyes as she spoke about killing him convinced me otherwise.

"Do you think she'll try to kill him?"

I turned to look at him. "She won't be able to."

He looked at me and then back at the road. "Why's that?"

"Because if I think for a second she's going to go through with that, I'll go to the judge myself and tell him everything. I'll make sure he's locked up so fast she won't have a chance."

"We won't know if she does it before telling us. She lives with him, Rush. She could do it tonight. Besides, you promised her you wouldn't tell anyone you saw Mom get shot." I could hear the trembling in his voice. "I won't let you tell. That family is crazy. They'll kill you."

"They won't know until after I tell them. What would be the point of killing me then?"

He scoffed. "Because they'll be angry! You're not telling, Rush."

"This could all be over if I just tell, Toby. Jorja shouldn't have to live with those kinds of thoughts in her head. She shouldn't have to feel like she has to murder someone to make things right. I can make this right so easily. That man thinks he can win this. He can't. I know what he was wearing that day. I know details that he wouldn't be able to deny."

He inhaled deeply and exhaled dramatically. "Can you just think about this a bit and not run to the courthouse first thing in the morning? And think of Brian. He was involved in that too, and Jorja would be devastated if he got locked up."

"I wouldn't mention Brian at all. And tomorrow is Sunday. It'd be Monday before I could go to the courthouse anyway."

"You know what I mean, stupid."

I laughed and nodded. I'd give it a day to ponder, but the more I thought about it on the ride home, the more it sounded like the best idea any of us had yet.

CHAPTER TWENTY-SEVEN

Jorja

"Are we still meeting everyone as planned?" I asked. After Tommy had picked me up, he'd asked if it would be okay to hang out with everyone after meeting the guys.

"Yeah, but question ... did you just kiss ma' boy True?" Tommy asked, teasing me as he drove.

I wanted to grin, but only a faint smile would appear. My bones felt unsettled. Something wasn't right. I mean, a lot of things weren't right, but it was more than all of that. More than me playing with the idea of murder. More than making Rush swear he'd never tell he was there when his mother was shot. Just ... more. Messy situations like this were always a web of lies and countless devious acts. Someone messing with my head, Rush and Toby's mother being killed, and Brian getting shot had to be only of the few things happening that we were aware of.

I pushed those thoughts aside to think about later. "Yeah ... I kissed him." I turned from the window and looked at him. Tommy was steady. He always wore his hair the same, combed to the side, his preppy clothes and his expression always on the verge of laughter, sort of like Rush. I liked that about him. He never changed. He's always just himself and oddly comforting in the midst of everything. I was lucky to call him friend.

"Are you serious or are you just playin' with him?"

If Tommy didn't know me so well, I would've taken offense to that. "I'm serious, but it's stupid with everything going on. And he hurt me. He should've told me the truth from the start, but I can't stay away from him, and my heart seems to forgive him. My head just has some trouble with it sometimes."

"Okay, so, what's ..." His eyes crinkled at the corners. "Never mind."

I narrowed my eyes at him. "No, say what you were about to say. I think we're all past keeping secrets now."

"Is there something going on between you and Toby, too? I mean, maybe this is some fantasy you're trying to fulfill with twins, and by all means be my guest, but—"

"Whoa, ummm. No. Pretty sure neither of them would go for something like that." I laughed and shook my head. "But ... Toby is complicated. He makes me feel looked after. Like an Avenger. Or a villain. Like Venom."

He chuckled. "But are there feelings there? If there are, don't lead Rush on. Right now is confusing for everyone. I just don't want anyone getting hurt with so much hurt happening already."

The way he asked made me think about two things. One, he noticed something I didn't. Two, someone wanted to know, and he was fishing for answers.

I crossed my arms. "Who wants to know?"

He shrugged. "Me. Just lookin' out for everyone, ya know?"

"We have bigger issues than my love life." It's funny how we could even talk about this after discussing how I wanted to kill my da—*Jerome*. That was a silly idea, and I had only come up with that stupid plan on our way to meet the guys. I talked it out with Tommy who also found it just as insane as Toby and Rush.

"Oh, I know that. I just see more that could be added to the fire. Just don't want problems to happen that could otherwise be avoided. I worry about all of you."

"Well, you shouldn't. I'm sorry you've been brought into all of this. You know you can tap out anytime, and I'll understand." I took my phone out of my back pocket and started scrolling through Instagram to busy myself with mindless things. It was nice the messages from Peter had stopped and that drama was behind us now. But a part of me still wanted to talk to him, as contradicting as that may be. I had so many questions for Peter. He was my half-brother, after all.

Tommy chuckled. "I'm here for it all, Jorja. It's entertaining as hell."

I grabbed a pen from the cup holder and threw it at his head, making him laugh. "Jerk. Nothing entertaining about any of this."

I could feel the truck hit gravel and knew we were getting close to our spot at the lake. I looked out the window and could see smoke in the distance. They had already started a bonfire which made me smile. This felt normal. When he parked alongside Beck's truck, I got out and warmed my hands in the pocket of my hoodie. Days were starting to get warmer since it was getting closer to spring, but nights were still chilly. I waited until Tommy came to walk with me, and we headed over to the fire with Beck and Becca.

"Where's Wren and Jena?" I asked as I hugged Becca.

She pulled back and frowned. "Their parents wouldn't let them come."

"Why?"

"They said their parents didn't think it'd be a good idea to hang out with you right now." She sighed. "I'm sorry, Jorja."

I shrugged, pretending that didn't hurt. "I get it. I seem to bring trouble lately."

Beck came over and hugged me. "Hey, how are you? It's good to see you getting out of the house."

I hugged him back and then took a step back. Becca still watched us closely, and I didn't blame her. "It feels good to get out of the house, and I'm okay. Just overwhelmed."

Beck nodded. "I'm sure." He put his arm around Becca's waist and pulled her close to him. "Tommy, did you bring anything to drink?"

Tommy grinned. "Have I ever come without?" Tommy went to his truck and opened the back door. He dug around for a minute and came back with Styrofoam cups and a large thermos. We each took a cup and he poured.

"I'm ready for summer and Tommy's peach sangrias," Becca said after taking a sip.

"I'm so pumped for summer," Tommy said as he poured his own cup. He set the thermos near a log.

Beck held his cup up. "To bikinis."

Tommy collided his cup with Beck's. "Hell yeah!"

"We have to make our next two summers ones to remember. College will be here before we know it,"

Becca chimed in. "Especially when all this stuff with Jorja's family blows over. We'll have something to celebrate. Right, Jorja?" She smiled softly at me.

I took a long drink and kicked a few small rocks. "I hope so."

"It'll happen. We'll all be sure of it." Tommy stood beside me and put his arm around my shoulders.

I forced a smile before taking another long drink. The four of us looked toward the road that led there. I could see headlights and heard the sound of wheels crunching against the gravel. They were getting closer. Tommy moved until he stood in front of me. Beck joined him, and Becca and I stayed hidden behind them. We weren't expecting anyone, and surely Toby and Rush knew better than to come there when I'd made it clear we weren't supposed to hang out in the open. I heard the vehicle park. It didn't sound like their truck. I stood on my tiptoes but still couldn't see because Beck and Tommy blocked my view. Short girl problems. I heard the door creak open then shut.

"Is Jorja Bonovich here?" I heard an older man's voice ask.

I handed my cup to Becca and squeezed through the middle of Beck and Tommy. Toby and Rush's dad stood before us, towering over us all. I looked at his cop car and then at him. I had seen him in the office when he picked up Rush after he beat the hell out of Peter but didn't pay close attention to him. Rush and Toby looked just like him, just younger. Damn, they were going to age well.

I chewed on my lip, the buzz of the cider settling in. It didn't take much to make my head feel fuzzy. When he looked at me, his brow furrowed, and he scratched his dark beard.

"Everything okay, Officer True?" I asked, wrapping my arms around myself.

He took the walkie-talkie from the holster on his belt and pressed the button, causing a moment of static and a loud beeping sound. "I've found Bonovich."

"Found me? I'm not lost." My frown deepened.

"According to your mother you are. She said she couldn't get in touch with you."

I took my phone from my back pocket and saw her missed texts telling me I needed to come home. I sighed. "She's being dramatic. She knew I was out."

"Well, I have to bring you home."

"I can drive her," Tommy said with a smile. Maybe he'd go for that since he knew Tommy from him and Rush hanging out.

Officer True chuckled in a "nice try" kind of way. "I'll be bringing her home." He looked at our cups with curious eyes but didn't say anything about them.

This felt awkward. Officer True knew I had been to his house with Rush and Toby without him there. I wondered what he thought of me and his sons hanging around such trouble. I looked at my friends before walking to his car. He opened the front passenger door and waited until I was in before shutting the door. I watched as he got into the driver's seat and cranked the engine. I looked out the window and spotted my friends, giving them a small wave.

"It's a good thing I have this car tonight. If I had brought my regular, you would've had to sit in the back like a criminal. Not all cop cars are set up like this. Most have a laptop taking up the front seat."

I blinked a few times, not really sure why he was informing me on the logistics of cop cars. Maybe he was just trying to break the ice. "I guess that's good then."

I wondered if he could smell the alcohol on me, even though I didn't have much. Cops seemed to have enhanced capabilities in detecting not-so-right situations. I looked out the window.

"How'd you know where I was?" I asked.

"I know all of the hangout spots. It's kind of my job."

"My mom didn't tell you?" I kept my eyes on the window.

"She may have given me a hint." I looked at him and saw the familiar amused smirk Rush always held. His smile grew. "So, I hear my boys are pretty fond of you."

I couldn't tell if he sounded happy or confused about that. I smiled a little but didn't say anything.

"Don't be nervous. I hold nothing your family has done against you. I'm sorry you've dealt with so much merely because you are their daughter."

I looked out the window. "I'm my mother's daughter, and that's it."

"You've sure had some heavy burdens to carry growing up. I'm sorry, Jorja. I know it's a lot."

I was shocked no tears were forming. I could feel myself growing colder toward it all, though. That had to have been a good thing. I needed to feel this way to stay strong. "I don't want to go home," I whispered.

"I'm sorry, sweetheart, but you have to."

I sunk down and huffed. I rested my head against the seat and closed my eyes. We didn't say anything the rest of the drive. Instead, country music played quietly, helping drown out the silence.

I picked my head up and opened my eyes when I felt the car slow down. The gate and small office came into view.

Bill took off his hat and chuckled while shaking his head. When Mr. True rolled down the window, Bill *tsked* me. "Well, isn't this something? I can only recall one other time you've been brought home in a cop car, Jorja."

"She's not in trouble tonight. Just worried parents needing her home." Officer True showed him his badge.

Mr. Bill put his hat back on. "I was hoping for a better story than that."

I sat up straighter. "You know there's always a good story, just can't talk about it." I laughed.

Mr. Bill nodded. "Very true, dear. You both have a good evening."

Once the gate opened, Officer True continued driving down the road to my house. He stopped at the big iron gates. They looked larger tonight and mocked me with their intimidating size. They were put there to keep us safe, or at least make us feel safe. I had never been scared growing up about anyone getting past them to hurt us. Who knew the real intruders would be my own family. The gates were useless. Who knew that today I'd feel safer outside my home.

I grabbed the handle and partially opened the door before turning to look at Officer True. "Thanks."

"Jorja, if you ever feel as if you're in danger, call the station and specifically ask for me, okay?"

I nodded. "I will."

"I'm serious. Even if I'm not on call, someone can notify me."

My lips curled upward. "Yes, sir. I'm serious, too. I will."

He chuckled. "Good."

"Am I ..." I looked to the gates and then at him.

He nodded. "Free to go."

I got out and shut the door. He waited until I was inside the gate and a good way up the driveway before leaving. I hated that the first time we officially met was in a cop car.

I stopped walking when I noticed the lawyer's car in our drive. I looked at the time on my cell phone, and it was a little past nine. Weird time for the lawyer to be there. When I came inside, I veered off toward the kitchen and saw Mom pouring a glass of wine.

"You knew I was out with my friends," I said in annoyance.

"I know, I just hate knowing you're out there with all of this happening. I just feel better when you're home. Especially past dark." She took a sip.

"You could've come and gotten me instead of sending a cop."

She shrugged and took another sip. "I couldn't. I already took my meds and don't need to drive. You know me and those steep hills in the mountains don't get along."

"Why is the lawyer here?" I kicked off my shoes by the bar and sat down. "And you shouldn't be drinking with the anxiety meds."

She leaned against the counter and took a drink anyway. "I'm losing my damn mind, Jorja. Leave me be."

I raised a brow but didn't say anything.

She cupped the glass with both hands and stared at the red liquid. "And the lawyer is here working on things for the case."

"How's Brian?"

"He's slept a lot today." She swirled the wine in her glass before downing the rest of it. She poured another.

My stomach tightened. "Mom, this is better than seeing you laying around sick, but take it easy, okay?"

Her hands began to tremble making the bottle and glass shake as she poured. "I'm a big girl. I can handle it."

She set the bottle down and before she could take a drink from the glass, I reached across the bar and snatched it from her. "No. No more."

Tears fell down her cheeks. "I need to feel numb. Just let me take care of myself."

"No," I stated more firmly. I went to the sink and poured the glass down the drain. I then grabbed the bottle of wine and poured it out, too. "I need you sober and alive." I threw the bottle in the trash and rinsed the glass out, leaving it in the sink.

"I want to wake up from this terrible nightmare and your dad's trial to be over and us all just be a family again."

I scoffed. "You called what we were doing a family?"

"It was our normal. We're not typical, Jorja. We weren't ever meant to be."

I narrowed my eyes at her and used some colorful words to describe what this family was.

Her eyes mimicked mine. "Watch your mouth."

I couldn't understand how she could be this delusional. Maybe it was the Xanax mixed with wine giving her rose-colored glasses or her unexplainable love and loyalty to Jerome. Either way, it was annoying. "I'm going to check on Brian. No more alcohol and meds. Promise?"

She nodded but didn't meet my eyes. I left the kitchen and headed up the stairs to Brian's room. I lightly knocked on his door and then went inside. He looked at me, but was just lying there, staring at nothing in particular.

"Hey," I whispered as I shut the door behind me. The lamp on his computer desk was dim and the only thing illuminating his room.

"Jorja?" The crackle in his voice sounded like it hurt.

"Yeah, it's me." I walked closer until I stood next to the bed.

He grabbed my hand hastily and squeezed it. "Jorja?"

"Brian, it's me. Are you okay?" I held tightly to his hand and knelt down so I could be eye level with him.

"I remember," he said with wide eyes. He seemed more awake now, but still out of it. Almost like a crackhead high on meth.

"Remember what?"

"Where am I?" He blinked several times, the whites in his eyes were bright red.

"You're home. You've been here for a few days now. You knew you were here yesterday. You're scaring me, Brian."

He never let go of my hand. "Jorja, we ... have to get out of here."

"What are you talking about?" I used my free hand to get my phone from my back pocket in case I needed to call for help.

"Put the phone away. Jorja, listen to me," he begged in a loud whisper.

"Brian, you're freaking me out." My voice shook.

"I know who shot me."

I stopped unlocking my phone and met his eyes. "Who."

His hand trembled. "It was Dad."

I dropped my phone and every muscle constricted. "What?"

"He did it. He tried to kill me." His eyes closed as he mumbled something in whispers that weren't audible. He started to fall asleep.

"Why?"

His eyes opened. "Because I took him." He took a deep breath. "I drove him to kill that woman. He heard he was ..." He took a few steadying breaths. He tried to sit up but struggled to even move a leg. "We have to go."

I put my hand on his arm. "You're not supposed to be up and moving around. Why do you think he shot you, Brian?"

"I know he did! He heard talk about being arrested for her murder, and he told me not to say a word. I wouldn't have said anything, but he got scared and thought I'd be easy to break and tell. He's killed so many people, Jorja. I've been there for a lot of them." His breathing started to get slower. "I'm so tired."

"Are you positive? You seem very out of it right now. Are you sure you're getting it right?"

"He came in here earlier with his lawyer. They gave me ... something." He started sounding sluggish again. He let go of my hand and tapped his upper arm. "There. Some ... thing," his words slurred together.

Oh. My. God. I saw his shoulder and noticed a fresh prick with a dab of dried blood where a needle had been.

As moments passed, he fell into a deep sleep. I watched the rise and fall of his chest but knew something was terribly wrong. If I understood correctly, they had given him something and I tried to tell myself it was just his pain meds to help him sleep, but my better judgement told me otherwise.

I picked up the phone from the floor, almost dropping it again with how badly my hands shook, and dialed 911. I put the phone to my ear, staying close to Brian and watching as his breathing became more labored. Little did Officer True know, but he'd be getting that phone call I promised him tonight.

CHAPTER TWENTY-EIGHT

Rush

"She's coming here?" I asked Dad in shock. Toby stood close by listening to Dad on speaker.

"Yes. Her brother is back in the hospital, they took her father into custody again, and her mother requested she stay somewhere where she is protected. Between the three of us we can offer that."

"What happened?" I asked.

"Brian told her that their father tried to kill him and possibly attempted again tonight."

"Another plot twist," Toby mumbled under his breath. "What the hell is wrong with her family?"

I wanted to punch him for his unnecessary sarcasm. I narrowed my eyes at him as I spoke to Dad, "She can have my room. I'll take the couch or stay in Toby's room."

"No, she'll have my room, and I'll take the couch. There are going to be ground rules. I mean it, boys. I don't know how long she'll be staying with us or much of anything right now. If I thought there was a better place for her to go, I'd send her there, but there isn't."

Toby chuckled, making Dad snap. "You boys better think with your real brains and keep your dicks in your pants. There won't be time for any stupid stuff. I mean it."

"What if we have to pee?" Toby asked, trying so hard to hold back laughter.

I couldn't help it, I laughed.

"You both are going to wish you were dead," Dad warned.

We both closed our mouths tightly.

"I'm about to head back into the hospital and tell her it's time to go. She didn't want to leave Brian, but I finally convinced her to come with me. I'm going to swing by her house and let her grab some of her things, then we'll head back to the house."

I looked at my brother and wished I could read his mind. "Okay, Dad. We'll get things ready for her." I hung up.

Toby raised a brow. "Why are you looking at me like that?"

"Because she's coming here. To stay with us." Surely, he could read between the lines.

He laughed and shook his head. "If you're worried about me trying to come between whatever it is you two have going on, I'm respectfully bowing out. You heard Dad. No stupid stuff. Jorja doesn't need two guys fighting over her. She needs safety and nothing else to confuse her. She just found out her dad not only killed our mother but also tried to kill his own son. You'd be smart to tone down your inner Romeo." He pointed his thumb over his shoulder. "I'm gonna go get Dad's room ready for her." He turned and left the kitchen.

I started working my way around the house to make sure everything was clean while I thought about what my brother said. He wasn't wrong, but the selfish side of me wanted to use this time to prove to her that no matter what, through all this stuff, we could still work.

I stood from the couch when Jorja and Dad walked in. He had two large suitcases in his hands and Jorja had a backpack slung over her shoulder. I noticed Dad looking around the room and knew he was looking for Toby.

"He's already in bed," I stated before he could ask.

He nodded and looked at Jorja. "I'll show you to the room."

She looked at me and then at Dad. "Okay," she said quietly.

It felt like days had passed rather than just a couple of hours since last seeing her. Her smile was gone, and mascara was smeared under her eyes. She was a total wreck and with reason. I wanted her in my arms, letting her cry and lean on me for support. She felt too far away though she was within reach.

I followed her and Dad into the room. He had the biggest room in the house, with its own bathroom. It was none of the things that she was used to, but I was sure that'd be the least of her worries. I reached for her backpack, and she took it off and handed it to me. I set it near the dresser while Dad explained how to operate the TV like she was from another planet. She intently listened to him ramble on like he was really teaching her something and she had never operated a TV before. It was adorable.

"Dad," I interjected with a chuckle.

He stopped talking and looked at me. "Yes?"

"She knows how to work a TV."

He laughed and scratched his forehead. "Right. All you youngins know more than us old folk." He handed her the remote. "I know this isn't much, but you'll be safe here, and we'll feed you. Me and my boys are great cooks."

"Thank you for letting me stay here." Her voice was still so quiet and timid.

"Of course. You'll still go to school as normal, but you have to come straight here after. You can ride with Rush and Toby. I've already talked to them about the rules, so they know they are to be complete gentlemen, right, Rush?" His eyes were like daggers.

I saluted him. "Sir, yes, sir." I had hoped that would make Jorja laugh, but it didn't. She only blushed, probably at the thought of all the reasons why my dad laid down rules. If only he knew things between us had always remained PG.

He drummed his fingers on the dresser. "Well ... I think that's it. I'm sure you know how to work a bathroom, and towels are in the small closet in there. If there is anything you need that you don't have, me or the boys can take you to get what you need."

She nodded and sat on the edge of the bed.

"If you want, Rush can stay in here with you for a little while, but the door stays open." He cut his eyes at me.

Jorja started to take off her shoes. "I'm actually really tired, and I think I just want to go to sleep."

My heart sank. That's a nice way of saying get out of here and leave her alone.

"If you need anything," I said, wishing she'd look at me, "I'm just down the hall."

She nodded but never looked up from the shoes she had placed beside the bed.

"We cook every Sunday morning, so if you're hungry when you wake up, there will be plenty to eat." After I said that, I noticed Dad had left the room. "Will you at least look at me? I don't know what all happened between seeing you several hours ago and now, but whatever it is, I'm sorry. I want nothing more than to fix this for you."

Her eyes fixated on mine and her lips pressed tightly together.

"O-kay." I ran my fingers through my tousled hair. "You know where my room is if you need anything."

Her hands were fists around the end of her sleeves and tears wet her cheeks. Still no words escaped her. Anger filled me. Not because of her, but at everything and everyone that led to the broken girl sitting in front of me. I was on that list of those who did this to her. I was a damn idiot to ever put the idea in Peter's head to mess with her to get to her family.

"I want to fix this," I said as I slowly made my way to the door. I leaned against the door jam and sighed. "Talk to me." The crack in my voice surprised me. I was usually good at suppressing emotions when I needed to appear strong, and I wanted to be strong for her.

"I'm tired," she whispered. "And confused. And scared."

Though her words were nothing I should have been happy about, they were words I could work with and were much better than silence. "But you don't have to do this alone."

"When I leave your home, when they say it's safe, you need to forget about me, Rush."

My lips parted to speak, but she cut me off by holding up her hand.

Her hand fell back to her lap. "I'm serious. You don't have to agree, but I've made the decision for you. My family brings nothing but trouble and if anyone ever finds out—" she lowered her voice "—you were there when your mother died ..." She swallowed hard and looked down at her hands. "Just forget about me. If you want to do anything for me and help me like you say, you'll forget about me."

"Jorja, your father is in custody now. He's being accused of the murder of my mother and now the attempted murder of Brian. He can't hurt me now. He can't hurt anyone else."

She threw her hands up. "You don't understand! Do you live in a bubble? People work for him! All he has to do is give an order, and he can do that from prison! He has connections everywhere!" She rubbed her forehead and closed her eyes. "No matter what, no matter what great ideas you think you may have, this thing with you and me will always be nothing but trouble, and I'm tired, Rush. I'm so tired, and I just can't do this anymore. I just want out. I don't anyone else ruining their life over this. Over me."

"Well." I smirked, refusing to let her win this. "Good thing I'm more stubborn than you."

Her lips formed a faint smile before fading completely. "Doubtful." She picked up one of the two pillows and fluffed it. "Goodnight, Rush."

I looked over my shoulder to make sure no one was around. "My dad's a heavy sleeper. I'll come back here in a couple hours." She went to argue, and I shook my head. "You're not calling the shots anymore, Jorja."

"But my feelings and boundaries are logical."

"They're stupid and self-centered," I challenged with a raised brow. "You don't get to decide who I care about, want to help, or be around."

She didn't argue with that, but the fire in her eyes told me she wanted to so badly.

"You're not in this fight alone. If I'm making a big mistake, then it's my mistake to make. My choice."

She didn't argue with that either.

I walked over to her, kissed the top of her head, and then her cheek. "Night." I left the room. For now, anyway.

CHAPTER TWENTY-NINE

Jorja

Rush was a man true to his word. I lifted my hand and brought it close to his face, trying to talk myself out of my next move. I let my index finger lightly trail down his cheek. I smiled a little when he smiled in his sleep. My attraction to him was no secret, but I liked to suppress it every time I could feel myself slipping into something that couldn't be. There were small, infrequent moments I allowed myself to be vulnerable and intimate with Rush. It was all innocent, but even the slightest touch and I could feel myself falling into the deep well of feelings I had for him and would be easily consumed by them with no way out. A silent drowning.

It's scary falling so hard for someone that would always know the worst parts of your story. I wanted nothing more than to get out of Grove, and to start a new life where no one knew who the hell Jorja Bonovich was. Find someone to love the delusion of the person I'd make myself be. It'd never be that way with Rush. He knew my wounds and deepest scars now.

At any given moment his dad could come in here and he'd be pissed, but Rush wouldn't be Rush if he followed the rules. But, I wanted the least amount of confrontation right now, so I whispered his name and gave his shoulder a gentle shake. He laid his arm over his face and groaned.

I laughed quietly. "Rush, you need to go back to your room."

He slowly peeled his arm away from his face and cocked an eye open to look at me. "My dad probably already knows I'm in here if that's what you're worried about." He closed his eyes and stretched. The way the sheets slid off him a little, revealing his bare chest, made every inch of my body heat up.

He grinned as he put his arm around my back and pulled me closer to him. "I could get used to this."

The honest truth was I could, too. "Well, don't," I whispered against his neck.

The door jerked open, and we both froze, still tangled together. I hid my face against his chest.

"Are you kidding me?" Officer True's voice boomed. "Rush, out! Now!"

Rush sighed and slowly got out of bed. "She's fully clothed, Dad. Nothing happened. I just didn't want her to sleep alone. She needs to feel safe."

I turned over and sat up, keeping the covers over my lap. Rush lied. I was in a large t-shirt and panties. I wasn't fully dressed. I didn't even have a bra on.

Officer True raised a brow in my direction. "Morning."

I could feel my cheeks redden. "Morning. I had nothing to do with him coming in here. He did that all on his own. In my defense, I did try to get him to leave."

He looked at Rush. "I'm well aware he's at fault because he knows the rules. Rush, she is a guest in our home. One, you're not supposed to be in here. Two, and most importantly, if she asked you to leave you should have. You never make a woman uncomfortable. If they ask you to leave you leave. Understood?"

Rush gave a mischievous grin, making me nervous for what would come out of his mouth next. "Pretty sure she was enjoying my company. If it weren't for your rules, she would've asked me to stay and not leave."

His dad looked at me with raised brows. It made me stutter and stumble over my words, making Rush's chest puff out a little, proud that my lack of sentence formation confirmed what he said.

His dad rubbed his forehead and let out a heavy sigh. "Rush, just get the hell out of the room. I promised her mother she'd be safe here."

Rush frowned. "She is safe."

His dad looked at him with narrowed eyes. "Not if you get her pregnant. Out. Now."

My mouth fell open. Pregnant? Does he think we've had sex? I wanted to crawl into a hole and die.

"We'd make pretty babies," Rush mumbled.

"Out!" he shouted. I swear the pictures on the wall rattled.

"Yes, sir." Rush left the room.

"Nothing happened or will happen," I said quickly. His dad needed to know that before he left the room.

He stopped in the doorway. "Yet is the silent word there. I know you two have feelings for each other, and I knew that'd be a challenge with having you stay here. I just need you both to follow the rules while you're here. It is my actual job to keep you safe, Jorja. If something happens that shouldn't while you're under my protection, I could be fired. It would cause a lot of issues that none of us need right now. I need you to keep him level-headed."

I laughed. "Ummm, have you met him? He's stubborn."

He chuckled and nodded. "Oh, trust me I know. His brother can be that way too. Keep me in your prayers because raising these boys may kill me."

"You'll be at the top of my prayer list." We both laughed.

"Breakfast will be ready in about an hour if you feel like eating with us."

I nodded. "Thanks."

He smiled and shut the door. I fell back into bed and cursed. I stared at the ceiling, reflecting on the past twenty-four hours, and sighed heavily. As comfortable as I was living in the lies of my family, it kind of felt good that things were out in the open. Maybe things could finally be resolved.

Toby walked into the living room where I was watching a movie. I looked for Rush to come in too, but he didn't. I looked at the plastic bag Toby sat on the coffee table in front of me.

"Where's Rush?" I asked, looking from the bag to him.

"On the phone outside. Something about going to get his belongings from Mom's. It was a crime scene for a while, so he could only grab a few things when he came here. I think he's only worried about getting his truck back, though." He motioned his hand toward the bag. "Open it."

I untucked my feet from under me, placed them on the floor and leaned toward the bag. I opened it and smiled when I saw a phone box. "You got me a phone?" I took the box out of the bag and opened it to see a purple Samsung Galaxy. "I thought you were going to just get a cheap prepaid phone."

"Well, this one screamed Jorja, and I got a phone, too. It was actually cheaper to just add lines to Dad's account."

I took the phone out of its box and powered it on. "I'm used to my iPhone. It might take me forever to learn an Android."

He laughed and sat down beside me. "Well, we can learn together, then. I got one, too."

If you had told me a month ago that Toby and I would have been bonding over a cellphone, I would've called you crazy. I looked at him and smiled. "Thank you."

He nodded and took his phone out of his hoodie pocket. "The only thing I know how to do is add a phone number. Rush had to show me how to do that."

I picked up my original phone from the end table to my left. "The only numbers I'll add are yours, Rush's, your dad's, Becca, Beck, and Tommy's."

"Why not Jena and Wren?"

"Their parents don't want them talking to me right now. Plus, they struggle keeping a secret." I started adding in the phone numbers.

Just as I started to enter Rush's number in, I got a text.

I noticed the name, My Favorite True Twin, and raised a brow at Toby. "You already put your number in my phone?"

He laughed. "I had to be the first. Since I'm your favorite and all."

I looked at the message.

Toby: You look beautiful today.

I looked at him and then typed a message back.

Me: Why not just say it out loud?

Toby laughed at the phone. "Alright." He looked at me. "Jorja Bonovich, you look absolutely beautiful today."

"Your brother won't like you flirting with me, Tobias True."

He shrugged. "And my brother can be a possessive jackass. He'll live. Besides, I'm not flirting with you."

"You're not? Then what do you call what you're doing exactly?" I set the phone on my lap and crossed my arms.

He shook his head. "Nope." His lips curled. "I call it simply stating a fact."

There was nothing wrong with that except one thing—I felt disappointed he wasn't flirting.

CHAPTER THIRTY

Rush

I came into the house through the carport door which led into the kitchen. I could hear Toby and Jorja laughing and talking from the living room. My heart started to race, though it shouldn't have. Toby said he wouldn't pursue her, and Toby never broke a promise. I hated being so territorial, but I'd never wanted anything as badly as I wanted Jorja. When it came to her, my better judgement left me and the claws came out.

Seeing them sitting so close their heads were touching made my blood boil. It was all innocent. They were looking at their phones and she was teasing him about how bad he was with technology as she showed him how to do something on his phone. Maybe what bothered me the most about it was that they were so consumed with what they were doing that no one even noticed I had entered the room.

I cleared my throat and they both looked at me.

Jorja held up the shiny purple phone we'd gotten for her today. "Toby got me a phone, so now we can be secret with our conversations."

I looked at my brother. "That Toby got you, huh?"

Toby rolled his eyes and looked at Jorja. "I guess he helped pick it out."

"I hear you get your truck back. Finally," Jorja said so cheerfully, I assumed it was an attempt to break the tension.

"Yeah, I have to get it, some of my other things, and Mom's stuff I don't want sold in the estate."

"When do you have to leave to go do that?" she asked, scooting away from Toby a little.

"Soon." I looked at Toby. "I'll need you to drive me there, and I'll just drive back in my truck."

Toby nodded. "Alright. What about Jorja?"

"I called Dad and asked if she could come with us, but he said it was best if she stayed here."

Toby frowned. "But she shouldn't be here when we aren't home and Dad's at work."

I sighed. "I know. Dad said he'd bring the pager home and work from here if he needed to."

Jorja didn't look happy at all. "How long will you two be gone?"

I shrugged. "A day. Two tops. I can't think of much I want, so it shouldn't take long. But I'll need my truck and Toby's to haul stuff if I decide to take anything or I'd just fly there and drive back."

Her lips formed a hard line. She gave a slight nod but didn't say anything. I knew she wouldn't like this. Hell, I hated it, too.

"I can try to talk my dad into letting you come again," I offered.

She shook her head. "No, that's okay. I understand why he doesn't want me to."

"I guess we need to figure out when we're going." Toby said as he stood from the couch.

"The sooner the better. The quicker we leave the faster we get back and get it over with." The thought of going into the house, reliving the moment my mom was shot, how I held her as she died, made me sick to my stomach. I remembered standing there covered in blood watching the medics confirm she was dead. I etched the image of Jerome Bonovich's face into my mind forever. At that moment, I had made a promise to myself that I would avenge her death somehow. That was when the plans to bring the Bonovich family down started with Peter. I never expected to fall for the daughter of the man who killed my mother. I truly was sorry that my initial plans brought all of the terrible things her father had done to light and Jorja was suffering through it all. I wouldn't take the blame for it, though. Peter couldn't be to blame either. Jerome Bonovich secured his own fate, and, unfortunately, brought his family down with him.

I'd made a new promise to myself. I wouldn't let Jorja's life be ruined because of this. I'd protect her at all costs and see that she got a happily ever after when all of this was over, even if it wasn't with me, as hard as that was to stomach. I didn't know what all that meant—protecting her at all costs—but I would no matter what.

"Tomorrow? I know it's Monday, but missing school for a couple days won't hurt my feelings," Toby said, pulling me from my thoughts.

I looked at Jorja and then at him. "Fine with me."

Jorja's shoulders sagged, making my heart drop to the pit of my stomach. "We'll make it fast. I promise."

She put on her bravest smile and nodded. "I know. I'll be fine."

"You sure?" Toby asked her.

She looked away from me and at him. "I'm sure. Just be careful and hurry back."

Toby looked at me. "I guess we should start packing a few things and tell Dad."

"We can tell him at dinner." I went and sat on the other side of Jorja. "Let me see this new shiny phone of yours."

She bounced a little and started showing me all the things it could do, including taking a selfie of me and her to show off the camera. That turned into a hundred more hilarious photos and videos of the three of us playing with the different filters on Snap. By the end of the day, she talked me and Toby into downloading SnapChat, even though both of us had no interest in having social media. Her pout was extremely convincing, which meant I was in big trouble. But I already knew that.

I went into the house first, Toby followed behind me. I knew it wasn't going to be easy. I swallowed hard, but it didn't help the lump in my throat. Toby's hand gripped my shoulder.

"I'm fine," I lied.

"Twin intuition is a real thing you know."

I nodded and walked farther inside. I wanted to avoid the spot in the living room where she died, but you couldn't get to the rest of the house without walking past it. I kept my eyes forward and not on the floor. The lawyer warned me that blood still stained the floor that would soon be replaced now that the investigation was over.

Toby followed me into my bedroom. I looked at him once we were in the room. "I'm gonna grab a few things, then we can leave to go to the hotel. Do you want anything from your room?"

I don't think he ever considered the fact that he had things here for when he would come stay with us. He shook his head. He'd always hated coming here. Well, until last summer when he met my friend Annie and they were inseparable. That relationship ended when summer did.

I set my bag on the bed and started putting things I wanted in it, like my football from the year we won the state championship. Mom was always my biggest fan. Even more than Dad. She never missed a single game—high or not, she was there.

The more I packed, the angrier I got that she was gone. She wanted to do better. She promised me that she'd stop. She died the same day she promised me that. I guess that promise was fulfilled in a sick way. She couldn't do drugs anymore because she was dead. She also wouldn't get the chance to be a better mom. She'd never meet Jorja or be at any of my games. She wouldn't see Toby or me get married one day or meet her grandkids if we had any. She loved life. She just made bad decisions. She wanted to get better, but the drugs got their way.

"Rush, you alright?"

I turned to look at my brother over my shoulder. "Huh?"

"You've been staring at the wall for a solid three minutes."

I wasn't okay. Not in the slightest. It was easier to conceal my struggles in Grove, where I was constantly distracted by being there for Jorja. There, in that room, all I had were memories and thoughts. Nothing else to distract me from it all. All the hurt was surfacing and backing me into a corner.

"It's not fair," I said quietly.

"It's her fault, Rush. She made her choices."

I glared at him. "She wanted to get better!"

"Statistics show that a drug head never gets better. They go through periods of doing okay before they—"

I took the hat off my head and threw it at the wall. "Screw statistics!"

Toby pressed his lips together and looked at his shoes. "Fine. Screw statistics."

I became more aggressive as I shoved things into my bag. At that point, I wasn't even paying attention to what I was grabbing. Toby came over and grabbed my arm to stop me.

"What the hell are you doing?" I snapped.

"You just put a hanger in your bag. I think it's time to go."

I didn't want to go there at all, but it scared me to leave so fast. I needed to soak the place in one more time. Just sit there and remember her. Everything was the same as if she'd be coming in from work at any moment. The only sign that she was really dead would have been that blood stain in the floor.

"Give me a few minutes longer." Tears filled my eyes, and I wasn't strong enough to keep them from spilling down my cheeks.

"I think it'd be best to get you out of here, Rush."

"You don't know what's best for me! You didn't even care about Mom!"

"That's a lie, and you know it. I cared, but I couldn't get past the fact that she didn't care enough about you and me to stop her bad habits."

"She was going to quit!"

He scoffed. "She told that lie several times, Rush. You were always too delusional to stop believing her."

"She loved us, Toby. You never gave her a chance!"

He picked up my black 49ers hat—it was my favorite, and he knew I'd be pissed if I left it behind. He narrowed his eyes as he handed it to me. "She did love us, but not enough. I gave her too many chances until I was finally done."

I finally broke, and when the violent sobs started, Toby hugged me. Maybe her death wasn't what I was really upset about. Maybe it was the fact that Toby was right. That all I ever wanted was for her to love me and my brother more than cocaine or meth. That she would've never quit but continued to fill our heads with lies so we didn't abandon her. Truthfully, she was gone before she ever died.

When the crying stopped, I moved away from Toby and sat down slowly onto the bed. "Sorry." When I looked up at him, I noticed he was crying, too.

He shook his head and wiped his eyes. "Me, too. I'm sorry if I was harsh, but I can't feed you with bullcrap or sugar coat what she really was."

I looked around the room one last time. "You're right." I stood and zipped my bag. "Let's get out of here."

"You sure? If you need to stay, I'll stay as long as you want."

"Positive." I put the bag over my shoulder, and we left.

CHAPTER THIRTY-ONE

Jorja

I woke up to the cell phone the guys gave me ringing. I saw Toby's name and quickly answered it. It was two in the morning, making me worry something bad had happened. They promised me they'd stay the night and not drive back right away.

"Is everything okay?" I blurted out before he could even say hi.

"Yes. Why?"

I let out the breath I had been holding. "It's two in the morning."

He laughed. "Is it?"

I paused for a moment. "Yeah. You scared me to death! You guys aren't driving, are you?"

"Nope." He started laughing again. "My baaad." His words slurred together a little.

I scrunched my nose. "Are you drunk?" I asked, sitting up in bed.

"Maybe a little."

I rubbed the sleep from my eyes and ran my fingers through my hair to get it out of my face. "I didn't know you drank."

"I don't. Not usually. Rush was having a hard time and we met up with some of his friends. One drink turned into four. No five. No six. Definitely seven."

I laughed quietly. "O-kay. And you decided to call me? You do realize I have to get up early for school tomorrow. It's Tuesday."

"Eh ... umm ... oops. Sorry 'bout that. I didn't think about the time. I only thought about how I wanted to call you."

I had to pull the phone away to look at it to make sure I was really talking to Toby. I put it back to my ear. "Why?"

"Because you've been on my mind all day," he said quietly.

My heart started to race. "Toby, you can't say things like that. We're just friends."

"I call bullcrap. There's more to us than just friends, and you know it. We just keep fighting it because of my brother."

I swallowed hard. "We can't have this conversation."

"Can't?" he scoffed.

I sighed. "Shouldn't."

"Can't or shouldn't? Which one is it, Jorja?"

I frowned and contemplated hanging up on him. I put the phone back to my ear. "Are you trying to piss me off?"

"Are you mad because you know I'm right?"

I sighed dramatically and pinched the bridge of my nose. "Where are you?"

He laughed coldly. "Why? Are you scared Rush is around?"

Heat rushed to my cheeks. "You need to stop."

He was silent for a moment. "Fine ... I'll entertain that lie. If that's what you want. But I know it's not what you really want."

"What lie?"

"That there's nothing more to us than friends."

I closed my eyes. "No one is lying."

But are you, Jorja?

His hushed laughter pissed me off more. It wasn't funny.

"Toby," I breathed out. "Just friends don't call at two in the morning talking about how they've been thinking about them all day. This can't happen again. Because that's what we are. Just friends."

"Then what am I allowed to call and talk to you about so early in the morning?"

This felt like I was sneaking behind Rush's back even though we weren't even dating. "I don't know, Toby. If you have feelings for me, maybe you shouldn't call at all. It would only complicate things."

"Things are already complicated. You tell me that you really believe we're nothing more than friends, and I'll never speak of my feelings again. I'll move past it, and we'll be friends that don't call each other at two in the morning."

I wondered how drunk he was, or if he'd even remember the conversation after he slept a while. Part of me hoped he didn't, and part of me hoped he would.

Why the hell was I taking so long to answer him?

I fought the fact that he's right. But it was wrong. I shouldn't have been feeling something for two guys at the same time and coming to terms with the fact that I was doing exactly that was a hard pill to swallow. I never meant for this to happen. It had been easy keeping those feelings buried until right then. I would've never mentioned it out loud like Toby had.

"Jorja?"

"I'm here," I said quietly.

"Just friends don't take forever to respond to a question like that. Just friends would have had an answer already."

I started getting really tired of hearing him say *just friends* because the more he said it, the more it sounded like a lie. So, what did my dumb ass do? I hung up, which was stupid because that only proved he was right. He was so right, and I didn't know what to do about it.

Nothing.

You'll do nothing if you're smart.

I fell back into bed and laid the phone on my chest.

Idiot.

I rubbed my forehead and cursed several times. I never had intentions of falling for two guys, but why did it have to be brothers? Shame on Toby for calling me and saying those things. How selfish of him. He knew I was in a tough place. The last thing I needed was to end up in some twisted love triangle with two guys I cared deeply about. I'd lose one of them if I chose one or the other, and I just wasn't willing to let that happen.

My phone rang again. I didn't want to look at it because I already knew it'd be Toby calling back. I looked at the phone and silenced it when I confirmed it was him, but he kept calling back. Over and over.

"What?" I finally answered.

"I'm sorry. I shouldn't have been so forward like that. This is why I don't drink. It makes me say things I shouldn't. It's why I swore off that stuff the first time I got drunk."

I scoffed. "You don't have a filter when sober, Tobias."

"Don't call me that. Call me Toby. Tobias sounds like I'm in trouble."

I picked at some fuzz on the comforter. "Maybe you are."

He chuckled softly. "You know, you're wrong about the filter thing. I do have one. A very thin one, but it's there. I say things because they need to be said, but I think about it before I speak. I say things that others don't say but want to. However, I do keep things to myself that don't need to be said, like how I feel for you. I'm a tad drunk, but that's no excuse. This is why phones and alcohol are stupid. Had I not had this stupid phone while drinking, I wouldn't have called. I would've thought my thoughts and kept my mouth shut when I woke up with a sober mind. So, I'm sorry, Jorja. If I made you uncomfortable or upset you, I'm sorry for that, too. The last thing I want to do is make things harder for you. Just forget I said it."

I chewed on my lip. "How the hell am I supposed to forget it? Please tell me because I have no idea."

"I ... I don't know. I guess it's out there now, huh?"

"It'd be like trying to put toothpaste back in its tube."

"That was the stupidest thing our science teacher ever did to try to hook us on a lesson." The warmth in his voice hinted he was smiling.

I laughed. "Wasn't that in Mrs. Landry's class?"

"Yeah, before that lesson on how we should treat others. I couldn't get past the fact that she wasted an entire bottle of Crest on the table and actually tried to shove it back in. She didn't have to go to that extreme to make a point to middle schoolers who know what being mean to others can do."

"I guess it was a tad bit dramatic."

He chuckled. "Yeah. I really am sorry, Jorja. I shouldn't have said the things I did."

Tears filled my eyes because I would have been lying if I said I wasn't happy he did say it. It killed me that I couldn't say what I really wanted to, so I gave him what words I thought were the safest.

"I'm a mess of a person right now, Toby. I don't want to drag anyone down with me. Not you. Not Rush. I need to be nothing more than a friend to anyone right now. Maybe forever."

He didn't respond, but I could hear him breathing, so I knew he was still there.

"Did you hear me?" I asked gently.

He sighed. "Yes, I heard you." His voice sounded so brittle.

"And you don't have anything to say to that?"

He paused. "No."

I huffed. "Liar."

"You were mad thirty seconds ago about me saying how I felt, and now you're upset that I'm done talking about it like you wanted me to?"

"See?" I frowned. "I told you I'm a mess right now."

"I think we've both said enough tonight, Jorja. Get some rest. I'm sorry I woke you."

This time he hung up, and I knew better than to call him back. He had probably already turned off his phone. I laid my phone beside the pillow. How the hell was I supposed to go back to sleep after that?

After school, I decided to walk to the Trues' house instead of getting a ride from Tommy. Since I was staying with them, I never got my car which I didn't want anyway. That car was purchased with money that ruined so many lives. If I could have walked around naked, I would have. I hated my clothes and anything Jerome purchased.

I thought a walk would help me clear my head before the guys made it home. Just me and my thoughts and Camila Cabello on shuffle. Of course, "Never Be the Same" was the first song to play. If I had listened to this song before the two-a.m. conversation with Toby, I would've thought about Rush. So, why was I thinking about Toby now? I didn't know him like I knew Rush. I was just getting used to actually getting along with him, so where the hell were these feelings even coming from? With everything going on, Toby was not what I needed to be thinking about. But in the midst of all the chaos, I did feel something there. A pull of some sort, but I ignored it because it was easy since he was never around. But now, being around him more, I wondered how much longer I'd be able to pretend it wasn't there.

I pulled the earbuds from my ears. I didn't need music making the struggles in my head louder. I looked at my phone as I kept a steady pace down the sidewalk. Mom was supposed to call me with updates on Brian that afternoon. Last I'd heard, they were still trying to determine what was in that shot that was meant to harm him, and that was yesterday. The doctor said whatever was in it was on the way to shutting down his organs and he had been given it more than that one time. No one could tell us how long he'd be in ICU or if he'd be able to pull out of this at all.

The new phone started to ring, so I put my phone in my pocket and answered the other without looking to see who it was. On this phone, it could only be a handful of people and only people I actually wanted to talk to.

"Hey." Rush's voice sounded so tired. "You at the house?" I cursed myself for being disappointed it wasn't Toby.

"No, not yet. Where are you guys?"

"Driving. We have about three hours before we make it home. Toby is following behind me."

I almost asked him about the party with his friends last night, but then I'd have to tell him Toby called. "You sound tired." Maybe I should tell him about the phone call because hiding would be wrong, right?

"I am. I met up with friends last night and we got wasted. Bad idea, by the way. Not the smartest decision when you have to make a long ass drive." I heard him yawn.

"Be careful. If you get too tired, you should stop and rest."

He chuckled. "I'll be fine. Any word on your brother?"

"Not really. Still waiting on Mom to call me today."

He yawned a second time. "What are you doing?"

"Walking to your house."

"Why are you walking?" He sounded more awake now.

"I wanted to."

"With everything going on, that's not a good idea."

I frowned. "With everything going on, nothing is a good idea, Rush."

"Are you okay? You sound irritated."

I rubbed my forehead. "Just a lot on my mind. I'll be fine. I'm ready for you guys to be home." I crossed the street and made it to the block where his house was. "I'm about two minutes from your house."

"Good."

I looked over my shoulder to be sure I was alone. He was right, walking wasn't the best idea. "How are you? I mean, after seeing your mom's place after all this time."

"It sucked, but I'm okay. I talked to Beck earlier, and he mentioned hanging out this weekend."

"Yeah, Becca and I talked about it at lunch. Sounds fun."

I looked down the street and saw my mom's black Corvette and Officer True's cop car parked on the street in front of the house. I picked up my pace. "Rush, I ... I need to go. My mom is at your house."

"Why?"

"I'm not sure. I'll call you back." I hung up the phone and jogged down the sidewalk until I was there.

I opened the front door and came into the living room where Officer True and my mom were sitting on the couch talking. They stopped their conversation and looked at me. I looked at Mom.

"What are you doing here? Is everything okay?" I set my backpack on the floor.

She nodded and forced a smile. "You're coming home."

My eyes widened. "But all of you said—"

"I am aware of what we said." She stood abruptly. "Get your things."

I looked at Officer True. "Is it safe?"

He looked at his hands, at my mother, and then at me again. "Your father was let out of jail today. Apparently, they found the one who killed Sheila."

That was the first time I'd ever heard Rush and Toby's mother's name.

"What?" I swear I stopped breathing. "But he did it! He tried to kill my brother, too!"

Mom cleared her throat. "Your brother was just delusional from all of his meds. It came back that he was taking too much pain medicine. The shot was drugs. He was trying to kill himself, Jorja."

I shook my head and tears filled my eyes. "He told me! Brain told me himself what that monster—"

"Brian lied!" she shouted.

I wasn't buying it. "He wouldn't lie to me."

"Well, he's the one who shot and killed your friend's mother. He was trying to cover his tracks by blaming it on your father." She looked at the gold watch on her wrist. "We need to go."

I refused to concede. "Then who shot him? Himself? Mom, this is crazy! I know you don't believe this!"

She stood as tall as she could, holding her head high. "Yes, he did shoot himself. He was going to try to make it look like your father did it. Get your things, we're going home. Now."

"My father?" I scoffed. "He's not—"

"*He is your father!*"

I shook my head adamantly. "What are you even saying? You told me yourself that he wasn't!"

"I said no such things. Now let's go." She pulled the sunglasses from her head and put them over her eyes. "Now. We need to get home. Your father is very upset and wants us home."

"Where's Brian?" I cried.

"In the hospital. Dying, as he should. He should be ashamed of himself."

"You don't mean that," I whispered.

"Forget getting your things. You have plenty at home and we can buy more. Let's go."

I refused to take a single step. "No." My eyes begged Officer True to help me.

My mother started to say something, but he cut her off. "Jorja, there's nothing I can do, even if I don't believe it either. She is your mother, and she has the right to take you home."

I still refused to move, so she came over, picked up my backpack, shoved it into my chest until I was holding it, and dug her nails into my arm, forcing me out the door with her. I cried and begged the entire way to the car. She opened the passenger door.

"Get in."

I dug my heels into the ground. "No!" I shouted.

"Jorja, if you don't get in, I will have Officer True come put you in this damn car!"

I looked over my shoulder and saw him standing on the front step. He didn't believe her either. Why was he letting her take me? Surely there was something he could do.

"Jorja, get in," he said gently, even though his eyes told me he didn't want me to. "It's going to be okay. I'll make sure of it."

And I trusted him. I jerked my arm out of my mother's grip and got in. I put my backpack in my lap and made sure the phone Toby got me was hidden in the side pocket.

When she got in, she broke out into sobs as she gripped the steering wheel. "I'm sorry," she cried.

"What's really going on?" I asked, crying too.

She threw her sunglasses onto the dash, wiped her eyes, and hit the steering wheel. "You will comply with everything your father says to do, do you understand me? If you don't, he will kill me and everything you and I love. We are going to go home and act as if we are the happiest family in Grove."

"I am not—"

"You will!" She hit the steering wheel again. "Dammit, Jorja! You will do this to save those you love.

If you don't, he will make sure they are dead one by one. He will not go down without taking everyone down with him."

I opened my mouth to speak, but she shook her head.

"No. There will be no discussion. This is our life, and we will go on as if all of this were a misunderstanding and your brother is a murderer getting what he deserves."

I laid my head back and closed my eyes. I felt like I was going to be sick. "I don't believe this."

"Well, you better, and you will comply. He has hits ordered on your friends, their families, you name it if you don't do as he says. And when we get home ... when ... when he puts a gun to my head as he explains the terms of this agreement, I need you to be brave. Don't cry. Don't get angry. You agree and hold your head high."

"Mom ..."

" *You will!*"

I wiped my eyes and looked out the window as she started to drive.

CHAPTER THIRTY-TWO

Rush

I couldn't wait to get inside and see Jorja. I barely had the engine cut off before I was getting out of the truck and rushing inside. I walked straight past Dad even though he said something and hurried toward her room.

"Rush! Wait, son!" I only stopped because he grabbed the back of my shirt.

"She's not here!" he said quickly, before I tried to pull away.

"What? Where is she?" I turned around to look at him.

"What do you mean she's not here?" Toby asked as he came into the hall.

He rubbed his neck and sighed. "Well, boys, things have taken a turn for the worse. Her father got out of jail."

"That man is not her father," Toby stated firmly.

"Not the point right now," Dad said through an exaggerated sigh.

My forehead creased as I processed what he said. "How the hell did he get out, and where is Jorja?"

Dad shook his head and shrugged. "My only guess is the man has some damn good connections and is very convincing through violent methods. All I know is her mother came here and got her. Man, is that woman off her damn rocker ..." He shook his head.

"Where is she?" Toby asked before I could a third time.

"At her house." Toby and I both went to take a step, and Dad held up his hand. "You're not going over there. I need you boys to go sit down and let me explain what I know."

I looked at my brother before following him into the living room. I sat down next to him on the couch and we both looked at Dad, waiting for him to explain. My hands shook so bad I had to ball them into fists.

"After they left, I started to call my contacts that can dig for info. Brian is being charged with the murder of your mother. They are also saying he drugged himself, trying to kill himself because he didn't want to go to jail."

"But he was shot at the dinner party," I said, fuming.

"They are saying he shot himself or had it planned in a way it wouldn't kill him so he could say his dad tried to kill him to take the heat off him."

"I saw Jerome Bonovich kill Mom!" I stood and started to pace. "This isn't right! I'll go. I'll go now and tell the authorities. I can end this."

Dad pointed at me. "Sit down! You're not going anywhere and telling anyone a damn thing! They will come after you so fast, and I will not bury a son over this!"

"But—"

"Sit!" he shouted.

I closed my mouth and sat down next to Toby. My heart thudded so hard I thought it might burst from my chest. I looked at Toby and knew that look. He was already thinking of a way to get to her.

"I need you to think with level heads right now and know that this man, his empire, is not one to mess around with."

"Are you saying we have to stay away from Jorja?" Toby asked calmly. I was glad he could at least stay calm because I was freaking the hell out.

"No, that's not what I'm saying. I'm saying you tread lightly. You don't talk about it. If she wants to talk, you listen and report what is said to me. Most of the cops here are on the Bonovich side, but I have other connections that can help me with this investigation. I don't want you two doing anything stupid. Promise me."

Toby and I stared at him without promising a damn thing.

Tears filled Dad's eyes. "I don't think you boys understand how dangerous and reckless this situation is. It's bigger than your minds can dream up, I promise you that. *Please.* Please don't do anything that will get you both killed."

"And what about you? If you start messing around with this case, won't they come after you?" I asked.

Dad wiped his eyes. "It's my job. You boys know I put my life on the line every day."

Toby scoffed. "It's Grove, Dad. It's not that dangerous of a place."

"And Jerome Bonovich was almost brought down, making Grove extremely dangerous now. You boys don't need to worry about me. I'm trained to deal with this stuff, and I know others who are even better at it than me."

I inhaled deeply before letting it out. "If Jorja is in danger, I can't make the promise I'll stand down."

"Same," Toby added.

I looked at my brother, but he didn't look at me. He kept his eyes on Dad. When did he become chatty Kathy when it came to Jorja? I shook my head. Right then wasn't the time for me to worry about what the hell was going through his head.

Dad sat down in his recliner and put his head in his hands. "Okay," he said quietly. He ran his hands down his face and looked at us. "Just do your best to stay out of harm's way if things get ugly."

Toby and I nodded. "Yes, sir," we said in unison.

"You boys act as if everything is normal. Not a word unless she initiates the conversation."

I didn't know how he expected us to do that, and Toby must've wondered the same because neither of us had a response for that. I watched Dad stand. He thought for a moment before looking at us again.

"I ordered pizza, and it should be here in an hour. I figured no one would feel like cooking tonight." He left the room, went down the hall, and I heard his bedroom door shut.

I looked at my brother who was texting. "Who are you texting?"

"Jorja," he said, never looking up from his phone.

"What are you saying?"

He continued to text. "Asking her if everything is okay. It's on the phone no one knows about, so it should be fine."

"Unless her dad already found it."

Toby looked at me. "Too bad, it's already sent."

I sighed heavily. "Dammit. This is messed up." I rubbed the tension in my neck. "What are we gonna do?"

Toby looked at his phone. "Oh no."

"What?"

He handed me the phone.

Jorja: Everything is great! So happy to be home and know my dad is innocent and Brian was caught! Did you and Rush make it home?

I handed him the phone back. "Do you think that's her texting?"

"Maybe. I don't know."

I let out a shaky breath. "Are you gonna respond?"

He nodded, and I watched as he texted. When she responded, he handed me the phone again.

Toby: That's cool and yeah we made it home. Will you be at school tomorrow?

Jorja: Yup! Can't wait to see you guys! I gotta go. Family dinner and my parents may kill me if I don't hurry up.

"Was that last part a hint of some sort? Is that what it felt like to you?" Toby asked, his voice trembling.

"Something definitely isn't right. We'll know when we see her tomorrow."

He nodded and gripped his phone tightly. "I'm going to take a shower." He stood and left the room.

I sat there, frozen, trying to decide my next move. I could tell my side of the story. I could fix this. Yeah, Dad was probably right that I'd just put a target on my back, but if that meant keeping Jorja safe, then so be it.

I felt my phone vibrate, and I opened a text from Jorja. It was from the number I hoped her parents knew nothing about.

Jorja: Don't forget your promise to me.

My hands trembled so bad it made it hard to type.

Me: And what is that?

Jorja: You swore you'd never tell, and you won't.

It was like she could read my mind, but she also wasn't an idiot. She knew what I'd want to do.

Me: That promise can go to hell with Jerome Bonovich.

Jorja: I'm deleting these messages. Don't text me back anything risky. I'll see you at school tomorrow.

Me: Just tell me you're safe so I can talk myself out of coming over there.

Jorja: I'm safe right now. Gotta go. I came to the bathroom to text you. Delete these messages just in case. I'm hiding this phone again.

I cursed and stood. I went down the hall to the bathroom. I heard the shower going. I knocked on the door several times.

"Toby," I said loudly.

No response.

"Toby," I said louder.

No response again. I opened the door and pulled the shower curtain open. He wasn't there.

Dammit.

I hurried back down the hall and outside. His truck was gone. My chest tightened, and I had to remind myself to breathe. I remembered in my rush to see Jorja I left the keys in my truck. I got in, started it up, and took off in the direction I figured he was going.

If Jerome Bonovich didn't kill us tonight, Dad surely would.

CHAPTER THIRTY-THREE

Jorja

I pushed the food around on my plate. Mom and Jerome hired a new housekeeper who believed we should eat nothing with salt or seasoning on it. At least, that's what I had determined from this bland food. Mom didn't like it either. She'd pulled Natasha into the dining area and had been complaining for the past five minutes and giving her "orders" for the next meal.

"You're free to go clean now," Mom said with a swish of her hand as if to shoo the poor woman away. I looked back down at my food and attempted to eat every bit of it after seeing my mother belittle Natasha so badly.

My head felt like someone was taking an icepick and stabbing every inch of my brain. When we got home this afternoon, Mom was right, Jerome slammed her body against the wall, put a pistol to her temple, and stared me dead in the eyes while telling me what I would do and wouldn't do. I realized in that moment someone could be so brave and a coward at the same time. Mom didn't flinch or fight him. She closed her eyes and let him do what he felt like he needed to do to get my attention. When he released her after I agreed, she straightened her red dress, fluffed her hair and kissed him with a smile like all was okay. She was brave in the sense that she was doing this to protect those she loved, but a coward for following suit with what he said to do. I guess that made me both of those things, too.

"Jorja, you haven't said a word to me since you've been home." Dad vigorously covered his food with salt and pepper. When he saw I was looking at him, he smiled with all of his teeth. If only he knew I was contemplating all the ways I could kill him.

All those years of training to kill and hide the evidence would come in handy. This stupid idiot created the perfect weapon, and it'd be the one to kill him. I didn't know when or how yet, but it would happen, even if I died trying.

"What would you like me to say?" I asked quietly, my eyes turned to slits. If I had the ability to set someone on fire, I believe my eyes could have done it at that moment.

Jerome's hands turned to fists on the table. "I know this is hard, but I do this because I want my family safe and to have all the things they could ever want. This is bigger than me, Jorja. Bigger than all of us. If I end up in prison, there will be a war against our family because we bring in so much revenue for the cartel," he said in a whisper while Mom made sure Natasha wasn't within listening distance.

"There is no *we* in this. I want no part of it," I said in a harsh whisper.

He picked up a steak knife and wiped it off with a cloth napkin. He grabbed Mom's hand and turned it over, laying it flat on the table. He ran his thumb over her wrist and looked at the knife.

"Is this what you want?" he asked all while staring me dead in the eyes.

Tears began to form, and I shook my head.

He smiled and let her wrist go and lowered the knife. "I didn't think so. So, how was your day?"

"Fine," I said through my teeth.

"I hear you're very fond of those True boys. You should invite them for dinner sometime." He laughed around a fork full of green beans. "Tell me, are you screwing them both or one and not the other? Man, if the latter part of what I said is the answer, I bet the one not benefiting is pissed."

Every bone in my body rattled. I pushed my plate away. "May I be excused now?"

He shook his head. "Not until you eat all your food."

I watched as Natasha walked in to refill glasses. As she filled Jerome's glass and Mom took her sleeping pills, the idea hit me. That was how I'd kill him.

He would have a glass of whiskey before bed in his study. As a matter of fact, he'd have the maid fix one before she left so it'd be there waiting on him with stone ice cubes that'd kept it cold but not water it down. He was a creature of habit, which I'd use to my advantage. I took a bite of my food. The sooner I finished the food and was excused, the quicker I could sneak into his study and lace his whiskey with enough crushed up sleeping pills to kill an ox.

I finished my food and pushed the plate away. "Now?"

Mom started to yawn. "Go ahead."

Jerome motioned his hand for me to get up. "Now, come give your dad a hug."

I took a deep, steadying breath, and made my way to him. I hugged him as requested.

"I truly do love you, Jorja. I hate I've had to go to these extreme measures, but these are the types of things you do for those you love."

I gave him a slight smile, hoping it looked legit. "I think I'm starting to understand."

He nodded. "Good. Your brother is the one we are angry with. He did this to our family."

I wondered if Natasha was hearing and seeing all of this. Her shift would be over as soon as the kitchen was cleaned and the whiskey was poured, and I wondered if she would go talk about what happened tonight. If she were even aware. Jerome and Mom made sure she was nowhere within listening distance, and we all knew which parts of the house it was safe to talk in when the maids were there, but I hoped somehow she heard and saw it all.

I left the dining room and went upstairs. I quickly made it to my parents' bedroom and into the bathroom. I went to the wall-length counter with two sinks and mirrors and opened Mom's, grabbing the sleeping pills. She'd already taken them for the night with dinner. She always grabbed the ones she'd need before heading down to eat. She wouldn't notice them missing. Not that night at least. I closed the mirror and hurried to my room. Mom and Jerome would most likely have dessert, leaving me a small window of time to get the pills crushed and in the drink then pray like hell it worked.

Is it bad to pray your plan of murder works?

Once in my room, I went to my bathroom, poured the pills on the counter, counting twenty, and started crushing them with the handle-end of one of my makeup brushes. I set the makeup brush in the sink and started running water over it.

I thought about where I could put this to make it easier to put into the cup with no chance of a mess.

Paper.

I turned off the water and went into my room. I found my backpack, took out a notebook, and tore a piece of paper. I went to the bathroom, raked the powder on the paper and folded it.

I almost talked myself out of the whole thing, but with light footsteps down the stairs, discreetly making sure Mom and Jerome were eating dessert in the dining room, and seeing the glass of whiskey on his desk in the study, I did it. I poured every bit of the powder into the drink, watched it dissolve, shook it around enough that not a trace could be seen, and threw the paper into the fireplace, thankful it was cold enough to have a fire going.

Then, all I had to do was go to my room and wait.

I paced my room, trying to talk myself into going downstairs to the study. An hour had passed since he had gone in there. What if he could taste it? What if he figured out his drink was poisoned and he came upstairs and killed me before I could kill him? He shouldn't taste it, though. He taught me that a strong drink would hide the taste.

I jumped and grabbed my chest when I heard a knock on my window. I could see a dark shadow, maybe two, on my white sheer curtain.

"Jorja," I heard Rush's voice from the other side of the window.

I hurried over, pulled back the curtain, and opened the window.

I took a step back. "What the hell are you doing here?" I gasped when Toby came in behind him. "Have you both lost your mind?" I cursed, realizing I forgot to whisper.

"I believe we have," Rush said, looking at Toby and then at me again. "Are you okay?"

I stumbled over words before giving up and shaking my head.

Toby tilted his head to the side as he studied me. "Jorja, what did you do? You did something. I can see it all over your face."

I ran a shaky hand through my hair. "I ... uh ..." I chewed on the inside of my cheek and looked toward my bedroom door. I looked at the guys again. "I may or may not have killed Jerome."

"What!" Toby almost shouted but quieted himself down.

My breathing picked up, and I started to panic a little. "It may have not worked. I don't know. It's been an hour since I laced his drink with sleeping pills," I whispered.

"Dammit, Jorja." Rush facepalmed.

"Where is he?" Toby asked quietly.

I shrugged. "If it worked, he should be in the study. If not, I guess in bed."

"And what is your plan if he is dead?" Toby asked, rubbing his forehead.

I chewed on my bottom lip. "Get rid of his body. Duh."

Both guys stared at me, blinking a few times.

"And how do you expect to do that on your own? He's over six feet and you're like, what, five-two?" Rush groaned. "What the hell were you thinking, Jorja?"

I folded my arms behind my back and rocked on my heels. "Well, I guess it's a good thing you both are here to help me. You guys have impeccable timing." I smiled sweetly.

"And if he's dead," Toby whispered, "what do we do with the body exactly?"

I walked over to my dresser and took the boat key out of the top drawer. "I have a boat." I tossed Toby the key.

Toby caught it and sighed. "Of course you do."

"And ..." I walked over to the lounge area of my room and pulled up the corner of the rug and pulled up the loose boards. When I pulled out gloves, large trash bags, rope, and weights, both guys cursed. I looked at them from the floor as I put the boards back in place.

"I told you two not to get involved with me." I stood. "I need to go see if it worked. You both stay here."

"Like hell—" Rush started to say.

"I will go down there alone. I've been trained to do this kind of stuff. You guys stay here, and I will come get you if he's dead. If he's not, you both need to leave."

When they went to argue, I glared at them. "Stay."

I quietly left the room and made my way discreetly to the study. When I peered around the corner and saw the door was open, I took a few steps forward to get a better view of his desk. His hand still gripped the empty glass, and his body was slumped over onto the desk. I went into the room farther, hoping he wasn't faking it, just waiting for the one who did this to come to make sure it worked so he'd know who to kill. His shoulders didn't rise and fall to indicate he was breathing. The closer I got, the faster my heart raced. I swallowed hard as I approached him. I took a deep breath before putting my fingers to his wrist. I let out a relieved sigh when I felt no pulse.

I almost screamed when the guys came into the study.

"What did I tell you two to do?" I whispered.

"Is he ...?" Toby asked as he made his way over to me.

I looked at Jerome and nodded. It all felt too easy, but maybe this was the universe's way of giving this monster what he deserved and all the stars aligned for this to go as smoothly as it did. But it wasn't over yet. We still had to get rid of his body without getting caught.

"Damn," Rush scratched his forehead. "Where's your mom?"

I didn't take my eyes off Jerome. "Sleeping. She's out, I promise."

"Anyone else here?" Toby asked.

I shook my head. "We need to get him upstairs."

"Then what?" Rush asked nervously.

"I can't believe this crap," Toby mumbled as he ran his hands down his face.

I looked at them both. "I need you two to calm down. If you don't want to help me, I understand."

"We're neck deep in this mess now, Jorja. It's too late to back out. Tell us what to do," Rush looked away from Jerome. "I think I might be sick."

Toby chuckled quietly. "Just pretend he's sleeping."

Rush's mouth opened slightly as he gawked at his brother. "I'm extremely worried that you're able to laugh right now." He covered his mouth with his fist. "What's that god-awful smell?"

Should I tell him?

I laughed a little. "When someone dies, they use the bathroom."

"How do you know this?" Rush asked, gagging again.

"I work in a morgue in the summers. We own a funeral home." I smacked my forehead. "Never mind. We need to focus."

"Tell us what we need to do. Rush will be fine." Toby walked closer to me.

"We get him upstairs to my room. Once there, we put him in a bag and get him out the window."

"Out your window?" Rush screeched.

I stared at him. "Yes. Out my window. Where are you guys parked?"

Rush put his hands on the top of his head. "I can't believe we're having this conversation right now." He looked at me and dropped his hands to his sides. "On the highway. We walked through the woods to get to your house. We figured it'd be the best way than to come through the gate."

With the help of Toby and Rush carrying Jerome and me going ahead of them to make sure we were in the clear, we got him up to my room, put on the gloves, put the body in the bag, and tied it up with rope.

"We don't take off the gloves yet. We wear them the entire way and we will burn them later." I put my hands on my hips and looked over the bag and made sure everything was done just right. "Let's get him out of here."

"I'll go down and try to catch him as you put him out the window," Rush said to Toby.

"Then what?" Toby asked.

I looked at him. "We hope like hell we get him to the highway, in the back of one of your trucks, and to the boat without being caught."

"Can't we just put him in the bed and make it look like he died in his sleep?" Rush asked.

"No," I said, shaking my head. "They'll do an autopsy and know he was poisoned. That will only make him look more innocent like he was trying to do."

Rush cursed a few times and went out the window. I helped Toby lift the body. I groaned and my muscles strained as I helped raise him high enough to get him over the windowsill. With a hard push, his body went tumbling down the roof, and when I heard a loud thud, Toby and I looked out the window to see Rush didn't catch him, instead, the body fell on top of him. Rush pushed him off, stood, and bent at the waist with his hands on his knees.

Toby got out of the window, and then helped me out. I shut the window and followed Toby to the ground.

"You okay?" Toby asked Rush who was dry heaving.

Rush held up a finger. "Give me a second. When he fell," he gagged, "all of his bones snapped. I think his neck is broken. I could feel them break." He gagged again.

I patted his back. "Suck it up, buttercup, we gotta hurry."

Toby chuckled.

"Not funny, asshole," Rush barely got out through gagging.

Toby shrugged. "Kind of is. Pussy," he mumbled.

Rush growled. "I hate you. I'd like to see a body fall on you."

Toby raised a brow. "Do I get to pick the body?"

"Of course you'd be thinking dirty right now." Rush rolled his eyes.

I covered my face so Rush wouldn't see me smiling.

He took a few deep breaths and looked at me. "How the hell are you so calm?"

"Because I was trained to do this. It's nothing more than a job right now. Let's go."

Everyone grabbed a piece of the rope I had tied to make handles and we started to make our way through the woods.

I stared at the water, the moon and stars reflecting off it, making it look like the sky was endless and we were floating through space. The lull of the rippling water, making the boat rock gently side to side, calmed my nerves. We did it. *I* did it. I killed Jerome Bonovich.

"Now what?" Rush asked as he stared out into the water.

Many different things could happen at this point. Jerome would be listed as a missing person. My home would be investigated again, so I'd have to be sure I cleaned up every bit of evidence the second I got home. If they found him, I'd be surprised. The weights we tied to him would keep him in the deepest part of the river forever. With the fast current, his body would drag across the bottom, never staying in one place. And if they did find his body, there'd be no trace of me or the guys.

The cartel would come after me and Mom and take everything we owned to make up for lost sales. Brian could fight for his innocence if he made it out of the hospital alive, but then he'd have to worry about the cartel coming after him. If they got to him, they could possibly make him run the business as Dad did. There were so many different scenarios, some a bit more severe than the others, but at that moment, nothing felt greater than knowing that monster of a man was dead. Whatever was to come would be worth it.

"Jorja," Toby said, pulling me from my thoughts.

I looked at him.

"Rush asked you a question."

I nodded. "I know, and I'm going to answer it. Just give me a second."

As they both patiently waited, I thought about what I should say to them. Thank you, for starters. They didn't have to help me. I'd always wondered what it would feel like to kill someone and have something so heavy on your conscience, but I felt nothing but relief. Not sad. Not scared. Relieved. They'd have to keep this a secret. Could they live with the guilt?

I looked at them both. "Thank you for helping me. I know this is going to be something that stays with you forever, and I'm sorry for whatever terrible emotions you go through because of this. I owe you guys everything. But, what we do now is keep this a secret. Take it to your grave type of secret. No one can know. Ever. Are you both capable of keeping it a secret and can swear you'll never tell a soul?"

"If we don't, will you throw us overboard, too?" Toby asked, his lips curled at the corners.

I smiled a little. "Just swear you guys will keep this a secret."

Rush made a cross over his chest with his index finger. "Cross my heart."

I looked at Toby as he stared into the water. He rubbed the back of his neck, looked at me, and nodded. "Swear. Not a soul."

I nodded. "Good." I stood and made my way to the driver's seat and cranked the motor. "Let's all get home. I have evidence to get rid of, and we have school tomorrow."

"But how do we go to school tomorrow after something like this?" Rush asked.

"After something like what, exactly?" I asked, crossing my arms in front of me.

Rush looked at me like I was insane. "Ummm ..." He motioned his hand toward the water.

I shrugged and smiled. "Go out for a boat ride on such a beautiful night?"

Toby chuckled. "The breeze is nice."

I raised a brow at Rush. "Are you sure you're going to be able to keep this a secret?"

He nodded. "Yeah, it's just gonna take me some time to process it all."

"I'll help you through it," I said as I gripped the throttle. "We should go."

Rush and Toby took their seats, and the entire boat ride back to the dock was silent.

If I learned anything that night, I'd learned that monsters can creep into your house, the place you thought you were the safest and pull at you until you fall into the deepest and darkest pits of hell. Once they have you where they want you, you have two choices: Succumb to their will, or throw them over a boat.

THIS LITTLE SECRET: BOOK 2
COMING SOON!

ACKNOWLEDGEMENTS

I am deeply grateful to all of my amazing BETA readers. To Rebecca and Lauren for reading multiple times, their insightful feedback and unwavering support were instrumental in shaping this novel into its best form.

A special shoutout to my editor, Wendi, whose keen editorial eye and skillful guidance whipped the manuscript into its polished state.

And let's not forget cover designer Emilt Wittig, whose artistry brilliantly captures the essence of mystery that dwells within these pages.

Together, you have all contributed to the enigmatic soul of this book, making it a journey worth taking.

Thank you.